Sixteenth Summer

MICHELLE DALTON

SCHOLASTIC INC.

With special thanks to Elizabeth Lenhard

For Paul, for six summers and counting . . .

This book is a work of fiction. Any references to historical events, real people, or real locales are used fictitiously. Other names, characters, places, and incidents are the product of the author's imagination, and any resemblance to actual events or locales or persons, living or dead, is entirely coincidental.

No part of this publication may be reproduced, stored in a retrieval system, or transmitted in any form or by any means, electronic, mechanical, photocopying, recording, or otherwise, without written permission of the publisher. For information regarding permission, write to Simon Pulse, an imprint of Simon & Schuster Children's Publishing Division, 1230 Avenue of the Americas, New York, NY 10020.

ISBN 978-0-545-89910-9

Copyright © 2011 by Simon & Schuster, Inc. All rights reserved. Published by Scholastic Inc., 557 Broadway, New York, NY 10012, by arrangement with Simon Pulse, an imprint of Simon & Schuster Children's Publishing Division. SCHOLASTIC and associated logos are trademarks and/or registered trademarks of Scholastic Inc.

12 11 10 9 8 7 6 5 4 3 2 1   15 16 17 18 19 20/0

Printed in the U.S.A.   40

This edition first printing, September 2015

Designed by Karina Granda
The text of this book was set in Berling.

June

The first time you lay eyes on someone who is going to become *someone* to you—*your* someone—you're supposed to feel the earth shift beneath your feet, right? Sparks will course through your fingertips and there'll definitely be fireworks. There are *always* fireworks.

But it doesn't really happen that way. It's messier than that—and much better.

Trust me, I know. I know how it feels to have a *someone*.

To be in love.

But the day after my sophomore year ended, I didn't know *anything*. At least, that's the way it feels now.

Let me clarify that. It's not like I was a complete numbskull. I'd just gotten a report card full of A's. And one B-minus. (What can I say. Geometry is my sworn enemy.)

And I knew just about everything there was to know about Dune Island. That's the little sliver of sand, sea oats, and sno-cones off the coast of Georgia where I've lived for my entire sixteen-year existence.

I knew, for instance, where to get the spiciest low-country boil (The Swamp) and the sweetest oysters (Fiddlehead). Finding the most life-changing ice cream cone was an easy one. You went to The Scoop, which just happened to be owned by my parents.

While the "shoobees" who invaded the island every summer tiptoed around our famously delicate dunes (in their spotless, still-sporting-the-price-tag rubber shoes), I knew how to pick my way through the long, fuzzy grass without crushing a single blade.

And I definitely knew every boy in my high school. Most of us had known one another since we were all at the Little Sea Turtle Play School on the north end of the island. Which is to say, I'd seen most of them cry, throw up blue modeling clay, or stick Cheetos up their noses.

It's hard to fall for a guy once you've seen him with a nostril full of snack food, even if he was only three at the time.

And here's one other thing I knew as I pedaled my bike to the beach on that first night of my sixteenth summer. Or at least, I *thought* I knew. I knew exactly what to expect of the season. It was going to be just like the summer before it, and the summer before that.

I'd spend my mornings on the North Peninsula, where tourists rarely venture. Probably because the sole retail establishment there is Angelo's BeachMart. Angelo's looks so salt-torn and shacky, you'd never know they make these incredible gourmet po' boys at a counter in the back. It's also about the only place on Dune Island where you *can't* find any fudge or commemorative T-shirts.

Then I'd ride my bike south to the boardwalk and spend my afternoon coning up ice cream and shaving ice for sno-cones at The Scoop.

Every night after dinner, Sam, Caroline, and I would call

around to find out where everyone was hanging that night. We'd all land at the beach, the deck behind The Swamp, Angelo's parking lot, or one of the other hideouts we'd claimed over the years.

Home by eleven.

Rinse salt water out of hair.

Repeat.

This was why I was trying hard not to yawn as I pedaled down Highway 80. I was headed for the bonfire on the South Shore.

That's right, the *annual* bonfire that kicked off the Dune Island summer, year after year after year.

One thing that kept me alert was the caravan of summer people driving their groaning vans and SUVs just a little too weavily down the highway. I don't know if it was the blazing, so-gorgeous-it-hurt sunset that was distracting them or my gold beach cruiser with the giant bundle of sticks bungeed to the basket. Either way, I was relieved when I swooped off the road and onto the boardwalk.

I tapped my kickstand down and had just started to unhook my pack of firewood when I heard Caroline's throaty voice coming at me from down the boardwalk. I turned with a smile.

But when I saw that Caroline was with Sam—and they were holding hands—I couldn't help but feel shocked for a moment.

In the next instant, of course, I remembered—this was our new normal. Sam and Caroline were no longer just my best friends. They were each other's soul mate.

As of two Saturdays earlier, that was.

I don't know why I was still weirded out by the fact that Sam and Caroline had gotten together that night. Or why I cringed whenever they gazed into each other's eyes or held hands. (Thankfully, I hadn't seen them kissing. Yet.)

Because the Sam-and-Caroline thing? It was really no surprise at all. There'd always been this *thing* between them ever since Sam moved to the island at age eight and settled into my and Caroline's friendship as easily as a scoop of ice cream nests in a cone.

We even joked about it. When Sam made fun of Caroline's raspy voice and she teased him about his gangly height; when she goosed him in the ribs and he pulled her long, white-blond ponytail, I'd roll my eyes and say, "Guys! Get a room."

Both of them would recoil in horror.

"Oh gross, Anna!" Caroline would say, sputtering and laughing all at once.

Inevitably, Sam would respond with another ponytail tug, Caroline would retaliate with a tickle, and the whole song and dance of denial would start all over again.

But now it had actually happened. Sam and Caroline had become a Couple. And I was realizing that I'd kind of *liked* the denial.

Now I felt like I was hovering outside a magical bubble—a shiny, blissed-out world that I just didn't get. Sam and Caroline were inside the bubble. Together.

Soon after they'd first kissed, both of them had assured me that nothing would change in our friendship, which, of course, had changed everything.

Still, Sam and Caroline were sweetly worried about my third-wheel self. And they were clearly giddy over their fresh-hatched love. So I was trying to be supportive. Which meant quickly hoisting my smile back up at the sight of them looking all cute and coupley on the boardwalk.

I eyed their empty hands (the ones that weren't clasped tightly together, that was) and raised one eyebrow.

"Don't tell me you didn't bring firewood," I complained. "I hate being the only one who did her homework."

"Naw," Sam said in his slow surfer-boy drawl. "We already piled it on the beach. The fire's going to be huge this year!"

"We were collecting wood all afternoon," Caroline said sunnily.

I couldn't help it, my smile faded a bit.

I guess this is how it's going to be, I thought. Sam and Caroline collecting firewood is now Sam and Caroline On a Date—third wheel not invited.

Caroline caught my disappointment. Of course she did. Ever since The Kiss, she'd been giving me lots of long, searching looks to make sure I was okay with everything. I was starting to feel like a fish in a bowl.

"We would have called you," she stammered, "but didn't you have sib duty today?"

She was right. I did have to go to my little sister's end-of-the-year ballet recital.

So why did I feel this little twinge of hurt? I'd had countless sleepovers with Caroline that didn't, obviously, include Sam. And Sam and I had a regular ritual of going to The Swamp for giant buckets of crawfish that were strictly boycotted by Caroline. The girl pretty much lived on fruit, nuts and seeds, and supersweet iced tea.

But ever since Sam and Caroline had gotten together, a kernel of insecurity had been burrowing into the back of my head. All I wanted to do was shake it off. But like an especially stubborn sandbur, it wasn't budging.

This is stupid, I scolded myself. *All that matters is that Sam and Caroline still love me and I love them.*

Just not, the whiny voice in my head couldn't help adding, *the mysterious way they love each other.*

I sighed the tiniest of sighs. But then my friends released each other's hands and Sam plucked the firewood bundle out of my arms. He hopped lightly from the boardwalk onto the sand and headed south. Caroline hooked her arm through mine and we followed him. I ordered myself to stop obsessing and just be normal; just be with my friends.

"Cyrus is already *so* drunk," Caroline said with a hearty laugh and an eye roll. "We have a pool going on how early he's going to pass out in the dune grass."

I pulled back in alarm.

"There's beer here?" I asked. "That's, um, not good."

The bonfire was not more than a quarter mile down the beach from The Scoop, where my mom was working the post-dinner rush. And when you make the most to-die-for ice cream on a small island, everybody's your best friend. Which meant, if there was a keg at this party, it would take approximately seventeen seconds for the information to get to my mom.

Luckily, Caroline shook her head.

"No, the party's dry," she assured me. "Cyrus raided his dad's beer cooler before he got here. What an idiot."

Down the beach, just about everybody from our tiny high school was tossing sticks and bits of driftwood onto a steadily growing pyramid. By now, the sun had been swallowed up by the horizon, leaving an indigo sky with brushstrokes of fire around its edges. Against the deep blue glow, my friends looked like Chinese shadow puppets. All I could see were the shapes of skinny, shirtless boys loping about and girls with long hair fanning out as they spun to music that played, distant and tinny, from a small speaker.

But even in silhouette I could recognize many of the people. I spotted Eve Sachman's sproingy halo of curls and Jackson Tate's hammy football player's arms. It was easy to spot impossibly tall Sam. He tossed my firewood on top of the pyre, then waved off the laughter that erupted when most of the sticks tumbled right back down into the sand.

I laughed too, and expected the same from Caroline. She was one of those girls who laughed—no, *guffawed*—constantly.

But now she was silent. So silent, I could swear she was holding her breath. And even in the dusky light, I could see that her heart-shaped face was lit up. Her eyes literally danced and her lips seemed to be wavering between a pucker and a secret smile.

I looked away quickly and gazed at the waves. The moon was getting brighter now, its reflection shimmering in each wave as it curled and crashed. I zoned out for a moment on the sizzle of the surf and the ocean's calming inhale and exhale.

But before I could get really zen, I felt an *umph* in my middle, and then I was airborne.

Landon Smith had thrown his arms around my waist, scooped me up, and was now running toward the waves.

If I hadn't been so busy kicking and screaming, I would have shaken my head and sighed.

This is what happens when you're five feet one inch with, as my grandma puts it, "the bones of a sparrow." People are always patting you on the head, marveling at your size 5 feet, and hoisting you up in the air. My mom, who is all of five feet two and a half, says I might grow a little more, but I'm not betting on it.

Landon stopped short of tossing me full-on into the surf. He just plunked me knee-deep into the waves. Since I was wearing short denim cutoffs and (of course) no shoes, this was a bit of an anticlimax. I looked around awkwardly. Was I supposed to shriek and slap at Landon in that cute, flirty way that so many girls do? I hoped not, because that wasn't going to happen. After a lifetime of tininess, I was allergic to being cute.

I'm not saying I cut my hair with a bowl or anything. I'd actually taken a little extra care with my look for the bonfire. Over my favorite dark cutoffs, I was wearing a white camisole with a spray of fluttery gauze flowers at the neckline. I'd blown out my long, blond-streaked brown hair instead of letting it go wavy and wild the way I usually did. I'd put dark brown mascara on my sun-bleached lashes. And instead of my plain old gold hoop earrings, I was wearing delicate aqua glass dangles that brightened up my slate-blue eyes. (Or so my sister Sophie had told me. She's fourteen and reads fashion sites like some people read the Bible, searching for the answers to all of life's problems.)

While Landon laughed and galloped doggily back onto the dry sand, I said, "Har, har."

But instead of sounding light and breezy, as I'd intended, it came out hard and humorless. Maybe because I was just realizing that Landon's shoulder had gouged me beneath the ribs, leaving a throbbing, bruised feeling. And because everyone was staring at me, their smiles fading just a bit.

I felt heat rush to my face. I wanted to turn back toward the ocean, to breathe in the cloudy, dark blue scent of it and let salt mist my cheeks.

But that would only make everyone think I was *really* annoyed, or worse, fighting back tears.

Which I *wasn't*.

What I was feeling was tired. Not literally. That afternoon I'd downed half a pint of my latest invention, dark chocolate ice cream with espresso beans and creamless Oreo cookies. (I *might* have eaten the cream from the cookies as well.) My brain was buzzing with caffeine and sugar.

But my soul? It was sighing at the prospect of another familiar bonfire. Another same old summer. A whole new round of nothing new.

Except for this restlessness, I thought with a frown.

That *was* new. I was almost sure I hadn't felt this way the previous summer. I remembered being giddy about getting my learner's permit. I dreamed up my very first ice cream flavors, and some of them were even pretty tasty. I graduated from an A cup to a B cup. (I'm pretty sure all growth in that area has halted as well.) And I was thrilled to have three months to bum around with Sam and Caroline. The things we'd always done—hunting for ghost crabs and digging up clams with our toes, eating shaved ice until our lips turned blue, seeing how many people could nap in one hammock at once—had still felt fresh.

But this summer already felt like day-old bread.

I shook my head again and remembered one of those first ice cream flavors: Rummy Bread Pudding.

If I'd turned stale bread into magic once, I could do it again, right?

It was this bit of inner chipperness that finally made me laugh out loud.

Because me channeling Mary Poppins was about as realistic as Caroline singing opera. And life was not ice cream.

Who was I kidding? Nothing was going to change. Not for the next three months, anyway. On Dune Island, summer was the only season that mattered, and this summer, just like all the others, I wasn't going anywhere.

After the bonfire was lit, I rallied, of course. It's hard to be too moody when people are skewering anything from turkey legs to Twinkies and roasting them on a fire the size of a truck.

I'd already toasted up a large handful of marshmallows and was contemplating the wisdom of a fire-roasted Snickers bar when Caroline trotted up to me. Sam was right behind her, of course. Since Caroline didn't like anything that tasted of smoke, she was just drinking this year's Official Bonfire Cocktail: a blueberry-pomegranate slushie garnished with burgundy cherries.

"This was a terrible idea," Caroline said, taking a giant sip of her drink. "Everybody's teeth are turning purple. But *mmmm*, it's so yummy, I can't stop."

She slurped noisily on her straw.

"Real attractive, Caroline," Sam joked. But from the uncharacteristic lilt in his monotone, I could tell he wasn't joking. He really *was* swooning.

Caroline responded by taking another slurp of her slushie, this one so loud it almost drowned out the crackling of the fire.

I threw back my head and laughed.

And then—because what did I care if I had purple teeth in this crowd?—I reached for her plastic cup to steal a sip of the slushie.

"Get your own, Anna!" Caroline teased. Holding her cup above her head, she shuffled backward in the sand, then turned and darted into the surf.

Laughing again, I ran after her, kicking a spray of water at her back. Caroline scurried back up to Sam, still cackling. She threw her free arm around Sam's waist and nestled against him. He slung a long arm around her shoulders. It was such a smooth, natural motion, you'd think they'd been snuggling like that all their lives.

I didn't want them to know that their PDA was making me regret all those marshmallows, so I grinned, waved—and turned my gaze away.

And that's when I saw him.

Will.

Of course, I didn't know his name yet.

At that moment, actually, I didn't know much of anything. I suddenly forgot about SamAndCaroline. And the too-sweet marshmallow taste in my mouth. And the fact that you don't— you just don't—openly stare at a boy only fifteen yards away, letting long seconds, maybe even minutes, pass while you feast your eyes upon him.

But I couldn't help it. It was like I forgot I had a body. There was no swiping away the long strands of hair that had blown into my face. I didn't worry about what to do with my hands. I didn't cock my hip, scuff my feet in the sand, or make any of my other standard nervous motions.

There were just my eyes and this boy.

His hands were stuffed deep into the pockets of well-worn khakis, which were carelessly rolled up to expose his nicely muscled calves.

His hair—I'm pretty sure it was a chocolaty brown, though it was hard to tell in the shadowy night light—had perfect waves that fluttered in the breeze.

His skin looked a bit pale; hungry for sun. Obviously, he was a summer guy, though (thank God) he wasn't wearing shoes on the beach. And he didn't have that "isn't this all so quaint?" vibe that some vacationers exuded.

Instead, he simply looked comfortable in his skin, washed-out though it might have been. He shot a casual glance at the party milling around the bonfire, then looked down at his feet.

He did that thing you do when you're a summer person getting your first delicious taste of the beach. He dug his toes into the sand, kicked a bit at the surf, then crouched down and let the water fizz through his fingers.

He stared at his glistening hand for a moment, as if he was thinking hard about something. Then he looked up—and straight at me.

I wish I could say that I smiled at him. Or gave him a look that struck the perfect balance between curious and cool.

But since I was still floating somewhere outside my body, it's entirely possible that my mouth dropped open and I just kept on *staring* at him.

It's not that he had the face of a god or anything. At first glance, I didn't even think of him as beautiful.

But the squinty softness of his big, dark eyes, the strong angle of his jaw, a nose that stopped just short of being too thin, that swoop of tousled hair, and the bit of melancholy around his mouth—it all made me feel something like déjà vu.

It was like his was the face I'd always been looking for. It was foreign *and* familiar, both in the best way.

Looking at this boy's face made me feel, not that famous jolt of electricity, but something more like an expansion. Like this oh-so-finite Dune Island beach, which I knew so well, had suddenly turned huge. Endless. Full of possibility.

"Who's the shoobee?"

Caroline's voice brought me back with a thud. I must have been holding my breath, because it whooshed out of me.

I closed my eyes, then turned around. When I opened them,

I was looking at my friend. But I wasn't really seeing her. I was feeling the boy's gaze. It was still on me, I was sure of it.

"He's . . . he's not wearing shoes," I pointed out to Caroline. "Which means he's not a shoobee. Not technically."

Caroline shrugged and peered over my shoulder at him. I was dying—*dying*—to turn around and look too, but I bit my lip and made myself stay put.

"He's kind of hot, for a short guy," Caroline said idly.

"He's not short," I huffed.

"Hmm, maybe five nine," Caroline allowed. "Of course, compared to you, *everybody's* tall."

"And compared to Sam," I reminded her, "everybody's short."

"Maybe that's it," Caroline said with a giggle.

I gaped. Caroline did *not* giggle. She cackled. She brayed. Was *this* what love did to a girl?

Caroline's eyes widened slowly. Was she wondering the same thing?

If so, she didn't let on. Instead, her focus returned to the mysterious boy down the beach.

"You should go talk to him," she said.

"No!" That's when my heart actually did leap into my throat. But it wasn't a love-at-first-sight thing. It was abject terror.

Which Caroline didn't notice at all.

"Look, this is totally low-risk," she said. "I saw him checking you out, so he's probably interested. And if he isn't, or if you screw it up, well, he leaves at the end of the week and you can forget all about him."

"Thanks for the vote of confidence," I said dryly. "But have you considered the other possibility? That he doesn't leave until the end of the *summer*? And I run into him everywhere I go, my humiliation festering like an infected wound?"

"There is that," Caroline agreed with a laugh. I was happy to hear that she'd gone back to the bray. "Or . . . it could go really well."

Could it? As Caroline danced back to the fire, I glanced the boy's way again. He was sitting on the ground now. Clearly, he didn't care at all if he got those nicely threadbare khakis wet or gritty. His bare heels were dug into the sand. His forearms rested on his bent knees. They looked strong and a little ropey and were completely mesmerizing. To me, at least.

The boy was gazing out at the ocean. I didn't get the sense that he was itching to join the bonfire. Or, for that matter, that he was burning to talk to me.

At least, that's what I thought until I saw him sneak another glance in my direction.

Before I could look away, he caught my gaze. And then *neither* of us could look away.

Instantly, I felt like I *had* to know what color his eyes were.

I wanted to hear what his voice sounded like.

I needed to know his name.

Caroline was right. I really had no choice.

I was going to talk to him.

Unless I had a heart attack as I walked across the sand, I was going to talk to him.

One of my feet inched forward as if it were testing to make sure the sand hadn't magically turned quick, ready to suck me under.

I took another, slightly bigger, step.

The boy got to his feet.

The sadness that had been dragging at the corners of his mouth and eyes was gone. He was starting to smi—

"Will!"

The boy turned away. He squinted beyond the fire at a woman on the deck of one of the beach's smaller cottages. Even from this distance, I could see the weary sag in her shoulders.

"Will," she called again, "can you come back in? We've got three big suitcases left to unpack and I just can't face them."

The boy—Will—paused for a moment.

And then, without another glance at me, he began to tromp across the beach to the house. His mom had gone back inside to what sure sounded like a whole summer's worth of unpacking.

I stood there watching him go. Now I felt like a speck on this newly big beach, as invisible as one of the ghost crabs that darted around the sand waving their ineffectual little claws.

But then everything changed again.

When Will had almost reached the rickety little bridge that connected the beach to his cottage's deck, I got the second of the summer's many surprises.

He turned around and looked right back at me. He shrugged and smiled, a rueful, crooked *what're you gonna do?* smile.

Then he lifted his arm in a loose half wave. His smile widened before he turned and jumped gracefully onto the bridge. He crossed it with long, almost-bouncing strides.

Maybe that was just the way he always walked, I thought as I watched him bound away.

Or maybe, just maybe, *I* was the spring in his step. Maybe he'd seen something in *my* face that was foreignly familiar too.

In the coming days, I'd kick myself for just *standing* there as Will waved at me, too dumbstruck to wave back or even smile.

I'd play out different running-into-Will scenes in my head. It would happen back on the beach or in the nickel-candy aisle at Angelo's or under the North Shore pier.

I'd think of his name, Will, and wonder if it was going to move to the tip of my tongue.

So what if it wasn't fireworks the first time I saw Will? Fireworks are all pow and wow and then—nothing. Nothing except black ash dusting the waves.

But me and Will? I thought we could be something. If I was lucky. If he'd seen the same spark in my eyes that I'd seen in his. If, somehow, this summer was going to be different from all the others.

The possibility of that was much better than fireworks.

"Has *any*one seen my wrap?" I'd just stalked into the screened porch that covers the entire front of our house. My parents and sisters, Sophie and Kat, were at the long, beat-up dining table, munching buttered Belgian waffles (leftovers from The Scoop). My five-year-old brother, Benjie, was sitting on the floor feeding his breakfast to his pet tortoise.

Not one of them even glanced at me.

Sophie ignored me completely. My mom didn't seem to hear

me. Kat shrugged her shoulders. And my dad's eyes never left his smart phone as he said, "Nope!"

"Thanks for the help," I muttered.

It was Wednesday, four days after the bonfire (not that I'd been counting or anything), and I was *trying* to get ready to go to the beach. And yet I didn't seem to be getting any closer to the front door.

First, I hadn't been able to find my swimsuit top. I should have known to look for it in Kat's room. Lately, Kat, who was seven, had been obsessed with breasts. She kept stealing bras and swimsuit tops from the laundry room and trying them on.

Sure enough, I found my blue-flowered bandeau crumpled on Kat's bedroom floor. Only then did I realize that I didn't have my wrap!

And girls on Dune Island never went to the beach without their wraps. Unless they were shoobees, that was.

The summer people lugged all sorts of unwieldy stuff to the beach: folding chairs, umbrellas, voluminous beach towels, all piled on top of giant, snack-stuffed coolers on wheels.

Local girls took three things and three things only—big sports bottles of something cold and caffeinated, reading material, and our wraps.

Wraps were homemade and usually hemless, so their edges were always fraying. They were made of a light, crumply fabric that could stretch to the size of a small tarp or be wadded into your back pocket. We used them for everything. Your wrap was both beach blanket and towel. It was a sarong, a tube top, or even a long-tailed bandanna. When the noon sun got too sizzly, you could drench your wrap in water and tent it over yourself.

Every April, which was when the sun on Dune Island started to graduate from merely sultry to scorching, we all made new wraps. We wore them until they were shredded, which conveniently happened right around Labor Day.

I loved the wrap I'd made this spring. It was pumpkin orange with a white tie-dye design in the middle in the shape of a giant eye. I'd been going for a crescent moon, but when I'd gotten an eye, I'd shrugged and kept it. Sophie always dyes and re-dyes her wraps, going for perfect, but that's just too girlie-girl for me.

Sophie had *always* desired the feminine stuff I couldn't fathom—popularity, a fabulous wardrobe, boys raising their eyebrows when she walked by.

But me? I didn't know exactly *what* I wanted. Sometimes I wanted to dance and laugh with my friends until midnight, and sometimes I wanted to screen all calls and hide away with a tragic novel and a bag of candy. Sometimes I spent an hour trying to pretty myself up, and sometimes I could barely be bothered to comb the knots out of my hair before I left the house.

Sometimes I wanted to know what it felt like to tell a boy all my secrets. Other times, that seemed as impossible as waking up one morning to find myself fluent in a foreign language.

Sometimes I felt better alone than I did with people. And sometimes that just felt lonely.

It didn't seem normal to be so wishy-washy. That was a term my mom used a lot, and it always made me think of gray laundry water, swishing around and around in circles before it drained away. And as anyone can tell you, gray is the most invisible color there is.

Orange is better.

Orange is a color people notice, people like . . . Will.

And there I was, thinking about this stranger named Will *again*. I was picturing that smile, that half wave, and the way he'd looked in his khakis. It made me want get out of the house faster than ever.

It was irrational—actually, it bordered on crazy—but here's what I was thinking as I frantically searched my cluttered house for the wrap: *I'm late for The Moment.*

That's right. I was certain that somehow Will and I were supposed to meet—*really* meet—right then.

At that very instant, I was *supposed* to be on my way to the beach and Will was *supposed* to be somewhere along that way, and I was *supposed* to bump into him.

Then I'd actually, *finally*, get to talk to him and . . .

Well, I had no idea what would happen after that. Destiny? Bitter dejection? Or some vague place in between the two? *That* seemed like the worst fate of all. But at this point, I would've welcomed even a lame Will interface—say, in front of my parents or something equally mortifying—if it would just *happen* already.

But it wasn't going to happen, my newly superstitious mind was telling me now. Because while I was searching for my wrap, the magic window of time—in which a boy bumps into a girl at that perfect moment when her teeth are freshly brushed, she's wearing her favorite bikini, and she has the whole morning to herself—was closing.

I was late. I was going to miss him.

Just like I'd probably missed him the night before when I'd somehow gotten a big gob of sunscreen in my hair and had to quickly shampoo it before going out with Sam and Caroline. And the day before *that* when I'd completely forgotten about a fishing party at the southern pier and had instead spent the afternoon at home doing ice cream experiments.

Those ice creams, by the way, had all tasted wretched. Probably because the spot in my brain where deliciousness usually dwelled was filled instead with all these made-up missed connections with Will.

All this was why I was pretty darn grouchy when I began searching our cluttered screened porch for my wrap. I barely looked at the plate of fluffy waffles or the sweaty pitcher of minty iced tea on the table. I made eye contact with no one and sighed loudly as I pulled cushions off the couch and rockers, peered behind the porch swing, and even rifled through the magazine rack next to the hammock.

I could *not* find my wrap anywhere.

I almost considered leaving for the beach without it. But the thing was, when you'd low-maintenanced yourself down to a single item, you *really* needed that item.

I sighed louder. And finally my mother looked up from the Scoop accounting books. She'd been poring over them with a pained squint. (Not because business was hurting. Numbers just made my mother's head hurt. It was one of the things, besides shortness, we had in common.)

"What're you looking for, honey?" she asked, her eyes a little bleary.

"My wrap?" I said, trying to keep my voice from sounding shrill. "The wrap I asked you about fifteen minutes ago?"

Glancing up from her magazine, Sophie snorted.

"Okay, five," I allowed.

"Mmm." Mom cocked her head, thought for about half a second and said, "Pantry. Next to the bread."

Now Sophie laughed, and I heaved one more sigh, this one equal parts irritation and gratitude.

I had no doubt that the wrap would be exactly where my mother said it was. My mom is famous for random brilliance like that. Which is kind of a surprise because both my parents are—how to put this delicately?—a bit scattered. Their very existence on this island was sort of an accident. They came here from Fond du Lac, Wisconsin when my mom was pregnant with me. And then they just . . . never left.

They'd stumbled into the ice cream biz too, when a kitchen fiasco led my mom to invent The Scoop's most famous bestseller, Maple Bacon Crunch. (Trust me, it's much better than it sounds.)

My parents had added onto our house as they'd added more kids to the family, and now it kind of reminded me of Sam—a kid who'd grown too tall, too fast. With all the new nooks and crannies, our place was pretty much chaos. But it was a chaos that my mom had a mysterious mastery over.

She'd decorated with mismatched vintage wallpaper, funky estate-sale furniture, and painted floors. She'd added a fancy marble pastry counter to the kitchen, but kept the creaky, pink sixty-year-old oven. She stored everything from safety pins to sugar in old mason jars, then stashed them on random window-sills or bookshelves.

And this morning she could remember exactly where she'd spotted my wrap—but it had never occurred to her to move it to a place where I might *ever* have considered looking for it.

Like Maple Bacon Crunch ice cream, my mother's world should have been a mess, but instead it was sort of sublime. You can only imagine how annoying *that* was.

I gritted my teeth while I thanked my mother. Then I knot-ted my wrap around my waist and flew out the door.

But I'd been right about missing that Magic Moment.

Even though I took the most roundabout route possible to the North Peninsula, I didn't see Will anywhere.

So then I sped through the end of my novel, requiring a trip to the library for reinforcements. But Will wasn't there, either.

Finally I committed an act of desperation. I convinced Sam and Caroline to go to the touristy end of the boardwalk for lunch.

"Ah, Crabby's Crab Shack," Sam said sarcastically as we walked into the café. The screened-in dining room was art-fully distressed, with deliberately peeling turquoise paint, paper towel rolls on every table, and a big fish tank so crowded with pirate, mermaid, and fisherman figurines, I wondered how there was any room for the fish.

"My grandparents love this place," Sam continued. "So 'authentic.'"

"Oh, shut up," I said, looking around with shifty eyes. The tables looked way too shiny and the floorboards had been oddly swept clean of sand. "You know you love their curly fries."

"The cheesiest food *ever*," Caroline said.

She snorted so loud that all the sunburned shoobees twisted to stare at her before returning to their fried shrimp baskets. Not one of those flushed faces was Will's, I noted with a quick but thorough scan of the joint. I was both crestfallen and relieved.

If Will *was* at Crabby's Crab Shack, I wanted it to be ironically. Or because he'd been dragged there by a clueless parent. Or because he was laughing at, not with, the curly fries.

But I knew it was too much to hope that Will would understand all these requirements just a few days into his summer here. From my experience of shoobees, there was a *lot* they didn't understand about us, and vice versa.

Dune Islanders live inland in candy-colored cottages. Our houses hide like turtles' nests on twisty cul-de-sacs and overgrown dead ends off Highway 80.

The shoobees' vacation rentals on the South Shore stand on stilts above prime real estate. The houses stand shoulder to shoulder like a barricade. They face the waves, casting long shadows behind them.

When inlanders cross the highway to go to work in bike rental shops, boardwalk bars, beachmarts, and sno-cone stands, we don't see the ocean. Our view is of the summer people's trash cans.

Okay, that sounds a little dramatic. It's not like shoobees and inlanders are Sharks and Jets, staging rumbles on the beach. It's just that we live in separate worlds. They're on one side of the cash register, and we're on the other.

"If you're so desperate for Crabby's," Sam said after we'd settled into a table that smelled of cleaning solution and fish, "does that mean you're paying, Anna?"

"I'm not *desperate*," I said, glancing through the screen at the boardwalk. "I just need a change. I've eaten at Angelo's for the past four days."

"Yeah," Sam said with a grin. "The same fried shrimp you can get on the other side of the island, but for five bucks more? That *is* a refreshing change."

I would have responded with a crack of my own, but I was distracted by the faces passing by outside the screen. *Not Will, not Will, definitely not Will, two more not-Wills* . . .

"Hey, who are you looking for?" Sam blurted, jolting me back to our table. "Is it Landon Smith?"

"Landon Smith?" I said. My voice was as flat as an algae-covered pond.

"Landon Smith!" Sam said. "Hello?"

"Sam thinks he likes you," Caroline said. She glanced at Sam. He glanced back. His eyes crinkled into a secret smile, and her lips pursed into a gossipy grin. Clearly they'd already discussed the possibility of a romance between me and—

"Landon Smith?" I said with a little laugh. "I don't *think* so."

"The guy made a clear gesture at the bonfire," Sam insisted. I laughed again.

"Oh, would that have been this gesture?" I asked, swinging

my arms around like an ape. "I guess I didn't realize that was a declaration of like."

"Duh," Sam said.

"Maybe he should have made himself more clear," Caroline suggested, grinning at me. "He could have dumped a smoothie over your head."

"Or *broken* some of my ribs," I suggested with my own grin, "instead of just bruising them. Swoon!"

I clasped my hands under my chin and fluttered my eyelashes.

"I'm just saying," Sam said, "you should think about Landon. The guy digs you. I can tell."

But the preposterous idea of me-and-Landon evaporated from my mind almost immediately. As Sam and Caroline started chatting about something else, my gaze drifted back to the boardwalk and its seeming flood of not-Wills.

I'd been so sure that he'd "dug" me that night at the bonfire. But now, after days of not running into him on this very small island, I was starting to think that perhaps I just wasn't meant to see him again. Maybe Will's sweet smile and cute shrug had meant nothing, and the spark I'd seen in his eyes had just been a reflection of the dancing fire. Maybe the beach was the same size as always.

I decided right then that it was time to give up on this boy named Will. We didn't have a destiny together. We didn't have some Magic Moment.

Coming to this decision in Crabby's Crab Shack, across the table from my mad-in-love best friends, was so depressing that I ended up ordering an extra-large curly fries from the waitress in the pirate hat. *And* a fried shrimp basket with cocktail sauce. So when I stumbled into work at The Scoop after lunch, I had greasy skin and clothes that smelled like fried fish, not to mention a stomachache. After two hours of ice cream scooping, I was also sticky and sweaty, with my hair pulled back in a sloppy bun and an apron smeared with hot fudge.

So of course *that* was the moment—during the lull between the afternoon-snack crowd and the ice-cream-for-dinner crowd—that Will walked through the door.

Will was with another boy, who was the same height as him but with lighter hair, broader shoulders, and lots of freckles. Still, he was clearly Will's brother. They had the exact same pointy chin and the same squinty eyes. But Will, it had to be said, was much cuter.

I'd been right about Will's eyes. They were brown, but a much darker, richer, prettier brown than I could ever have imagined.

Will's brother didn't even notice me. Like most customers, he went straight for the glass cases, peering down at the tubs of Mexican Chocolate, Grapefruit Mint sorbet, and Buttertoe (a Butterfinger bar smashed into vanilla ice cream with some toasted coconut thrown in). I think he might have asked me if I preferred the Salted Caramel to the Pecan Praline. And I might have mumbled a reply.

But I'm pretty sure I just stared at Will and thought two things: (1) *It's him!* And (2) *Oh, crap!*

Will had clearly spent the day on the beach. He was wearing faded red swim trunks and a worn-to-almost-transparent gray T-shirt. I wanted to reach over the ice cream case and touch it. Luckily, that would have involved some not-terribly-subtle climbing up on the counter, so it wasn't too hard to restrain myself.

There was also the fact that as good as Will looked, that's how gross I felt.

Maybe, I thought with a mixture of hope and dread, *he won't even recognize me, with my hair up and ice cream toppings all over my apron. For all I know, I've got Marshmallow Fluff on my face.*

A quick swipe at my sweaty forehead came away Fluff free, but it was small comfort.

I glanced at my dad, who was sitting on a tall stool behind the cash register, his nose buried in a copy of *Time* magazine. I could only hope he'd stay this oblivious until Will left.

I managed to eke out a panicked smile at Will, then quickly spun around and pretended to attend to the chrome hot-fudge warmer. In actuality, I was peering at my distorted reflection in the silver cube. My face was supershiny. I grabbed a paper towel, blotted surreptitiously, then tucked a few errant strands of hair behind my ears. I would have loved to pull my hair out of its rubber band and whisk off my chocolaty apron, too. But that would have been ridiculously obvious, so I just took a breath and tried to recapture the feeling I'd had after my lunch with Sam and Caroline, when I'd written Will off and resigned myself to a summer without him.

A summer alone.

And yes, what I'd felt was sort of empty. Maybe even a little tragic.

But I hadn't curled up and died or anything. I'd survived.

So what did it matter that Will was here, and that he was likely to take one look at me and try to forget he'd ever smiled at me? (That was, if he even recognized me.) Since I'd already lost him, the stakes couldn't have been lower, right?

Then why was my face feeling hot (and probably getting even pinker and shinier)? And why was I having trouble getting enough oxygen into my lungs to make my brain work correctly?

Luckily, I could scoop ice cream in my sleep, so when Will's brother finally decided on a sugar cone full of Sticky Toffee Pudding Pop, I was able to dish it up without any disasters.

But then I had to look at Will.

I mean, he was the next customer in line. I had no choice.

Unlike his brother, Will wasn't studying ice cream flavors. Or searching for an open booth or admiring the hundred vintage ice cream scoops that dangled from the ceiling.

He was looking *right at me*.

His eyes were a little wide. And his hands were suddenly digging deep into his pockets, sending his shoulders up to his ears.

Oh yeah, he remembered me all right.

But I had no idea if this was a good or a bad thing.

"Um . . . ," I croaked out. "Ice cream?"

I gestured with my scoop at the bank of ice cream cases. You know, just in case he hadn't noticed the two tons of electronic equipment that stood between us, humming loudly.

"I . . ." Will's voice was on the froggy side, too.

Wait a minute. Was Will as tongue-tied as I was?

"I'm not really into sweets," Will said. "He is."

He glanced over at his brother with a shrug. The broader, blonder version of Will, meanwhile, was kind of moaning his way through his ice cream. Clearly, he was the sugar fiend in the family.

"I can't believe you don't want some of this," he said to Will with his mouth full. "It's the best stuff."

"Yeah, it is! My daughter invented that flavor!"

I froze. Was that actually my *dad* inserting himself into the most awful, yet potentially fabulous, moment of my life?

"Um . . . ?" I squeaked.

Dad had shoved his reading glasses up so they rested on top of his endless forehead. He was pointing his rolled-up *Time* at Will's brother's ice cream cone.

"Sticky Toffee Pudding Pop, right?" Dad said. "That's Anna's!"

Now he was pointing the magazine at me—at a shocked and mortified me.

"My daughter," Dad went on, getting off his stool, "is an ice cream genius."

He grabbed a tiny sample spoon, scooped up a little chunk of Pineapple Ginger Ale gelato, and thrust it over the counter at Will.

"Try it," he ordered Will.

"Dad, he just said he doesn't like sweets," I said. My voice sounded reedy, as if my throat had completely closed up. Because it had.

But Will gave a little smile as he took the spoon from my dad and popped the ice cream sample into his mouth.

I cringed. I assumed my dad had chosen Pineapple Ginger Ale because it was *his* favorite. I had to admit, it was one of my favorites too. When I'd come up with it a few months earlier, it had emerged from the churn both spicy and subtle, bubbly and sophisticated. It had been the first time that I'd felt like an alchemist in the kitchen, instead of just someone who messed around with cream and sugar, hoping for a happy accident.

Still, Pineapple Ginger Ale definitely wasn't for everyone. I wished my dad had picked something easier to love, like Peanut Butter Crisp or Mud Pie.

I watched Will's face as the ice cream melted in his mouth. His dark eyebrows shot upward. The corners of his mouth slowly lifted into a surprised, and very satisfied, smile.

He looked at me and said, "I'll have a double."

I bit my lip and looked down at my feet, trying to keep a dorky grin from erupting on my face. I failed completely, of course. But hopefully Will didn't see me beaming as I ducked into the ice cream case and dished up his two scoops. I hovered in the case for a moment, my eyes closed, feeling a cloud of sugar-scented coldness billow over my hot cheeks. It felt wonderful.

But it couldn't compare to the knowledge that Will loved my ice cream.

Or, I realized, he *didn't*, but had ordered it to be polite. Which you would do only if you really cared what the creator of that ice cream thought of you!

Either scenario seemed shockingly promising.

I carefully stacked Will's scoops into a deep brown waffle cone.

"It's a gingerbread cone," I explained as I handed it to him. "It really brings out the zing in the ice cream."

Will smiled at me for two beats too long, as if he didn't know what to say but wanted to say *something*.

I wanted to say something too. I felt my head buzz as I searched for the perfect witticism.

"I just don't understand people who don't like sugar," I blurted. "I'm obsessed with it."

Um, *what* was that?

I so badly wanted to bite my words back, I think I might have clacked my teeth together.

Of course, I couldn't take the words back. So for the next minute or so, I squirmed because I'd basically just called Will a sugar-hating freak. And Will took galumphing bites of his ice cream, probably thinking that the sooner he finished the stuff, the sooner he could get out of The Scoop and never come back.

We were saved from all this awkwardness by Will's brother, who spoke up once again as he paid my dad for the two cones. I liked that guy already.

"I know, right?" he said to me. "*How* does anyone not like sweets? Of course, you've never seen anyone more obsessed with salt than Will. He used to buy those giant soft pretzels on the street and cover them with mustard. Then he'd lick the mustard off, along with all the rock salt, and throw the pretzel part away.

It was like nails on a chalkboard listening to him crunch that salt between his teeth."

This made Will stop eating. His mouth dropped open and he gave his brother one of those *how am I related to you?* looks. I knew that look well.

I glanced at my dad, who was now cleaning out the milkshake machine, his *Time* open on the counter next to the sink so he could read and (messily) work at the same time.

Well, Will and I already have something in common, I thought, feeling shaky and exhilarated at the same time. *Familial humiliation.*

Will returned his gaze to me.

"We're from New York," he explained. "There's a lot of street food there."

"I know," I said quickly. "I love New York."

Which was true. I *had* absolutely loved New York during the three days my family had vacationed there when I was twelve. I'd loved it so much that my daydreams about my future self were almost all set there. I always pictured myself—taller and with shorter hair—striding down those impossibly busy streets. I carried a cute little short-handled purse under my arm and often ducked into one of those subway stairwells with the wrought-iron railings and the globes that glowed green or red.

What this future self was doing in New York, and how she would get there, was a mystery. More than that, really. It seemed just as fantastical as, say, becoming magic. People in movies and books did it *all* the time, but in real life? It just didn't happen. Likewise, it didn't seem possible that a girl who'd lived her entire life on a nine-mile-long island could end up in New York City.

"I never had a pretzel when I was in New York," I told Will. "But I remember having a knish from a street cart. It was delicious."

Suddenly, Will's mouth started twitching. He looked like his was trying mightily to suppress a laugh.

His brother didn't even try, though. He guffawed.

"It's *kuh-nish*," he said, correcting me. "Not *nish*."

"Oh . . . ," I choked out.

Will gave his head a little shake, then took a few more enormous bites of ice cream. The silence between us grew awkward. And *more* awkward, until . . .

"Did you know," Will blurted, making me jump, "that if you leave your beach towel on the sand at seven p.m., it'll pretty much be sucked out to sea the minute you turn your back?"

I shrugged and said, "Well, yeah. This time of year, that's right before high tide."

"High tide," Will said with a shy smile. "I always thought that was just a saying."

I was floored. Not only was Will (probably) choking his way through my ice cream just to be nice, but he'd admitted to flubbing something as basic as the tide.

Or, I supposed, as basic as the pronunciation of "knish."

And even though it's much cooler to be a big-city guy who's ignorant about Dune Island than a backwater babe for whom Manhattan is practically Mars, I decided that we were even.

So now I didn't even try to hide my smile from Will. I just laid one on him. A big, toothy smile.

Will returned the smile, and instantly, I was back at one end of that wire-thin connection I'd sensed between us. I was feeling the glow of the bonfire all over again.

And I wasn't just *wishing* I could hear Will's voice or see his eyes up close. I was listening and seeing—and feeling so floaty, I was a little embarrassed.

Until Will's brother broke the spell by grabbing Will's waffle cone.

"You're dripping," he said, helping Will out by taking several large bites around the base of the scoop.

"Gross, Owen," Will said, snatching the cone back.

Will's brother looked bewildered for a moment, then glanced at me. His eyebrows shot up and he murmured, "Ohhhhh."

Then he leaned over and whispered—good and loud—in Will's ear, "So *that's* the girl from the bonfire. I think the dad said her name is Anna."

"Shut *up*," Will hissed.

Owen just gave a little laugh, then strolled over to the bulletin board by the front door and peered at the rental flyers, lost cat photos, and join-my-band pleas.

Will avoided my eyes until his ice cream started dripping again and he had to scramble for a napkin from the box on top of the freezer case. I tried to make myself busy until he spoke again.

"That bonfire the other night," he said, "was it fun?"

"Oh, yeah." I shrugged. "I guess."

"So those people were . . ."

". . . pretty much everyone in my school," I said. "It was an end-of-the-year thing."

"Yeah . . . " Will said, trailing off. "And then where does everybody go? For the summer?"

I opened my arms and gestured to my right and left. Since The Scoop was smack-dab in the center of the boardwalk, there were cafés and candy shops, surf shops and beachmarts on either side of us. I probably knew a kid who worked in every one of the boardwalk's stores.

"Oh, yeah, I should have known that," Will said. "We usually stay home for the summer too. Other people go to the Hamptons or the Catskills or places like that, but we just stay in the city and sizzle. It's actually kind of fun. New York just empties out every August."

I didn't tell Will that *I* had been in New York in August—and thought I'd never seen so many people smashed into one place.

"So . . . ," Will said after popping the soggy end of his cone into his mouth. "I guess you're going to the thing tonight?"

"The . . . thing?" I was confused. Sam had said something about folks going to The Swamp to watch a Braves game later. But how did Will know about . . .

"The Movie on the Beach?" Will asked. "I think it's *Raiders of the Lost Ark*."

"Oh, *that*," I said. "That's a shoob—"

I caught myself, then said diplomatically, "That's the first movie of the summer. They happen every other week."

"Pretty cool," Will said, ignoring my squirming. "Where do they put the screen?"

"It's kind of funny," I said, leaning against the ice cream case.

"The guy who does it is a movie nut. He's the dad of someone I go to school with. And every year he tries a different screen placement. Once he put it on the pier, but the sound of the waves on the wood drowned out the movie. Then he put the screen on these poles literally in the water. But the wind kept blowing it down, you know, like a sail? So he had to cut these little semicircles all over the screen to let the air through. Ever since, the people in the movies looked like they had terrible skin or black things hanging out of their noses, or . . ."

I stopped myself. Once again I was putting my foot in my mouth, making fun of something that Will obviously thought was cool. He had no idea that my friends and I only went to Movies on the Beach when there was *absolutely* nothing better to do.

And when we went, we laughed at the holey screen, or drifted into loud, jokey conversation halfway through the movie, ignoring the glares and shushes of the summer people who found the whole scene so enchanting.

I could tell Will could see the lame alert on my face.

"So I guess you have something else going on tonight, then?" he broached.

I caught my breath. Had he just been about to ask me to the movie? And had I just completely blown it by being snarky?

Once again I became painfully aware of my father, who'd finished cleaning the milk-shake blender. Now he was loading a fresh tub of Jittery Joe into the ice cream case just to the left of me. He was so close I could feel a gust of cold air from the freezer. The blond down on my arm popped up in instant goose bumps, which only added to the shivery way I was feeling as I talked to Will.

"Um, well, my friends are kind of having a thing . . . ," I said weakly.

"Yeah, that's cool . . . ," Will said, stuffing his hands back in his pockets. "I heard about a party going on tonight, too, actually. It'd be funny if it was the same one."

I was incredulous. And hopeful.

"At The Swamp?" I asked—at the exact moment that Will said, "At the Beach Club pool."

"Oh," I said, deflating a bit.

Of *course*, Will hadn't heard of The Swamp. The dark little bar and grill, surrounded by an alligator moat, was hidden in a mosquitoey thicket off Highway 80. It had no sign, just a break in the kudzu and a gravel driveway. The only shoobees who ever found it were Lonely Planet types who tromped in with giant backpacks and paid for their boiled peanuts and hush puppies with fistfuls of crumpled dollar bills.

And the only locals who went to the Beach Club were the retirees who lived on the South Shore year-round. Mostly the Beach Club was filled with summer people from Atlanta who wanted to hang out with their country club friends—in a different country club.

Suddenly, it became clear that almost everything about The Moment was going *badly*. I was a muscle twitch away from just hustling Will out the door with a chipper, *Have fun tonight. Maybe I'll see you the next time you want some Pineapple Ginger Ale. Unless, of course, you hated it* and *you think I'm drippier than your ice cream cone! Ta!*

But before I had a chance, Will stepped closer to the ice

cream case. He rested a hand on top of it in a way that was probably supposed to look casual. The only problem with that was Will's hand was knotted into a white-knuckled fist.

I felt a prickly wave of heat wash over my face. He was about to say something. Something that mattered. I would have sworn on it.

"Why don't you come with me to the party?" Will blurted.

"Or to the movie, if you want," he added quickly. "But at a movie, you can't really talk. And it'd be kind of . . . nice. To talk. I mean, if you want to . . . and you don't mind ditching the, um, swamp?"

Then *I* was hanging onto the ice cream case for dear life, too. I felt another head-rushy wave, but it didn't feel at all bad.

Even so, I wasn't sure at first what I should say. As cheesy went, Movie on the Beach was a stack of American slices—so bad it was kind of good. But a party at the Beach Club pool was more like stinky French cheese—you could swallow it, but only if you held your nose. I definitely would have preferred pockmarked Harrison Ford to the fusty air-conditioning, horrid wallpaper, and uniformed "staff" of the Beach Club.

But Will wanted to *talk*.

Fuzzy though my mind was at that moment, my gut told me this was a good thing.

It was such a good thing that I sort of wanted to start the conversation right there. That very minute. But one sideways glance reminded me that my dad was still there, fumbling around the cash register and *so* obviously eavesdropping on me as a boy asked me out for the very first time.

And then there was Will's brother, Owen. He was still

stationed at the bulletin board but had his head cocked in such a way that it was *just* as obvious that he was listening in too.

And *then*, the wind chime on the screen door tinkled as a quartet of locals—most of whom I knew of course—came in for their sugar fix.

I had to make a decision and I had to make it immediately.

So I said yes to the Beach Club pool party. To a night of eating bad hors d'ouevres among an army of shoobees . . . and to a date with Will.

"Meet you there at eight?" I proposed.

Will grinned and nodded. Then grinned some more and nodded again until finally Owen came over and grabbed his arm, muttering, "I'm gonna save you from yourself, here, mm-kay? Let's go."

They left so fast, I barely had time to squeak out a "See you later." I was too floored to form complete sentences anyway.

After that, I nodded my way through four ice cream orders before I realized I hadn't heard a word the customers had said. After I asked them to repeat themselves, I got half the orders wrong anyway. But I didn't really care. How could I when all my hopes and dreams (at least, all my hopes and dreams of the past four days) had come true?

Will and I had had our Moment. Our weird, awkward, yet somehow amazing, Moment. It hadn't been destiny, but it *had* made me excited about going to the Beach Club of all places. So maybe it actually *had* been magic.

Time, I thought, looking anxiously at the clock over the screen door, would tell.

$\mathcal{I}$ had an hour and a half left in my shift. If I'd been keeping a log, here's how it would have read:

5:05: Went to the walk-in cooler and called Caroline to tell her I had a date. But hung up when I got her voice mail. Leaving this information on a message seemed jinxy somehow. A recorded declaration of swooning would only come back to bite me later, right?

5:07: Began a catalog (on a paper napkin) of all the date-worthy outfits I owned.

5:08: Despaired at lack of date-worthy outfits in closet. Began a catalog (on several paper napkins) of Sophie's date-worthy outfits.

5:14: Plotted sister bribery for that pale blue halter dress.

5:16: Decided the blue halter dress was trying too hard and I should just wear jeans.

5:18: Called Caroline to confirm. Hung up on voice mail again.

5:19: Okay, I would compromise with a skirt and top.

5:20: Realized I'd been in the cooler for fifteen minutes and was freezing. Returned to work. Dad was scooping away and messing up all the orders. I took over and Dad reminded me that *he* preferred to be the backstage operator at The Scoop, before slinking into the kitchen to make a batch of Strawberry Rhubarb.

5:44: Scooped for a group of shoobees who looked less like individuals than just a tangle of sunburned limbs and expensive sunglasses. Occurred to me that Will might not have been asking me out for a *date* per se. Maybe he'd just meant for it to be a group thing. A join-the-crowd kind of thing. That's what a party really *was*, wasn't it?

5:53: Called Caroline to confirm suspicion. Voice mail *again*. She was probably too busy making out with Sam (ew) to answer. Hung up. Again.

6:03: Certain now that I was delusional. Of course Will wasn't asking me out! It was just a "Maybe I'll see you at the Beach Club party" invitation. Right? What *were* his exact words? Obviously, goose bumps had impaired my hearing.

6:06: Considered asking my dad for his impression. Questioned own sanity. Ate extra-large scoop of Maple Bacon Crunch to calm nerves.

6:10: Worried about having bacon breath at party.

6:11: He was definitely not asking me out on a date. Wondered if I should even go.

6:15: Okay, I would go, but I wasn't dressing up.

6:17: Wait a minute, Dune Island was *my* turf. Decided I should just call Will and tell him I was going to The Swamp. "And maybe I'll see *you* there."

6:18: Realized I didn't have Will's number. Despaired.

6:19: Went back into the cooler. Breathed in stale fridge smell and tried to get zen. But goose bumps on arms reminded me of conversation with Will, so went back to work.

6:23: Epiphany! Called Caroline. Actually left a message.

6:29: Shift (almost) over! Tore my dad away from his backstage maneuvering and hightailed it out of there.

* * *

*J*ust as I was getting home, my phone rang.

"Is this The Scoop?" Caroline rasped in my ear. "I'd like one Nutty Buddy, please. Oh, wait, I've already got one."

"Oh my God," I said. "We don't have time for your corny jokes. I've got an emergency."

"So I heard after about eighteen hang-ups," Caroline said. "It was the other part of your message that must have gotten mangled in my voice mail. You didn't *actually* say you want me and Sam to come to a party at the Beach Club pool, did you?"

"*He* invited me," I whispered as ran up the stairs and into the screened porch. Kat was on the porch swing eating a bowl of bright orange macaroni and cheese.

"Ugh!" I said, looking away. I was already queasy, and watching Kat eat fake food as she swung in long, lazy swoops gave *me* motion sickness.

Kat pointed a bright orange fork at me and said, "That was rude!"

I gave her an apologetic shrug, then headed up the stairs. Hoping not to run into (and possibly offend) any other family members, I darted down the wide second-floor hallway, then ducked into the steep, narrow staircase that led to my room.

Meanwhile, Caroline was chattering in my ear.

"What 'he'?" she said. "*That* he? The he from the bonfire?"

"Yes!" I said as I flopped into my unmade bed. I stared through my skylight at a wispy, strung-out cloud. My parents had finished the attic for me and Sophie three years ago. Well, it was *their* version of finished, which meant floorboards painted with pink and orange polka dots to hide their unevenness, curtains made out of vintage bedsheets, and in the bathroom, a claw-foot bathtub that my parents had gotten cheap because someone had painted the entire thing lime green.

Sophie and I had been granted one wish each for our room. She'd wished for a walk-in closet, of course. I'd asked for a skylight over my double bed, so I could watch the stars blink at me as I fell asleep. I'd somehow forgotten about the flip side of stargazing—blinding laser beams of light waking me up every morning. But it was worth it. I loved looking through the glass dome just over my pillow. It made me feel like I was outside, even when I was in; like I could just float away, weightless and free, at any moment.

As I pulled the rubber band out of my hair, letting it fan over the cool pillowcase, the view of the sky calmed me. For a brief moment I forgot about my armoire full of non-datey clothes and about the fusty Beach Club.

I only thought about him.

"The he from the bonfire is named Will," I told Caroline. It came out as a sigh—the kind of simpering, love-struck sigh I usually mocked on TV.

But hearing the sigh in my own voice felt, strangely, kind of good.

It also brought all my nervousness rushing back.

"He asked you to the *Beach Club pool party*?" Caroline said. I knew she was curling her thin upper lip.

"Yeah, but I don't think he knows what it's like there," I said defensively. "I bet he just heard about the party from people on the beach."

"From the other shoobees he's been hanging around with," Caroline insisted. "Is that who *you* want to be with tonight?"

I thought about all the summer people who'd ever called me a "townie." Most of them didn't even know there was anything obnoxious about that word. They weren't malicious so much as clueless, which was somehow even harder to swallow.

If this date (or whatever it was) with Will was a bust, the presence of all those shoobees would only make me feel worse. That was why I needed backup.

"Look," I pleaded with Caroline. "I've basically been your third wheel ever since you and Sam got together. Now it's your turn. You guys *have* to go with me tonight. Just in case."

"In case of what?" Caroline said.

In case my heart gets broken, I thought.

Then I shook my head in disbelief. A broken heart? I'd never used that phrase in my life. I didn't believe in broken hearts. Or guardian angels, destined soul mates, or any of the other things that my sister and her friends giggled about when they rented romantic comedies.

I knew that the tide wasn't mystical; it was just the rotation of the Earth relative to the positions of the sun and moon. I knew that ice cream wasn't magic; it was an emulsion of fat, milk solids, and sugar. And I knew that girls like me became chic New Yorkers only in the movies.

I also knew another thing from Sophie's favorite flicks. The "townie" who got swept off her feet by a big-city boy usually found out she'd been played.

That was why I needed Sam and Caroline to come with me. Because if I'd misunderstood Will and this *was* a group thing, *they* were my group.

And if my heart did get shattered, they'd be my shoulders to cry on.

I pictured myself standing on the sand in front of the Beach Club with my head literally on Caroline's shoulder (because Sam's shoulder is impossible for me to reach).

The image made me smile through my nervousness.

But then I imagined Sam in this scenario. He'd be standing on Caroline's other side, holding her hand.

And that made me sigh wearily.

I slithered off my rumpled bed and went over to my dresser. The first thing I saw in the top drawer was the slightly crumpled camisole I'd worn to the bonfire.

The top was silky with thin, delicate straps. When I'd tried it on while I was getting ready, it had looked soft and romantic, like something a ballerina would wear with a long tulle skirt. It had made me feel pretty, almost *too* pretty for the Dune Island High bonfire. But if I'd stashed the camisole away for a special occasion, I might have found myself waiting forever to wear it. So I'd gone ahead and kept it on.

Little had I known, I'd been going somewhere special after all.

And maybe tonight I'd be surprised again.

"Can you meet me at the club at eight?" I asked Caroline.

Maybe she heard a change in my voice. I was no longer the girl who'd shrugged Will off over a plate of curly fries that afternoon.

Now I actually had something to lose.

And though it filled me with a sort of hopeful dread, I had to see this night through; see who this boy was who'd (most likely) lied about liking my ice cream and who'd asked me out in front of my dad.

He wasn't afraid to look foolish. So the least I could do was show up.

Even if it ended up breaking my heart.

I hadn't been to the Beach Club since The Scoop catered an ice cream social there two years earlier. As I walked in that night with Sam and Caroline, the entry hall smelled exactly as I remembered it—of slightly fishy ice and Sterno.

I knew the odor emanated from the ice sculptures and chafing dishes in the large main room. But I always imagined the smell came from the club's hideous wallpaper. The pattern, a burgundy and gold paisley with forest green borders, made me imagine horrible things usually seen only under microscopes. Just looking at it made my queasiness return. Or maybe I was just nauseous over the prospect of this nebulous perhaps-date with Will.

Sam wasn't exactly making me feel better.

"Anna, if you tell anybody I ditched the Braves versus the Padres to go to *this*," he threatened, "I'll seriously have to kill you."

"I'm sure there are plenty of guys out there who can tell you the score," I said, pointing at the wall of windows and French doors on the other side of the ballroom. Through them we could see the pool deck, packed with men in wheat-colored blazers and women in pastel shifts; boys in long shorts and golf shirts, and girls in tube tops and A-line skirts. It was like they'd all gotten an e-mail instructing them to wear a uniform. They skimmed back and forth on the other side of the glass like a bunch of extremely white fish in an aquarium.

"Yeah, right, I'll ask *them* the score," Sam muttered. He looked even more gangly than usual in the low-ceilinged foyer.

"You are going to keep it together, right?" Caroline asked Sam. "*Please* don't get in another fight."

"What are you talking about?" Sam said. "Fight?"

"You know what I'm talking about!" Caroline said. She'd been jokey at first, but now her voice had a bit of an edge to it.

"Anderson Lowell's party," Caroline and I said together.

"Last August?" Sam squawked. "Well, that was totally provoked!"

"What, a shoobee simply *showing up* at one of our parties forced you to punch him in the head?" Caroline said.

"What *was* that, anyway?" I asked, with one eye on the French doors. I still didn't see Will. "I always meant to ask you. I thought you Neanderthal boys always went for the nose or the chin. But you hit him on the *head*."

"I didn't mean to," Sam said, a semiproud smile tugging up one corner of his mouth. "The guy was so short, I couldn't reach his face."

"Oh my God," Caroline said, rolling her eyes. "I can't believe I allow myself to be seen with you in public."

She was joking, of course. But I could hear a thin shard of impatience in her voice.

And in Sam's there was a touch of wheedling as he said, "You know that's not me, Caroline. The guy was a complete jerkwad, throwing his weight around. It was just . . . a bad moment, I guess."

"Well, remind *me* never to make you have a bad moment," Caroline said.

"You could never . . . ," Sam began, but Caroline had already waved him off. She was peering out at partygoers.

"Looks like skirts were indeed the way to go, Anna," she said.

She and I were both wearing skirts, if not the A-line uniform of the shoobee girls. Caroline's was short and sporty. Mine was more flowy, tickling my ankles when the hem fluttered.

Even though we'd ditched our cutoffs for the evening, I knew Caroline and I didn't look like those girls. And it wasn't just because they had bleached teeth and manicures and we didn't. There was a shininess to the shoobees. And a chilly breeziness. In my mind, these qualities created a sort of force field around them that deflected funky odors and ugliness. Not to mention insecurities about vague date requests from strange boys.

I was the one who lived here year-round, yet in this "club," it felt like they owned the whole island.

"Oh!" Caroline rasped. She grabbed my arm and pointed through the windows to the left side of the pool deck. Thinking she'd spotted Will, I felt my stomach swoop.

"Daiquiris!" Caroline exclaimed. She was pointing, it turned out, at a bar where people were ordering frozen fruity drinks in voluptuous glasses. "I forgot this place serves the best virgin daiquiris."

"Caroline," Sam said. "There's nothing less cool than a virgin daiquiri."

"Of course there is," Caroline said, motioning to the entire pool deck.

Sam and Caroline both dissolved into snorts of laughter.

I wanted to swat them on the backs of their heads Three Stooges–style, but then I thought of the alternative: Caroline curling her lip at the shoobee girls, Sam swaggering by the shoo-bee guys, then everyone jumping down to the beach for a good old-fashioned fistfight.

A little derisive laughter, I decided, was definitely preferable.

"Listen, can you get me a drink too?" I asked Caroline. At that moment I had as little interest in a virgin daiquiri as I did in geometry. But I was pulling out the trick my mom always used on Kat and Benjie when they were acting insufferable—she distracted them with a task.

"I'll see you out there, okay?" I said, pointing vaguely toward the right side of the pool deck.

Then I headed across the ballroom to the French doors. Just before I reached them, I had an impulse to run to the ladies room, where I could check my teeth for food particles, blot my shiny face, and fruitlessly attempt to pee.

But at that point I was annoying *myself* with all the nervousness, so I just gritted my teeth and plunged through the double doors. They automatically swung shut behind me, actually making a little squelching sound as they closed. They reminded me of spaceship movies where people get sucked out of the airlock.

What am I doing *here?* flashed across my mind.

Then I was scanning the crowd dizzily. The people really did all look alike to me. But none of them looked like—

Will.

There he was, leaning against the pool deck railing. He wore a pumpkin-colored T-shirt and faded jeans. With the sand and darkening ocean behind him, he almost seemed to glow. In just four days on the island, he had gotten very tan. Somehow I hadn't noticed in the fluorescent lighting of The Scoop.

His brown hair had also gotten cutely frazzled by all the salty breezes.

But did Will have one of those shiny force fields around him?

That I couldn't tell yet.

When he saw me, though, he lurched off the railing so hard that an ice cube flew out of the Coke he was holding.

I couldn't help but laugh.

He laughed too as he hurried around the pool to come meet me. I relaxed a little as I wondered if he was as scared, and exhilarated, by this moment as I was.

If he *was* really different from the other shoobees.

And if this was going to be a night that I'd always remember.

* * *

"Hi," Will said as he sort of skidded to a stop in front of me.

"Hi," I said.

Then we both tried, and failed, to stop grinning unrelentingly.

Will smoothed down his flyaway hair with his palm and straightened his slightly wrinkled T-shirt. I marveled at how pleasurable it was just to look at him.

Then we started talking—and things spiraled downward from there.

"So," Will said as we found a couple of deck chairs to perch on, "it's pretty cool that this isn't a members-only club. Anybody can go, right? It's so different in New York. You can't even get into most apartment buildings without a birth certificate."

"Yeah . . . ," I said. I glanced at the Beach Clubbers as my voice trailed off. My smile went plastic. How could I tell Will—without sounding like I had a big, fat attitude—that the Beach Club *felt* like the most exclusive place in town? It was about the only place on the island where I didn't feel absolutely comfortable.

"So . . . how'd you find out about this party?" I asked. It was a lame conversation starter, but it appeared to be all I had.

"Oh, my brother, Owen," Will said with a laugh. "He found out about it from someone he met on the beach. Of course. The guy can't ride the subway without becoming best friends with everybody within five feet of him."

"Oh," I said. "That's not normal?"

In Georgia, when you pass someone on the street, you not only say hello, you ask after her mama and find something—*anything*—about her outfit to compliment.

"No way," Will said with a laugh that made me feel like a yokel. "You don't talk to anybody on the subway. Unless you're Owen."

Or, I thought, *me.*

"So . . . Owen's here with you?" I asked.

Yes, my wit was positively sparkling.

"Well, he wanted to come," Will said. "But I kind of didn't want him to."

He gave me a shy smile and I . . . had no idea how to respond. What did he mean? Had Will ditched his brother because he'd wanted to be alone with me? Or was it just because he and Owen didn't get along? Was Will trying to tell me that he sometimes felt overshadowed by Owen the Extrovert? I could totally bond with him about that! But how to broach this subject without potentially dissing his brother? What if they were actually *really* close and I offended him and . . .

Yes, as you've guessed, the silence that ensued while I pondered all these scenarios was long. And awkward.

Will swirled his ice cubes around in his glass—*clink, clink, clink*—until finally he broke the silence with some more (nervous, I think) chatter.

"Anyway," he said, "my mom roped him into going to this place for dinner. I think it's called Caleb's?"

"Oh yeah," I said. "Out on Highway 80. It's, um, nice."

Once again I was censoring myself. Caleb's, a restaurant in a semicrumbling, Civil War–era mansion, was more than nice. The food was so decadently Southern, it drawled. But I loved Caleb's because whenever my family went there for dinner, Sophie and I made up stories about all the ghosts that haunted the old house. As Kat and Benjie gripped their deep-fried drumsticks harder and harder, our stories got more and more grisly. Then one of the kids either cried or freaked out and we had to get our dessert to go.

It was tradition. Even my parents kind of liked it, despite the nightmares the kids usually had afterward.

But telling Will about these goofy family dinners would make me feel about twelve years old. It was out of the question.

"Well, all I know is my mom used to go there when she was a kid," Will said. "It's the only place from that time that's still around, so she decided she *had* to go. And Owen never, *ever* turns down a free meal."

I grinned, and Will pressed on.

"That's why we're here," he said. "My mom's on a nostalgia trip. She spent summers here when she was a teenager. We're even staying in the same cottage her parents rented every year. Of course, the place has been totally redecorated. Mom's kind of heartbroken that the owners got rid of the orange shag carpeting."

"My parents always go on about shag carpeting too!" I said, grateful that I finally had something to say, even if it did invoke my parents. I took comfort in the fact that Will had done it first.

"Oh, my mom's got it bad," Will said. "She gets all misty-eyed over everything from the good old boardwalk to the smell of the seaweed that washes up on the beach every morning."

"I ate seaweed once," I volunteered with a shudder. "In a sushi restaurant in Savannah. It tasted exactly like that stuff on the beach smells."

The moment the words left my mouth, I regretted them. First of all, gross. Second, could I sound like any more of a hick? New Yorkers probably ate sushi for their after-school snacks.

A waiter walked by with a tray of goat cheese mushroom puffs or some other fussy party food. I glanced at him and realized that the server in the red polyester jacket and too-short black pants was Jeremy Davison, a boy I knew from school.

Being spotted by Jeremy just as I'd revealed my sushiphobia made me feel doubly dumb.

At that point I pretty much clammed up—until Will gave a little jump, sending another ice cube flying.

"Oh my God, I just realized," he said, "you don't have anything to drink." He made it sound like this was a *really serious problem*.

"It's okay," I assured him. "I'm not thirsty."

Because you can't drink anything when your throat has closed up.

"But I invited you here," Will said, jumping to his feet. "I should have gotten you a Coke. Do you want a Coke?"

"It's okay," I said, getting up too. "I don't like . . . I mean, I don't *need* anything to drink."

"Here's your daiquiri!"

I closed my eyes for an agonized moment. Of course. That was Caroline, bouncing over—with the drink I'd requested.

The slushie she thrust into my hand was the color of a sunset.

"It's peach-raspberry," Caroline said. "*So* good. I got strawberry-lime. Want a taste?"

"No, thanks," I muttered.

"Um, hi?" Will said. He was clearly confused. He looked from Caroline to me. Then Sam strolled up, swigging a Coke from the bottle.

"This is Sam and Caroline," I offered lamely. "This is Will."

"Hey," Sam said, giving Will a floppy wave.

"Hi, Will," Caroline said. "How do you like Dune Island?"

"I love it," Will said, nodding for too long. He gestured politely toward the clubhouse. "This place is great."

All four of us froze.

Out of the corner of my eye, I saw Caroline squeeze Sam's forearm, warning him with a dig of her nails not to make One. Obnoxious. Comment.

I felt, bizarrely, like I might burst into tears.

And Will looked even more confused.

Then Sam shook off Caroline's claws and blurted, "Dude, *seriously?*"

"What?" Will said. His eyes went wide.

"You *like* the Beach Club?" Sam said. "*Nobody* likes the Beach Club."

"Sam . . . ," I said.

Will gaped at Sam. Then he glanced to the right as another waiter walked by with a tray of smoky-smelling Scotch glasses. To our left, a woman wearing a *lot* of jangly jewelry came through the French doors, bringing a gust of stale-smelling air-conditioning with her.

"So you guys don't hang out here," Will said. It wasn't a question.

As Will processed this information, I literally saw a crease between his eyebrows melt away.

"You know," Will said after yet another awkward beat, "a month ago I wiped out playing basketball on an asphalt court. I had this big scrape all down the left side of my calf. And when it scabbed over . . . it looked *just* like that wallpaper in there."

I blinked. Had Will just done what I thought he'd done?

When Caroline started laughing, I knew that he had.

From the moment this awkward date had begun, I'd felt like there was a barrier between me and Will—that invisible wall between the ice cream scooper and the guy paying for the cone.

But with one little joke, Will had batted that barrier away as easily as if he were slapping a mosquito. I laughed, as much from relief as from Will's quip.

Sam gave Will a friendly wallop on the back.

"So do you want to get out of here?" he proposed. "You heard of The Swamp?"

"I have, actually," Will said, looking at me. A smile played around the corners of his mouth, but it was only a small one. The rest of his face was not very smiley at all.

Will's eyes shifted quickly to Sam and Caroline, then back to me. Then they dropped to his glass of ice cubes. *Clink, clink, clink.*

With a sinking sensation, I realized I'd blown it.

This hadn't been a group thing.

It *had* been a date.

And I'd invited not one, but *two* friends to come along. All because I was worried that a date at the Beach Club had meant a date with a Beach Clubber.

I mean, would that even have been so bad? I thought. Now that I knew Will wasn't one of *them*, I was feeling magnanimous about the people at the party. I took a quick survey. A boy with eyelash-skimming bangs pulled a flask out of his pocket and dumped some clear liquid into his Coke. The girl who was flirting with him *flip, flip, flipped* her long, blond hair. An older couple laughed as they woozed their way toward the bar.

Um, yes, it would have been very *bad,* I told myself with an inward and, okay, smug giggle.

When I returned my gaze to Will, though, all self-congratulation ceased. I would have bet that Will wasn't sizing me up nearly this exactingly. He hadn't even smirked at my sushi gaffe. All he'd wanted to do when he'd asked me out was *talk,* but I'd been too freaked-out to be even remotely charming—or charmed.

Until now. Was it too late?

I wanted to find out. And I didn't want to do it with my friends at The Swamp. Pulling Will into my world felt like cheating somehow. No, I wanted to get to know him there, at the Beach Club.

Or maybe, I brainstormed, breaking out my first confident grin of the evening, *not* quite *at the Beach Club.*

"You know what, guys?" I said. I was talking to Sam and

Caroline but I was looking at Will. "You go on to The Swamp. I think we're going to do our own thing."

That "we" felt strange and wonderful to say. Maybe Will caught it too. His thick eyebrows shot up.

I didn't have to ask Sam and Caroline twice. Caroline gave Will a little wave as she slurped up the dregs of her daiquiri. Sam gave him a fist-bump. But Will seemed to be looking at *me* during the entire exchange.

Ever-watchful Caroline noticed and flashed me a quick grin.

It was official. My friends liked Will. It seemed like something I should be glad about. Everyone knew that was a classic sign of boyfriend worthiness.

But at that moment, I didn't feel in a position to be testing Will. Quite the opposite. I had some making up to do.

As Caroline and Sam drifted away, I tried to smile lightly at Will. I pointed to the railing at the edge of the pool deck, the one that overlooked the beach.

"Can you go wait for me over there?" I asked. "I'll be just a minute."

I was being cryptic, I knew. Will looked skeptical and I couldn't blame him. He probably thought I was sending him into another ambush—my parents, say, ready to hop out and interview him about his credentials and intentions.

But to Will's credit, he just shrugged and also tried to smile. Then he headed over to the rail.

I ducked into the crowd of partiers.

My plan took longer than I'd thought. By the time I headed back toward Will, a good ten minutes had gone by and I could see he was getting annoyed. He tipped his plastic cup to his lips, clearly forgetting that his ice cubes had melted long ago. Then he carefully knelt to put the empty cup on the edge of the pool deck, stretching his orange T-shirt tightly across his shoulder blades. He hadn't seen me yet, which was a good thing, because looking at his back made me stop and take a deep, wide-eyed, admiring breath.

Looking at Will was so *different* from looking at other boys. When you live on an island, you don't even think about see- ing boys' bodies. They're just always . . . there. I barely noticed when Sam whipped off one of his holey T-shirts to go galloping into the surf. My friends' tan skin, broad shoulders, and angular shoulder blades all sort of looked alike.

But here was Will, so fully clothed even his *ankles* were cov- ered, and I was practically hyperventilating.

Which was not good, given all the plates, glasses, and food- stuffs I was balancing in my arms.

When Will straightened up and glimpsed me, I could swear he gave his own little gasp. His smile was instant, and natural this time, lighting up his entire face from his crinkling eyes to his slightly scruffy chin.

He simply looked happy to see me, which, given all the con- fusion of the past half hour, seemed like a feat.

Suddenly I felt like the old independent me—the one who thinks nothing of cutting her friends free and committing acts of petty larceny all over the Dune Island Beach Club.

I found myself beaming right back at Will.

"Come on," I said, transferring a few of my more awkward items into Will's hands. I sat on the floor, swung my legs out, and inched beneath the railing's lowest bar until I'd landed in the sand below. I kicked off my flip-flops, then started collecting my loot from the edge of the pool deck.

"Am I supposed to come down there too?" Will said, glancing furtively over his shoulder.

"Yeah," I said. "Make a break for it before they notice all the stuff I took."

Will grunted as he squished himself through the railing. His T-shirt scrunched up to his rib cage and I tried not to stare. Instead I bent over and sidled under the deck, which was about four feet off the ground. The sand felt cool and slithery under my bare feet. I smoothed a patch of it into a makeshift table, then arranged on it all the dishes and napkin-wrapped bundles I'd collected.

"Has anybody ever told you," Will said, grunting again as he crab-walked under the deck to join me, "that you're really small?"

"Watch it, bub," I muttered with a laugh.

As Will settled in on the other side of my little sand table, I arranged votive candles in a circle around us. We were quiet as I lit them. The party chatter over our heads was muffled by the stone deck, but the crash/sizzle of the waves seemed to echo all around us. The candlelight danced on the blond fuzz on Will's arms and made my own hands look almost graceful as I pulled a burgundy cloth napkin off a dinner plate. It was piled with hors d'oeuvres.

"What's this?" Will asked, taking in the crab puffs, hot artichoke dip and crackers, spinach pies, and bacon-wrapped dates.

"A picnic," I said, using a toothpick to pluck up a crispy date for him. "A tremendously old-school picnic. I don't think the Beach Club has updated their menu since before we were born."

"When *were* you born?" Will asked with a curious smile.

That's when I realized—we didn't know anything about each other. I didn't know Will's age. I didn't even know his last name!

I looked down so he wouldn't see the momentary panic flutter across my face. I busied myself with cracking open a bottle of lemony sparkling water and pouring it into two champagne flutes. I felt a little sheepish about the flutes. When I'd filched them from the bar, I thought they were sophisticated and romantic. Now they seemed way too heart-shaped-hot-tub for comfort.

"I'm sixteen," I told Will.

"Seventeen," Will said, tapping his chest with his fingertips. Then he reached for the flute of fizzing water and said, "What's with these skinny glasses, anyway? I mean, where do you put your nose?"

Confirmed. The glasses had been a cheesy choice. I pointed at the pool deck above us. "So much of *that* just baffles me," I said. "I mean, a bathroom attendant to hand you your paper towel? *Really?*"

"You're right," Will said, popping the date into his mouth. "That's just dumb."

I skewered my own date and twirled the toothpick between my thumb and forefinger.

"Is that what it's like in New York?" I asked. "Poshness everywhere?"

Will shrugged.

"Eh, there's a lot of posh, I guess," he said. "Just not necessarily in *my* house. Especially lately . . ."

His voice trailed off and he took a quick sip of sparkling water.

"Um, what . . . ," I stammered. "Why. . ."

I didn't want to pry. But on the other hand, I *seriously* wanted to pry.

"It's nothing," Will said, still looking down at his crossed legs. "Just—my parents split up in February."

"Oh, I'm sorry," I said.

"It's okay," he said. "I mean, it wasn't a scandal or anything. My dad didn't slink out in the dead of night or leave my mom for a younger woman. He just moved into a studio a few blocks away."

"Did they fight a lot?" I asked. Which seemed *very* prying, but I couldn't stop myself.

"Naw," Will said. "That was one of the things that was weird about it. One of many, many things. They just—I think they stopped seeing each other, you know? Stopped talking. I had a feeling that when Owen and I weren't around, our apartment was just . . . silent. I could almost feel it when I got back home— this heaviness."

I thought about my own house, where the front door was always open, letting in the breezes from the screened porch. Where the floors were often crunchy with sand and dried dune grass and waffle crumbs. There was always chatter in my house, and cooking smells, clashing cell phone rings, and somebody calling up or down the stairs. Heavy, it definitely wasn't.

I braced myself, wondering if a barrier would rise up between us again. A wall with Dune Island on one side, New York on the other; big, happy family on one side, fractured home life on the other; inscrutable boy on one side, confused girl on the other.

And maybe that *would* have happened if I hadn't been so focused on what Will was saying. If my interest in *him* hadn't drowned out my own self-consciousness.

"After the divorce," Will went on, "my mom and Owen and I had to move, too. We rented a two-bedroom, which meant I had to share a room with my brother for the first time since we were little kids."

"I share a room with my sister too," I said. "It definitely can suck sometimes."

"Yeah . . ." Will picked up one of the triangular spinach pies. He peeled off the top layer of crispy phyllo. But instead of popping it into his mouth, he crumbled it between his fingers. I had a feeling he didn't even realize he was doing it.

"The truth is, and this is going to sound really dorky," Will said, "but it was actually kind of nice to share a room with my brother. He just graduated and he's moving out to go to NYU in the fall. So it was the last time we'd ever be living under the same roof in New York.

"Plus"—Will crushed up another layer of the phyllo before tossing the spinach pie back on the plate—"Owen's the only one who can understand what it's like to be in my family. To go out for sad Chinese food with my dad on Sundays or pretend not to hear my mom crying some nights."

I felt a little choky just imagining such a bleak scene.

Then I knew why I sometimes saw that melancholy dragging down on the corners of Will's mouth.

Of course, I hadn't seen it since we'd ducked under the pool deck, which made me feel a little thrill as Will kept on talking.

"My dad left right before Valentine's Day," he said. I had a feeling he hadn't talked about this very much and was sort of unleashing. I leaned forward a little, not nodding or going, "Hmm." Just listening.

"It was Owen's idea to take my mom out for an anti-Valentine's Day," Will said. "I never would have thought of it. We went over to the Bowery to watch the garbage barges. For dinner we had street meat, these disgusting gyros you buy from carts on the street. With extra onions, of course. Then we went to a horror movie."

"That's brilliant," I said with a laugh. "I hate Valentine's Day in general. But that one must have really been awful."

"Why do you hate Valentine's Day?" Will asked. He was looking at me seriously, almost sadly.

"Oh, well . . ."

Suddenly I felt stammery. How did I tell Will that I hated Valentine's Day because nobody had ever wanted me to be his valentine? Every year on February 14, my school was overrun by cheesy red and white carnations—the bigger your bouquet, the greater your social status. I'd gotten plenty of flowers, but they'd always been white, signifying friendship. Not love.

"Valentine's Day is so . . . schmaltzy, don't you think?" I said.

"And you don't like schmaltz?" Will asked. He lifted his

champagne flute of bubbly water and took a giant gulp. "Could have fooled me."

I felt myself turn bright red.

But then I looked at Will's eyes, which were all sparkly in the candlelight. They were also filled with warm humor, and not a speck of judgment.

So I decided to get over myself and just enjoy this okay-I'm-just-going-to-call-it-an-official-date.

Because I *was* enjoying it. Against all odds, I really, really was.

Will and I talked until the votive candles sputtered out. We emerged from our little cave under the pool deck and Will snuck back under the railing to return our plates and glasses.

I waited in the sand, feeling pleasantly overwhelmed by the big, black sky after the intense coziness of our picnic.

Or maybe I was whooshy-headed because I'd been chatting with a boy for over an hour and it had felt like five minutes. It had been as fun and easy as coasting my bike down an endless, gently sloping hill.

Will came back to the railing. This time, instead of sliding under it, he vaulted over it. He sailed over the rail so easily that he almost looked buoyant, as if he were in the water rather than the air. He landed in the sand, stumbled, then righted himself with a self-mocking grin.

Okay, there's the catch, I thought, trying not to laugh out loud. *He can fly. He's a superhero, like one of Benjie's action figures.*

Then I did end up snorting as I imagined Caroline shaking me by the shoulders and saying, "Get a grip, Anna. Just because you finally decide to like a boy doesn't mean he's Superman!"

The Caroline in my head was right. I was being an incredible dork.

"What are you laughing about?" Will asked as he kicked off his shoes. "Or should I say, what are you laughing *at*? Did I just look incredibly klutzy jumping down here?"

In quick succession, I thought:

1. No, he hadn't looked klutzy *at all*.

2. I loved that he'd even asked. And . . .

3. The fantasy Caroline in my head had been right. I liked Will. I really liked him.

And *that* made me feel so overwhelmed that I had to catch my breath.

Except that I couldn't. I continued to feel hopelessly breathless and giddy. So I ran. I ran down to the frothy edge of the surf, which was already cooling down for the night. Plunging my feet into the churning water calmed me, as it always does.

Will jogged up and joined me. We didn't make eye contact. Instead we both gazed out at the violet-black horizon. One point of light was twinkling brightly and I wondered if it was a star or a satellite. I decided it was a star.

I extricated a bit of hair that had flown into my mouth and smoothed it behind my ear. I scratched an itch on my neck. They were the completely mundane fidgets I did all the time and never noticed. But now, they felt *weird* because I was doing them next to this boy. Will was standing so close to me,

I could almost feel warmth radiating off his arm. It felt pretty amazing.

I wondered what Will had noticed about me. The fact that I walk just a tiny bit pigeon-toed? That my nose was peeling because I'd forgotten my sunscreen a week earlier? That I was having a pretty good hair day? I hoped he'd noticed that this silence between us wasn't awkward in the least. It was lovely, in fact.

"I love this feeling," Will said, looking down at his feet, which were planted ankle-deep in water that was rushing back out to sea. "The sand sort of sweeps out from under your feet and you feel weightless for a second, you know?"

"Yeah, I do," I said, looking down at my own legs, submerged to the ankle. They looked so twiggy next to Will's muscley calves. "I love it, too, now that I think about it."

"Do you know, when you walk on the sand," Will said, "you don't even stumble? It's like you're walking across a perfectly flat floor or something. How do you *do* that? I feel like I'm picking my way through wet cement out there."

He jabbed over his shoulder with his thumb, pointing at the part of the beach that was feather-soft, drifty, and seriously uneven.

So, I guess *that's* what Will had noticed about me. I smiled, feeling proud. So what if he was basically complimenting me on my ability to *walk*, which was a fairly basic skill.

"I think I took my first steps on sand," I said to Will with a shrug. "And pretty much took it from there. It's a local thing, I guess. But don't worry, you've got a whole summer to get the hang of it."

"Or you could just cast a voodoo spell to help me skip the pesky learning curve," Will suggested.

"What?!" I blurted with a laugh.

"Oh, come on," Will said, grinning. "You must have some spells going on at The Scoop, for instance, to lure in unsuspecting tourists. There's no way normal ice cream can taste that good."

"Oh yeah, that's it," I said with a sly smile. "Next time you come to The Scoop, just ignore that pentagram smeared on the door with chicken blood."

Okay, what was *that*?

That was me trying to be clever and quippy. That was my sushi comment all over again, but even more disgusting.

The only thing different was that it was two hours later. And I wasn't mortified by the dorky thing I'd said. I just laughed my way through it, the way I would with anyone I knew.

Sure enough, Will didn't recoil in horror. He just laughed and said, "Gross, Anna."

"You're the one who brought up the voodoo." I giggled.

I cocked my head and gave Will a quizzical look.

"Can I ask you something?" I said. "Are you glad to be here? I mean, you seem pretty *urban*. And it's for the whole summer."

"This place is a loooong way from New York," Will admitted. He glanced over at me. "I was a little anti at first. But I gotta say, Dune Island's growing on me."

I was glad it was so dark out. My blushing, I could tell from the heat on my face, was intense.

"Besides, I wasn't going to take this summer away from my mom," Will said, turning away from me and gazing out at the sea. "First my dad left, next Owen's leaving. She's kind of a basket case right now.

"So—the find-yourself mission," I said with a nod.

"Pretty much," Will replied. "The get-back-to-your-roots, find-yourself, and forget-your-ex-husband mission."

"My parents have basically been finding themselves my whole life," I commiserated.

"Oh, they're not from around here?"

"No way," I said. "They're refugees from Wisconsin. Every Christmas, they tell these epic tales of the awful Midwestern winters. You know, snowdrifts up to the roof, digging out the driveway, clunking radiators, the whole bit. And then they go on and on about the paradise that is Dune Island."

"Oh my God, that's *so* my mom," Will exclaimed. "If I have to hear once more how much better all the food tastes here in the fresh sea air, I'm going on a hunger strike."

"Besides which," I said, "there's no way we have better food than you do in New York."

"Well, they don't have Pineapple Ginger Ale ice cream in New York," Will said.

"Pineapple Ginger Ale," I said with a sly smile. "What kind of twisted mind came up with that?"

"That's what I intend to find out," Will said with a sly smile of his own.

I looked down and nudged the sand with my bare toes so he couldn't see how hard I was grinning.

"So I have a question for you," Will said, "now that we're on a last-name basis, Anna Patrick."

Last names had been one of the things we'd covered under the pool deck.

"What's that, Will Cooper?" I asked.

"Can I have your phone number?"

I laughed. Because his asking for my number *after* this amazing date seemed so backward.

And because I was overjoyed that Will wanted it.

And finally because I couldn't wait to see Will again. Yes, the night wasn't over yet and I could still enjoy the sight of Will's hair blowing into his eyes, the way his back muscles rippled under his shirt when he threw a clod of sand into the water, and the way the scruff on his chin glinted in the moonlight.

But I was already looking forward to more.

I wish I could say I dreamed about Will that night. But that would have made the date a little too perfect. Untoppably perfect. When you think about it, you really don't want that on the first date.

So I suppose I should have been grateful that when I got home a squeak after curfew, I stubbed my toe on the front steps because the porch lights were off.

Then I realized I was famished because I'd forgotten to eat more than a couple of dates during my picnic with Will. And when I went to the kitchen to grab a snack, I accidentally tipped over a glass of tea that someone had left on the counter.

After mopping up the spill, I grabbed a few crackers and tried not to crunch as I tiptoed up to my room. I didn't want to wake anybody and have to talk about my date. It would have broken the night's spell.

Or worse, someone (probably Sophie) might have pointed out that there had been no spell; that it had just been an ordinary night, complete with soggy spinach pies and more than a few verbal gaffes on my part. That I really had no reason to be so gaga.

Luckily, I made it to my room without waking anybody. When I slunk through the bedroom door, Sophie was breathing evenly, deep in her own dreams. I went straight to the bathroom, closed the door, then sank onto the round stool at the vanity. Sophie and I both loved our antique wooden vanity, which was ornate and curvy and had a slightly pink cast to it. It had lots of tiny drawers, niches, and cabinets where we used to stash things like Barbie shoes, gumball-machine jewelry, and illegal candy.

Now most of the nooks were taken up with Sophie's makeup and perfumes, but I'd staked out one drawer all for myself. In it I put keepsakes that only I could decipher.

I'd saved a piece of sea glass, for instance, that I'd picked up during my last beach walk with my grandfather before he died.

I had my childhood hair comb, the one with the mermaid on the handle, which I'd never been able to pass on to Kat.

There were pebbles, shells, and notes passed in class that I could sift through when I wanted to recall certain perfect afternoons, moments of hilarity, or even waves of sadness.

Now I pulled from my skirt pocket a green plastic toothpick.

It was shaped like a pirate's sword, with a D-shaped handle and a flattened, pointed blade. It was ridiculously cheesy and pure Dune Island Beach Club. I stashed it in my little drawer, tucking it under the torn-off bits of paper and the smooth, flat sea glass.

Then I reached across to the sink, soaked a soft washcloth, and dabbed it on my face. I felt too luxuriously dreamy to stand in front of the sink and be all efficient with my washing up. I stretched out my legs, gazed out the window, and enjoyed the feel of the cool, damp terrycloth on my hot forehead and cheeks.

As I swabbed off my neck, I glanced at myself in the vanity's cloudy round mirror. My skin was both summer gold and flushed from my bike ride. My hair was wind tousled. There was a speck of pale green artichoke dip on the scoop neck of my T-shirt.

I didn't look exactly ravishing but I *felt* sort of extraordinary. Not polished like one of the shoobee girls from the club or effortlessly buoyant like my sister or casually confident like Caroline. I suppose I felt like myself, only slightly shinier. Lighter. Happier.

And that was the girl who fell into a blissfully zonked, dreamless sleep that night. I didn't completely understand why Will and I had clicked so well. In truth, I couldn't fathom what exactly he saw in me.

But I was confident I would find out the very next day—as soon as Will called.

There was one problem with that little scenario.

Will *didn't* call the next day.

Which was perfectly fine at first. Good, even. That way I

could spend the morning floating around inside my own fuzzy head, replaying the entire date like it was my favorite movie. I could pause on Will's face when I handed him that silly champagne flute. I could fast-forward through the early, awkward bits. And I could scene-scan my way through all our conversations.

I also imagined what our phone call would be like.

In detail.

It went something like this . . .

Will: Nobody ever made me a picnic before.

Me: Oh, it's no big deal.

Will: True, the food *was* pretty bad . . .

Me: Hey, *I'm* not the one who chose the Beach Club and their antique artichoke dip.

Will: Well, at least I chose the right girl. You gotta give me credit for that, right?

Me: Oh . . .

Will: Anna? You didn't really think I cared about the food, did you?

Me: Oh . . .

Will: Tell me you'll have dinner with me again. A *real* dinner this time. Tonight.

I'd go on with my fantasy banter, but you're probably throwing up a little in your mouth right now.

Believe me, I was just as mocking of myself. I just *wasn't* a romantic. One time I found a yellowed bodice ripper in my parents' bookshelf and reading it had made me feel like I was eating corn syrup. Yet here I was spinning so much schmaltz you'd think my brain had been replaced by a cotton candy machine.

It wasn't that I wanted Will to be Prince Charming. I didn't, believe me. I guess this crazy dialogue was just my brain adjusting to life on the other side. On the other side of a fabulous first date.

On the other side of falling in like for the first time.

On the other side of Will.

Meanwhile, on the other side of Dune Island? Will continued to Not Call.

He didn't call while I was at the beach dishing with Caroline. He didn't call during my shift at The Scoop. He didn't call while I was in the shower or during *any* of the inconvenient moments when, Murphy's Law, he was *supposed* to call.

By that evening I resolved to call *him*. He'd given me his number, too, after all.

But first I needed sustenance.

Since my parents were both at The Scoop with Kat and Benjie, it was a fend-for-yourself night dinner-wise. I shuffled down to the kitchen and tried to decide if I wanted sweet (ice cream of course) or savory.

I decided spicy was better for my pre-call state of mind. It would wake me up, whereas ice cream always lulled me into a happy stupor.

As I was sizzling up some bacon for a sandwich, Sophie strutted in from the porch. She had her hot-pink wrap knotted around her waist and her sparkly pink cell phone clamped to her ear.

"Okay, so you're signing us up?" she was asking.

I heard a high-pitched voice on the other end of the phone. It reminded me of a mosquito's whine.

"I thought we decided the team name," Sophie said. "Summer Lovin', right? I know—love it! Okay, buh-bye, babe."

Strangely enough, I could completely translate that cryptic conversation.

"So that's the name of your team?" I said. "For the sand castle competition?"

The Dune Island tourist bureau staged the competition every August, just when things started to get impossibly sleepy around here. My sister and a gaggle of her friends entered every summer. Castle building was one of Sophie's random obsessions, along with gymnastics and a crocheted bracelet business she'd started with yet more of her friends. Sophie pretty much had people buzzing around her at all times. It made me claustrophobic just thinking about it, but she was one of those people who hated being alone.

I suppose that's why she hung around in the kitchen while I poked at the bacon strips on the griddle.

"Yeah, we're calling the team Summer Lovin'," Sophie said. "It's that song from *Grease*. Sung by *Sandy*? Get it?"

"Got it," I said dryly. "It's definitely better than Days of our Lives, from last year. Though I still think you're flirting with copyright infringement there."

"Um, *what*?" Sophie said, slouching into a chair at the kitchen table.

"Nothing," I said, shaking my head. "Do you want a sandwich? PBJ?"

"What am I, eight?" Sophie balked.

"Not *that* PBJ," I retorted. "It's peanut butter, bacon, and jalapeño. Very gourmet!"

"Ugh!" Sophie said. She flounced off her chair and headed to the walk-in pantry to forage for something else to eat. "Your diet is so weird. I don't know why you don't weigh a hundred and fifty pounds."

"The one perk of our genes, I guess," I said. Like me, Sophie was short and bird boned. Unlike me, she preferred her food bland, predictable, and in tiny portions.

"Come on, try my sandwich," I cajoled her. "It's like Mom's bacon ice cream. You think it's going to be awful, but it ends up being awesome. And don't worry, the jalapeños are pickled. They barely even burn."

"Guh-ross!" Sophie squealed.

I smeared some peanut butter on a butter knife, topped it with a crispy crumb of bacon, and thrust it toward her.

"So-phiiiiieee," I singsonged like a ghost out of one of our Caleb's stories. "Eeeeat me! Eeeeat meeee, So-phiiiiieee."

"Oh my God," Sophie said, dodging my sticky butter knife. "Why are you always trying to be so weird?"

I laughed, shrugged, and turned back to the counter. After I'd assembled my sandwich, I sat at the table with Sophie, who'd decided on a (boring) bowl of granola.

"You know, I don't *try* to be weird," I said after I'd taken my first (delicious, I might add) bite of my dinner. "Everyone *is* weird. *You're* the one who's trying to hide."

"Hide what?" Sophie demanded.

"You're trying to hide your inherent weirdness," I said. "It's futile, you know. Nobody's *really* normal."

"See?!" Sophie screeched, slapping her cereal with her spoon and sloshing milk on the table. "That's such an abnormal thing to say! That's what makes you weird!"

"Fine, Soph." I sighed. "Whatever you think."

I glanced at my cell phone, which was perched not inconspicuously on the corner of the kitchen table. If Sophie hadn't been there, I would have checked it to make sure the ringer was set on loud. But she was, and besides, I'd already checked the ringtone status. Twice.

"Are you waiting for him to call?" Sophie blurted. "That guy you went out with last night?"

Clearly, I hadn't been surreptitious enough for my sister.

"No," I said. "I mean, I'm not *not* wanting him to call. I'm just . . . well, I'll probably just call him. Just to say hey. No big deal, right?"

"Yes big deal!" Sophie cried. Suddenly, she sat up straight in her chair. "You can't call him."

"Um, yes, I can, Sophie," I said. "This isn't the movies and it's not 1950. You can call a boy after you've had a great time together."

"So it was good, then!" Sophie said. She raised her eyebrows.

"*Yes*, it was good," I said defensively. "Don't be so surprised."

Sophie waved off my bruised ego. She was too intent on issuing orders.

"First of all, you *think* the date went well," she said. "But you can never be sure. He could have a different story altogether. That's why you have to wait for him to call. If he does, you *know*. But if you call *him*, you never will. Plus you'll look desperate."

"Why doesn't it make him look desperate if *he* calls?" I sputtered.

That one stopped Sophie. She frowned, looked confused for a moment, and then got irritated (because she clearly didn't have an answer).

"This is just the way it is!" she declared. "I can't believe you don't know that."

Part of me was *glad* I didn't know that. I'd always zoned out a little when Sophie or Caroline dissected the latest social dramas at our school. I knew just enough of the "rules" to get through school without humiliating myself, but not enough to play all the little games. Because I'd always hated games. I read my way through whatever school sporting events Caroline and Sam dragged me to. And I could never get through more than a few minutes of Monopoly with my family.

Sophie, of course, adored Monopoly—and she always won. Which was why it was hard for me to completely ignore what she'd just said.

So I didn't call Will.

I didn't sleep much that night either.

And when I left for the beach the next morning, my wrap pulled around my shoulders like a dowdy shawl, I was officially depressed.

By the time I got to the North Peninsula, though, I was officially *mad*. I mean, *what* kind of boy asks for your number, then doesn't call? A boy who wants to mess with your head, that's who!

That must have been why *my* head felt hot and buzzy and the hair sticking to my temples was as maddening as a swarm of mosquitoes.

I tossed my wrap onto the sand, then ran into the surf. I dove head-first into a seething whitecap, then swam a few frantic laps back and forth along the shoreline. The hissing and churning of the water felt like a perfect match for what was going on inside me.

Only when I could dive beneath the surface and actually feel a hint of the peace I usually got in the water did I allow myself to stop swimming and just drift.

I dove down and skimmed my hands across the sand. My fingers felt floaty. The wet sand sifted through them, weightless and velvety. As I often did while swimming, I gave in to the illusion that I was part of the island, as elemental as the sea oats or the sandbars that emerged every day at low tide.

Still sifting, I uncovered a sand dollar. I zinged it from one hand to the other before flipping it back to the ocean floor. Then I swam by pressing my legs together and undulating them like a tail. My sister and I had taught ourselves to do that when we were little, imagining that we could go faster if we swam like mermaids. I'm not sure if it worked, but the habit had stuck with me.

Swimming like that now made me remember when mastering a mermaid kick (or a cartwheel or double Dutch) had seemed to matter so much and had been so *hard*.

They seemed easy now compared with all the mental gymnastics it took to just sit on my butt and wait for one boy to call me.

The thought of my silent cell phone got me simmering again,

and I pushed out of the water with a big splash and gasp. After blinking the ocean out of my eyes, I spotted Caroline on the beach, waving her pale blue wrap at me.

I trudged up to join her.

"Where's Sam?" I asked her as I collapsed onto the sand. I didn't even bother to spread my wrap out beneath me, but just let my soaked arms and legs get breaded like a fish fillet.

"Where's Will?" Caroline retorted.

The fish fillet gave Caroline the fish eye.

"He hasn't called?" Caroline asked with a little gulp that she quickly tried to cover up with a cough.

"So that's bad, right?" I said. I flipped out the straw on my sports bottle and took a big gulp of sugary, minty iced tea.

Caroline started to stay something, then reconsidered and clamped her mouth shut. Then she inhaled again, but cocked her head and clammed up a second time.

"What?!" I sputtered, breaking into the debate Caroline was having with herself. "Just say it! Will is blowing me off, isn't he?"

"That's the thing," she said with a helpless shrug. "I don't know *what* to say. I don't know if Will not calling is tragic or totally fine. I might have a boyfriend, but I haven't figured any of this stuff out yet. I mean, Sam and I didn't go through the mating dance when we got together because we already knew each other so well."

"Yeah, I guess it's different," I said. I'd been propped up on my elbows but now I flopped flat on my back, not even caring that I'd have to scrub sand out of my hair later. "Why couldn't I have given my number to someone *I've* known forever?"

"Because that's the whole point," Caroline said. She was sitting cross-legged on her wrap, picking at one of its many loose threads. "You don't know Will at all and *that's* the appeal. He's a mystery. He's nothing but possibility."

"Or *im*possibility." I sighed. "That's what's killing me. If this were Sam, I would *know* what was going on at his end. I'd know that he was working a double shift at the bike shop or having an emergency band practice for a gig. Or I'd know that the more caffeine he drinks at night, the later he sleeps the next day."

"Yeah, well, you never know *everything* about a boy," Caroline said before lying down herself.

I lifted my head and squinted over at her.

"Wait a minute," I said. "Is everything okay with Sam? Where *is* he, anyway?"

"What? Sam? Oh, everything's fine," Caroline said with a brusque wave of her hand. "He's just where you said. Double shift at the bike shop."

I plopped my head back down, then laid a hand on my stomach, which was feeling a little queasy.

"Uch," I said. "I think I sucked in too much salt water. Let's go to Angelo's for some sour candy."

"I'm way ahead of you," Caroline said. She pulled out a white paper sack filled with unnatural colors and flavors.

Angelo's was the closest beachmart to both Dune Island schools, so naturally, it was the island's best candy source. In fact, its bulk candy bins were legendary. During the school year, Angelo's was like a stock market floor every afternoon, complete with jostling, negotiating, and trading.

But in the summertime Angelo's was sleepier, so he was lazier with his stock. You might end up with nothing in your candy bag but popcorn-flavored jelly beans or Bit-O-Honeys.

"The pickings weren't that bad today," Caroline said. "I got a ton of sour straws. All the apple, cherry, and watermelons were gone, though. We have to make do with blue raspberry."

"Too bad Benjie's not here, he'd love that," I joked, fishing a long, cobalt-blue gummy straw out of the bag. The sour sugar made my mouth smart for a moment before the man-made deliciousness of the gummy took over. I took another bite before musing, "Remember when all it took to make us happy was mermaid kicking and some blue candy?"

"Um, no!" Caroline said. She stared at me and gave her head a frustrated little shake. "Anna, that stuff has *never* made you happy. You've always been waiting for something better to come along."

"I have?" I said. Now I sat up, feeling little rivulets of sand slide off my limbs. "What do you mean?"

"I don't know," Caroline said. "I mean, it's not extreme. You don't do that whole 'I hate my small-town life so I'm going to dye my hair matte black and start piercing myself' thing."

"So cliché," we said at the exact same time.

After we stopped laughing, Caroline got serious again.

"Sometimes it just feels like you're not completely here," she tried to explain. She pointed at the water. "When you swim laps out there, like you were just doing, sometimes I wonder if you want to just keep going. Like you wish you could swim all the way across the ocean or something. I mean, Anna . . . did you *really* think Dune Islanders were going to go for Cardamom Hibiscus ice cream?"

I laughed again.

"Holy non sequitur," I said. But Caroline only half smiled.

Of course, she was right about the ice cream. That lurid orange stuff had sat almost untouched in the ice cream case for two weeks before my dad had hauled the poor freezer-burned tub out and tossed it.

But just because I made some exotic ice cream didn't mean I wanted to run away to India tomorrow.

Right?

"Maybe that's why none of the Dune Island boys are good enough for you," Caroline went on. She looked down in her lap and fiddled with her gummy straw. "And why you were so instantly into this guy from New York."

"*Good* enough for me?" I said. "That's *so* not it. Especially since Will isn't even like that. He's way more like us than a shoo-bee. I *told* you what we talked about the other night."

"I'm just saying," Caroline said, looking away from my confused face and gazing out at the water, "it *is* possible to go out with someone you know. Someone who *would* call the next day."

My mouth dropped open. I had a million retorts to this, but also—none.

I'd never really thought about why the Landon Smiths of my world held no interest for me.

It also hadn't occurred to me that I might like Will simply because he was different; because he was from someplace else.

Especially since right then he couldn't have felt *farther* away and I definitely *didn't* like that. Already our date was starting to feel hazy to me and I wondered if I hadn't invented some of its swooniest parts. Maybe I'd been the only one who'd felt like the night had flown by in about five minutes—and left me wanting more.

I didn't know which was a more depressing thought. That I liked Will only because I was a pathetic small towner and he was a glamorous city boy.

Or that this boy I liked so much seemed to have forgotten about *me* entirely.

I crammed the last of my gummy straw into my mouth, then said, "It's hot. You want to swim?"

Caroline peered at me, one eye squinted shut against the sun.

"I promise not to make a break for England," I said with a forced laugh.

"Your lips are bright blue," Caroline said as we got to our feet.

I laughed, feeling a little bit better.

I mean, other than the black hole of rejection that was eating up my insides.

Perhaps to fill that hole, I reached into the candy bag for one more mouthful of sugar therapy before we headed into the water. Since the gummy straws were all gone, I popped three sticky Swedish fish into my mouth.

When I straightened up, I almost choked on them. Because walking toward me, with a bright red rental bike kickstanded in the parking lot way behind him, was Will. He was still far away, waving as if we were in a crowd on Fifth Avenue and not all by ourselves on this empty stretch of sand.

I grabbed Caroline's arm with one hand and waved weakly at

Will with the other. Then I began chewing like my life depended on it. It pretty much did. If Will walked over to find me—encrusted with sand, red-eyed from my salty swim—*and* with a mouth glued together with candy, I might have literally died.

Luckily, Caroline was my lifeguard. As Will approached, *she* spoke in my place.

"Well, hello, Will!" she called with a little too much joviality.

Then she crossed her arms over her chest, and my sigh of relief got caught in my throat. Because Caroline's stance was the same one she takes before a varsity volleyball game or a debate over fossil fuels with her dad—or before putting annoying shoobees in their place.

The annoying shoobee of the moment was clearly Will.

I started chewing much faster, hoping I didn't look like a rabbit.

"Hey!" Will said. He was trying to be polite and look at Caroline, but he kept peeking at me. I tried to chew between glances, promising myself that if I was *ever* able to swallow these ridiculous gummy fish, I'd never eat candy again.

Well . . . not in front of boys at least.

"That bike looks familiar," Caroline said, pointing at Will's shiny red beach cruiser. She wasn't smiling.

"Yeah!" Will said. It looked like the blue laser beams Caroline was shooting him with her eyes were making him a little sweaty. "I went to rent it and there was Sam!"

"And he told you where we hung out," Caroline provided for him.

"Uh-huh," Will said. He turned to check out our almost-empty beach (while I *finally* swallowed). There was nothing there but Angelo's and its cracked parking lot, a spindly looking fishing pier, and a big, sloping dune that hid all of it from Highway 80. "This is amazing. So this is why I don't ever see you at the south beach."

Caroline shrugged.

"Sam and I sometimes hang down there," she said, "but Anna's a loner."

"No, I'm not!" I protested. "I'm a . . . reader."

I pointed wanly at my novel, which was tossed into the sand next to my wrap.

"*Beloved*?" Will said. "Kind of heavy for the beginning of the summer, isn't it?"

"Have you read it?" I asked. "I love it. When it's not, you know, tearing out my soul and stomping on it."

"I had to read it for school," Will said. "I go to this kind of intense private school because my mom teaches there. They're always making us read books that feel like they're in a foreign language, even though they're in English. But *Beloved* was one of the ones I actually really dug by the time I finished it. Writing a term paper on it? Not so much."

I felt a pang. So Will dug impossible books like *Beloved*? Even if he'd read it reluctantly, that was definitely another checkmark on his growing list of pros.

Caroline rolled her eyes at my lit-geekery and stepped in again.

"I'm just curious," she said to Will, "what brought you to the bike shop?"

Will shrugged.

"Just wanted to do some exploring, I guess," Will said. "I still have a lot of the island to see. I didn't even *know* about this peninsula. It's awesome."

"I know somebody who could have given you a tour," Caroline said. Her folded arms tightened. She was practically a pretzel. "But you'd have to have, you know, *called* her."

"Caroline," I whisper-shrieked.

"Oh yeah?" Will said. "Dune Island does seem to have a lot of, like, *really* passionate volunteer types. Especially those people who camp out to protect the sea turtle nests? I met one the other night. She was a little scary, I've got to admit . . ."

"Not as scary as *some* people I could name," I said, glaring at Caroline.

"You know what's scary?" Caroline said, glaring back at me, then shifting her laser beams to Will. "Being caught in a new place without a *phone*. I mean, you're practically paralyzed if you lose your cell phone. That ever happen to you, Will?"

"Um, no . . ." Will was looking at Caroline in confusion. Then suddenly his eyes went wide. He'd realized what she was *really* talking about.

He looked at me in alarm.

"Wait a minute," he blurted. "My brother told me not to call you for thirty-six hours."

"Thirty-six hours?" I said. Now I was confused. "Is that like not swimming for a half hour after you eat? Because you know that's a myth, right?"

My voice was as flat as my feelings. I wondered if Will's

thirty-six-hour spiel was going to be more or less lame than a couldn't-find-your-number one.

"It just seemed like . . . what you're supposed to do," Will said.

"Why?" I blurted. Just as I had with Sophie.

"Because . . ." Will shook his head as if he had a sudden case of fuzzbrain. "You know, it seemed like a good idea at the time. But now . . ."

Will looked at me. And his expression was something I'd never quite seen before. Call it a meeting of delight and nausea.

Which was pretty much exactly how I'd been feeling ever since our date.

Could that be what smitten looked like?

I glanced at Caroline. Her blue laser beams had softened and her mouth was slowly widening into a big grin of recognition.

The next thing I knew, she was scooping up her wrap. She whipped it around her waist so fast that she covered both me and Will with a spray of sand.

"I just remembered," she said, "I told Sam I'd meet him for coffee on his break."

Sam didn't drink coffee. I was about to point this out when I stopped myself—and smiled slyly.

Caroline, of course, *knew* that Sam didn't drink coffee. She was speaking in code, which seemed almost as silly as Owen's thirty-six-hour rule. It also felt, somehow, very sophisticated. If the language of love was French, the language of dating seemed to be some sort of spy code. Like being in the CIA, boy-girl relations were all about intrigue and subterfuge and wearing cute outfits.

"Well, tell Sam thanks," Will said as Caroline began to walk away. "I never would have found this beach if he hadn't pointed me in the right direction."

"You should really call that tour guide," Caroline said, grinning at Will. She gave the knotted waist of her wrap one more tug, then strode over to her bike, which was propped next to mine in front of Angelo's.

After Caroline left, Will and I stood in uncomfortable silence for a moment. And suddenly I became painfully aware of what I was wearing.

A bathing suit.

A bikini, to be specific. And nothing else, unless you counted a whole lot of sand. When Will had arrived, I'd been so focused on my mouthful of candy that I hadn't even thought to consider the rest of my body and every curve, freckle, and scar on it—all just laid out there for Will to size up.

Now it was my turn to whip my wrap off the ground. I quickly sausaged myself within it while simultaneously dusting sand off my arms and legs.

"My brother . . . ," Will began.

"Oh, say no more," I said, holding up my hand.

Which was sort of a mistake, because he *did* say no more. At least for a minute.

But when Will finally found his voice again, what he said made my jaw drop.

"Nobody's ever made me a picnic before," he said.

He paused to look even more queasy/delighted—and I gaped at him. He hadn't *really* just said that, had he?

It sounded much less cheesy than it had in my daydream. It was just straightforward and sweet. I was starting to think that Will would make a terrible spy.

I pointed at his bike.

"So are you renting that by the hour?"

"Sam actually gave me a deal on it for the summer," Will said. "Even if I knew how to drive, we don't have a car here, so . . ."

"You don't know how to drive?" I said.

"I know, it's embarrassing," Will said. "But, listen, it's impressive that I can even ride a bike! A lot of people I grew up with can't even do that because their parents never lugged them over to Central Park to teach them."

"I can't even remember not being able to ride a bike," I said. "I don't know what I'd do without Allison."

I pointed over in the direction of Angelo's.

"Oh, is that who taught you to ride?" Will asked, following my gaze.

"Um, no, that's my bike, Allison Porchnik," I stammered, suddenly realizing how dumb that sounded. "You know, from *Annie Hall*, the Woody Allen movie?"

I'd always named my bikes, from my first trike (Lulu) to my old green Schwinn (Kermit) to my current gold cruiser with the white seat and the super-wide handlebars. The bike was so seventies fabulous that I'd *had* to give her a name from that era. After watching every movie in my parents' Woody Allen collection one rainy weekend, I'd come up with a perfect one: Allison Porchnik, one of Woody's dry-witted, golden-haired ex-wives.

Will was giving me a funny look.

And suddenly I realized something else.

"Oh my God," I said, covering my mouth with my hand. "My mouth is bright blue, isn't it? Caroline got us these horrible gummy straws and—"

"No, no." Will waved me off. "It's just . . . Woody Allen. The guy from New York?"

"Um, he's kind of more than 'the guy from New York'!" I said. "He's like the best filmmaker ever. Or he was, anyway . . ."

"Yeah, decades ago." Will shrugged.

"Yeah, that's when he was at his best!" I insisted. "You know, 'especially the early, funny ones'?"

Will looked at me blankly, and I smiled and rolled my eyes. So much for us having an instant private joke.

"That was a line from *Stardust Memories*," I told Will. "You *have* to rent it sometime."

"Well, if I *have* to," Will said, teasing me. Then he glanced over his shoulder at his bike.

"So," he added casually, "do you and Allison Porchnik want to go for a ride?"

I looked down at my toes so he wouldn't see how hard I was beaming. Who cared about private jokes? I was about to go on my second date with Will Cooper.

*I*t had been a long time since I'd ridden the entire nine miles of Highway 80. I usually was too busy getting from point A to point B to just tool around for the pleasure of it.

But it was fun listening to Will's amazed exclamations as we skimmed down the endless stretch of asphalt. On our right was a prairie of swamp grass, emerald green and practically vibrating with cicadas, frogs, and dragonflies. On our left was the ocean, shooting flashes of gold at us every time the sun hit a wave.

With Will beside me, I slowed down, and not just because his red bike was a heavy clunker. The traffic was sleepy and we rode side by side, with me playing tour guide.

"We could go to the lighthouse at the south end of the island," I said. "That's what the chamber of commerce would have us do."

"Ah yes, the lighthouse from all the T-shirts and mugs and mouse pads?" Will said. "I've been there already with my mom and her *Let's Go* book."

"Dune Island's got a travel book?" I gasped.

"Um, no," Will said with a laugh. "It's more like three pages *in* a travel book. But they're a really packed three pages!"

I laughed.

"Well, does the travel book mention our water tower on the west side?" I asked. "Because I think it's a much better view than the lighthouse. If you ask me, the swamp is a little more interesting from that high up. Every time you go up there, the tidal pools are in different places. They make a picture."

"Of what?" Will asked, lazily looping his bike back and forth across the highway.

"I usually see Van Gogh," I said. "You know, all those swirls and swoops like in *Starry Night*? Most people just see Jesus."

"Seriously? Like the people who see him in cinnamon buns and water stains on the wall?"

"Will," I said gently, "Remember, you're in the South now. There's a *lot* of Jesus down here."

"Believe me," Will said. "I can tell just by talking to you."

"What?!" I sputtered. "I don't have a Southern accent. My family is from up North."

"Um, I hate to break it you . . ."

Will lifted one hand off his handlebars to give me a helpless shrug.

"Okay!" I admitted. "So I say 'y'all.' I suppose that sounds pretty Southern. But come on. 'You guys'?! That just sounds so . . . wrong."

"Yeah," Will agreed, "if you have a Southern accent."

I coasted for a moment, staring at the glinty ocean.

"Well, that's kind of a big bummer." I sighed.

"Why?" Will asked.

"Because everyone thinks that people with Southern accents are dumb," I complained. "Even *presidents* are totally mocked for their Southern accents."

"Well, you're not dumb," Will said. "Anybody who talked to you for more than two minutes would know that."

It took my breath away, it really did. Will said these things to me so matter-of-factly, as if he wasn't giving me the most lovely compliment but simply stating the obvious that anybody could see.

He didn't know that, up until then, nobody else had.

"And besides," Will added, "I like your accent."

See what I mean?

"My second favorite view," I said, pedaling harder so I could get a bit of breeze on my now flaming face, "is from the biggest dune on the island. It's way south, past the boardwalk. But you can't go there at this time of year. The panic grass is just sprouting, so it's too delicate to even *look* at."

"Maybe *I'm* dumb because I didn't understand a word you just said," Will said. "You call that dune grass 'panic grass'? Why?"

"That's just what it's called," I said. "I don't even know why, actually. All I know is, as soon as you learn to walk on this island, all you hear from your parents is, 'Watch out for the sea oats! Mind the panic grass!' Maybe that's why. They sound so *panicky* about it. I mean, if you thought the turtle nest sitters were scary, wait until you meet a dune grass guard. They're very, very passionate about erosion."

"Well, after Toni Morrison books, erosion is my favorite subject," Will cracked, with that half smile that was already starting to feel sweetly familiar. "I mean, I could go on and on and on."

I threw back my head and laughed.

And then we did talk on and on and on. Not about erosion, of course. Mostly Will asked me questions about Dune Island. Like why the gas station at the south end of the island is called Psycho Sisters. (It's a long story involving the Robinson twins, a sweet sixteen party, and a way-too-red red velvet cake.)

"Okay, and why, when I went to the library," Will asked, "was there an entire shelf with nothing but copies of *Love Story* on it? There were fifteen! I had to count them. I mean, that many *Love Story*s in a one-room library is pretty weird."

"Oh, yeah, the *Love Story*s." I sighed. "There's an island-wide book club, and someone had the fabulous idea of having *that* be the selection a couple of summers ago. Everywhere you went, women were reading this cheesy book and just *crying*."

Will had started laughing halfway through my explanation and I had to laugh too. It was kind of fun recounting these random little Dune Island details that I'd always just known and never thought twice about.

Before I knew it, we were at the southern tip of the island, which was as different from the North Peninsula as could be. The north juts out into the Atlantic with absolutely nothing to shelter it. It's craggy and lunar and feels as deserted as, well, a desert if you turn your back to the beachmart and the pier.

But the southern end of the island hugs the coast of Georgia like a baby curling against its mother. There's a sandy path there that leads into a giant tangle that my friends and I have always called the jungle. It's lush with out-of-control ivy, dinosaur-size shrubs, and big, gnarled magnolias, palms, and live oaks. The sun shoots through breaks in the greenery like spotlights, and the sounds of bugs and frogs and lizards spin a constant drone. In the middle of the jungle is a clearing, and in the middle of that are some half-decayed tree trunks arranged into a sort of lounge.

Without even discussing it, Will and I got off our bikes and walked down the path toward it.

For the first time in a while, Will didn't ask me any questions. I was quiet too. This cranny of the island suddenly felt special. Not just someplace to go with my friends to break the monotony of our beach/Swamp/Angelo's loop, but like something out of a fairy tale—my very own Secret Garden.

I hadn't done anything to make all this teeming life happen, of course. Still, showing the jungle to Will, like the rest of the island, made it somehow feel like mine. So instead of rustling quickly over the path, just trying to jet to the clearing, I found myself lingering over things. I stroked feathery ferns with my finger, enjoyed the dry, green scent of an elephant ear plant brushing my cheek, and pulled a dangling swatch of palm bark free from the trunk that was still clinging to it.

It was all very romantic, until Will started cursing under his breath and slapping at his calves.

"Oh, the mosquitoes," I said. "I can help with that. Come on."

We hiked back to the head of the path, and because we were hurrying against the drone of the bugs, we got there in only a few minutes. I pulled a little plastic box out from beneath my bike seat. In it I had an emergency stash of sunscreen, bug spray, and sno-cone money.

I held out the spray bottle, but instead of taking it, Will cocked his leg in my direction.

I hesitated for a moment, then dropped to one knee to spritz the fumy stuff on Will's ankles and calves. I tried not to fixate on Will's muscles, the hair on his legs that was somewhere between light brown and sun-bleached gold, or the way his frayed khaki cutoffs grazed the top of my hand when I stood up to mist his arms.

I guess I held the bottle a little too close when I sprayed the back of Will's neck, because the repellant pooled up in a little froth just below his hairline.

"Man, that's cold!" Will said.

"Sorry!" I giggled, then used my fingertips to rub the stuff in.

Touching Will's neck seemed shockingly intimate. Part of me wanted to jerk my hand away. Another wanted to put my other hand on his neck too, and maybe give him a little massage.

But instead I just swiped the bug spray away quickly and said, "You know, my shift at The Scoop starts kind of soon. I should probably . . ."

Will nodded, smiled, and walked toward his bike.

I had no idea if he'd thought of that moment as A Moment— or if he'd just been grateful for the bug repellant.

Either way, I felt calmer as we walked our bikes back to the highway and headed to town.

Because whatever that moment had been, I now felt pretty certain that it wouldn't be our last.

Over the next couple of weeks, Will and I fell into such a comfortable groove, it was almost hard to remember that day and a half of *will he call or won't he?* Because Will did call, whenever he felt like it.

Or I called *him*.

One morning he wandered over to the North Peninsula with a beach towel, a paperback book, and a giant iced coffee, just because he knew I'd be there.

And one evening I stashed some ice cream in a cooler and

drifted over to the crooked little boardwalk that connected his rental cottage to the beach, because he'd told me that he liked to sit there at night, dangling his legs over the tall grass and listening to music.

We covered every corner of Dune Island, me on Allison Porchnik and Will on Zelig. That's the name, from another Woody Allen movie, I'd come up with for his chunky red bike.

But with each day that went by, I realized we hadn't given our bikes the right names at all.

Unlike Zelig, the character who traveled the world pretending to be all sorts of people he wasn't, Will was incredibly honest—but sweet about it. (For instance, he eventually told me that he *had* noticed my blue lips that morning on the beach. But he also told me he'd thought they were cute.)

And after Will chucked Owen's thirty-six-hour rule, I never felt like jilted Allison Porchnik again.

It was thrillingly comfortable being with Will.

But also uncomfortably thrilling.

Every time I saw him, I felt like my eyes opened a little wider and my breath got just little quicker. I felt *intense*, like I was getting more oxygen than usual. And even though this was preferable to the way I'd felt when I'd first met Will—and couldn't get enough air *in*—it still made me a little self-conscious.

I worried that I looked like a chipmunk in a Disney cartoon, all fluttery lashes and big, goofy smiles—basically, the worst incarnation of cute.

But I couldn't stop the swooning. Every day I discovered

another little bit of Will. One afternoon he told me he'd been the resident haunter in his old apartment building. Every year on Halloween, he'd dressed up in a different creepy costume to scare the sour candy out of the kids trick-or-treating in the hallways.

Another time he reminisced about spotting his dad one day eating alone at a diner. He said he'd almost burst into tears, right there at 66th and Lex.

All these layers made me like Will more and more.

But was I *falling* for him?

That was the big question—that I had no idea how to answer.

"How did you know?" I asked Caroline one day. It was the third week in June and the heat had gotten to that point where you could see it waving at you as it shimmied off the hot asphalt. We were sitting on a shaded bench at the far end of the board-walk, eating coconut sno-cones. We shoveled the crushed ice into our mouths, trying to eat it before it melted into syrupy puddles.

"How did I know what?" Caroline slurred. Her tongue was ice-paralyzed.

"That Sam was *it*," I said.

Caroline looked down into her Styrofoam cup, then smiled a private smile, remembering.

"You're gonna think it's dumb," she said.

"Caroline," I said urgently. "This is research. I'm totally objective."

She gave me a funny, searching look, but then went dreamy again as she thought about Sam. About their Moment.

"It was almost nothing," Caroline said. "We were out at the Crash Pad."

The Crash Pad was Caroline's dad's bizarro version of a play set. He had this ancient Airstream trailer that the family used to take out for long camping trips. But when Caroline was eight, her mom had put her foot down and said she'd rather live in a yurt made from recently slaughtered yak skin than spend one more night in that camper.

So Caroline's dad had moved the Airstream into the backyard. Then he'd put an old trampoline next to the camper and connected the two with a slide.

And *that* was what we'd grown up playing on. Now the camper was completely taken over by kudzu and the slide was no longer slippery, but the huge trampoline still had some bounce. We'd named it the Crash Pad, the perfect place to look at the stars through a halo of crape myrtle branches or to just goof around, jumping between snacks and snacking between jumps.

"We were just sprawled on the trampoline, talking about some school drama," Caroline reminisced. "I don't even remember what it was. But then a wind came and blew all these pink crape myrtle blossoms all over us. A bunch of them stuck in my hair and Sam started pulling them out. He was so gentle, so careful not to pull even one strand. And when they were all out, he made this tiny bouquet out of them and handed them to me."

I wanted to laugh, because this was just the sort of goofy thing that Sam did all the time.

But obviously, this time it had been different. It hadn't been a joke. And somehow they'd both known it.

"For me," Caroline said, "it was kind of like when my dad got new glasses. He wandered around for two days just so happy because everything suddenly looked more clear and crisp and colorful. Well, suddenly *Sam* looked, not *different*. Just more vivid, I guess. More interesting. More *Sam*."

My own eyes went wide. That sounded a *lot* like what I was feeling for Will.

"I just *knew*," Caroline said with a happy shrug. "And somehow he *knew* that I knew and he told me that he'd loved me for more than a year!"

"Really?" I gasped. "He kept it a secret all that time?"

"Well, what if I hadn't felt the same way?" Caroline posed. "Can you imagine how crushing that would be?

Yes, *that* I could imagine.

Like Sam, I didn't know how Will felt about me. Of course, I knew that he liked me. But did he like me like *that*?

Had he gone shivery all over when I'd touched his neck, or had he forgotten it before his mosquito bites had even healed?

And how much of all this time together was happening because there was nobody *else* here for him hang with except his brother and his mom?

The only time I asked myself these questions, though, was when Will wasn't around. When we were together, I was having too much fun to think about the nuances of his feelings. We could be bobbing in the waves, talking, and suddenly two hours had gone by and I was a total prune, late for my shift at work.

We'd get lunch and I'd be too busy talking to eat it.

Strolling down the boardwalk, he'd make me laugh so hard I'd forget that I hated attracting the attention of nosy islanders.

Will didn't mind people looking at him. He seemed to actually like the fact that we couldn't go anywhere without people saying, "Hey, Anna! What's the flavor du jour?" Or, "Anna, tell your mom Kat left her goggles at our house." Or especially, "Anna, who's your friend?"

"At home," Will told me as he was walking me to work one afternoon, "you're always walking through this sea of strangers. Here it's like everyone's family."

"Yeah," I said. "And what does family do? Nose into your business, remind you of embarrassing things you did when you were four, and never fail to let you know when you need a haircut. You don't know how good you have it."

"Yeah, well . . ." Will drifted off as we arrived at The Scoop. He looked through the window and as I followed his gaze, I cringed.

My entire family was inside.

Sophie was behind the ice cream case with a friend, sneaking samples. My dad was settling Kat and Benjie at one of the kiddie tables with some sorbet, and my mom was scooping for a small crowd of customers.

They looked like, well, my family. Chaotic and dreamy and . . . happy.

And *together*.

They were everything Will's family wasn't. And I'd just stuck my big, sandy foot in my mouth.

While I was wondering if I should apologize or if that would just make things worse, Will opened The Scoop's warped screen door and went inside.

I froze.

This was new. Will had walked me to work once before, but I'd said a quick good-bye before we'd arrived. I hadn't wanted to subject him to my dad's clueless questions, my mom's big, over-eager smiles, or God forbid, Sophie scanning him from head to toe for fashion appropriateness.

Plus, bringing Will home to meet my family (because The Scoop was home just as much as our house was) seemed so old-fashioned. So girlfriendy. And we weren't there.

Yet.

Yet?

I watched Will pause inside the door and glance back at me with a look that said, *Aren't you coming in?*

There were a million ways I could have analyzed Will walking into The Scoop. But I tried (really hard) not to.

Whatever was happening between me and Will—whether it was a "relationship" or just a friendship—would make itself clear soon.

It has to, right? I asked myself. *How many dates can you have without any handholding, kissing, or sappy declarations of like before you realize that they're non-dates? They're just two friends (one of whom has an unrequited and possibly tragic crush) hanging out.*

Something would happen, I told myself, or *not* happen, soon.

And I just had to keep myself together until then.

With that I gulped and went with Will as he met my entire family.

*　*　*

My peace-love-and-gelato parents are not exactly the types to give boys bone-crunching handshakes or a threatening mention of my eleven o' clock curfew. When I introduced them to Will, they only wanted to foist heaps of ice cream on him.

"Will, I want you to taste this," my mom said from behind the counter. Her voice sounded a little shrill and overenthusiastic. I was both touched and mortified that she was trying to make a good impression on Will. My parents hadn't asked me much about this boy I'd been spending so much time with, but clearly they'd been curious. As my mom mixed up something at the marble slab, she kept shooting Will quick, probing glances. She must have been wondering if this introduction to Will Meant Something.

Of course, I was wondering the same thing.

Mom plopped a huge, shaggy scoop of ice cream into a bowl and placed it on the counter.

"This," she told Will, "is a mix-in I've been playing around with."

"Mom," I interjected, "I don't think—"

"Looks good, Mrs. Patrick," Will interrupted, giving me a nervous glance. "I'll give it a try."

I didn't know whether to laugh at all this posturing or leap in to save Will. My mother was an ice cream genius, but somehow her mix-in ideas were almost always awful.

Will took a very large first bite. He started chewing. And chewing. His eyes practically watered from the effort.

"Mom?" I quavered. "What's in there?"

"Maple Bacon Crunch ice cream with mandarin oranges and sliced almonds," my mom announced proudly. "It's my play on duck a l'orange."

"But," I sputtered, "bacon is *not* duck. And anyway, *duck ice cream*?"

I think it took Will a full minute to choke his mouthful down.

"You don't have to eat any more," I assured him. "My mom won't care, right, Mom?"

"Well, I guess not, sweetie," Mom said. "But, Will, maybe you should tell us what *you* think."

She looked at him eagerly.

I watched Will's jaw tense. Either he was trying to figure out what to say, or he was working the horrible taste out of his mouth.

"Well . . . ," he said carefully, "it's very, um, textured. Yeah. A *lot* of textures going on in there."

"Do you want a palate cleanser?" my dad offered. He jumped off his stool behind the register. "Some sorbet?"

"No!" Will burst out. Then he reddened. "I mean, no thanks . . . sir."

At this Sophie and her friend dissolved into giggles. I had to stifle a laugh too as I grabbed Will by the elbow and pulled him into the kids area.

"*Sir?*" I said.

"Well, like you've said," Will said defensively, "it's the South. I figured where there's a lot of Jesus, there are probably plenty of ma'ams and sirs, too."

"That's true," I admitted, "but believe me, not with my *dad*."

"Oh," Will said. He shook his head wearily. And then . . . he shrugged it off. He pointed at the doodles Kat and Benjie were making on their chalkboard table.

"Hey, what's that you're drawing?" he asked. "Is it an Ewok?"

An instant later Will was sitting with my brother and sister, doing a Darth Vader voice. He seemed completely recovered from the duck a l'orange, not to mention meeting my parents.

So what does that mean? I started to ask myself. But before I could even begin to ponder that question, I gave my head a little shake.

Don't analyze, don't analyze, don't analyze, I ordered myself. *Just because he isn't traumatized after kind of bombing with Mom and Dad doesn't necessarily mean he's not interested in me.*

After another few minutes of amusing my brother and sister, Will stood up to leave.

"So my brother wants us to try ghost-crabbing tonight," he told me.

"Ah, yes," I teased. "For those who don't like cow-tipping, there's always ghost crabbing."

"You know I have to do it," Will said. "It's so Dune Island."

"Yeah, you kind of have to," I agreed with a grin. "Well, you and Owen have fun."

"Um, Anna," Will said, clearing his throat. "That was sort of me asking you if you wanted to come."

"Oh!" I said, rolling my eyes and grinning. I hesitated before answering, though. A date with a boy and his brother was definitely a non-date, wasn't it?

Just like this powwow with my family seemed to be too.

It was all just so *friendly*.

My heart sank a little bit. But then Will grinned at me, and he shrugged his bony, broad shoulders and I noticed a small hole in the neck of his faded navy T-shirt. It all made me feel that familiar Will-induced intensity once more.

So what could I do? I said yes. But in the back of my mind, I was also steeling myself.

Crabbing with Will's brother isn't exactly a setup for a first kiss. I might as well face it—it's not going to happen tonight.

I didn't want to think about the bigger picture, though, which was this: If we didn't kiss soon, there was clearly not going to be any romance between me and Will Cooper.

"Wow," I said to Owen and Will that night on the beach. "It's a good thing I'm here. You guys *really* don't know anything about crabs."

Both of them were crouching next to a little hole in the sand, shining their flashlights down it. They looked at me, bewildered.

"Yeah, where *are* they?" Owen said. "It's eight thirty and finally cooling off. I heard this was prime ghost crab time."

I laughed, walked over to the brothers, and turned their flashlights off.

"Give your eyes a minute to adjust," I said. "Then listen . . ."

The three of us stood very still.

Except I didn't feel still.

Ever since I'd made that secret pact with myself at The Scoop, I'd felt buzzy. Like a quivering pitch fork. Like a ticking timer.

All I wanted was for Will to put his hand on my arm or shoulder, to quiet all that nervous vibration.

But he didn't—because Owen was there, cracking jokes.

Or maybe Owen was there so that Will would have the perfect excuse to keep his distance.

Maybe this was his signal.

Maybe this was how it was going to be. Me and Will—and Owen. And Caroline and Sam and my parents and siblings . . .

Maybe we would just be friends.

I was trying to be fine with this. I mean, this evening had been fun so far. Until I'd turned off their flashlights, Will and Owen had been splashing water on each other and romping on the beach. Like all boys, they reminded me of dogs. (In a good way.)

Also, Owen—who would apparently do *anything* for a laugh—had actually checked out one of those *Love Story*s from the library. He kept tossing the book's cheesiest lines out at the most perfect moments, cracking us all up.

And I'd forgotten how ridiculously fun ghost-crabbing could be.

That was, if I could get the crabs to actually recover from Will's and Owen's flashlights.

I told Owen to stop talking.

"Just listen," I whispered.

Then I heard that familiar crunchy skittering and my

instincts took over. I snatched Owen's flashlight out of his hand and clicked it on, illuminating four tiny crabs zipping sideways over the wet sand.

If not for their darting, spidery movements, we never would have seen them. Ghost crabs were often smaller than your palm and a mottled beige, the exact color of the beach. They camouflaged themselves so perfectly, they were always a surprise, even to ghost crab lifers like me.

"There!" I shrieked.

"Aaah!" Owen and Will yelled together as the crabs scattered. Will grabbed the tin bucket they'd brought with them, pounced at one of the crabs, and scooped.

Which left him with a bucket of sand, water, and probably some crab poop.

"Oh my God," Owen huffed, bending at the waist and putting his hands on his shins. "Those things are *scary*. And so fast! I mean, they're worse than roaches."

"Naw, they're cute!" I said. "Let's try again. This time let me do it."

While Will laughed at Owen, we turned off our flashlights. Soon the creepy crawling sound returned and I leaped into the fray. Cornering one crab, I hopped around it, blocking its escape with my ankles. Then I scooped it up. You had to hold ghost crabs carefully on the sides of their bodies. Their front claws were little, but they could still pinch you until you cried. I thrust my little crab toward Owen and Will and it wiggled its many limbs in annoyance.

"That was simultaneously the most ridiculous and cool thing

I've ever seen," Will said, cracking up as the crab writhed in my hand. I put it down and it darted into the water.

"I'm so freaked out right now," Owen said, glancing at the sand nervously. "Keep your lights on so they don't come back!"

"You should see him when there's a spider," Will said. "He screams like a little girl."

"I do not," Owen started to say, when his phone buzzed.

"Oh my God, Mir," he said as he answered. "You would not believe what we're doing right now . . ."

Owen wandered down the beach as he talked.

"So much for Owen," Will said. "That's Miriam, his girl-friend. They'll be talking for the next hour at least."

I cocked my head. Will didn't sound disappointed.

"Clearly, he can't handle the crabs, anyway," Will said. He grinned and I could see his teeth shining in the moonlight.

"So you're the bug killer in the family," I said. "So am I. Well, except for spiders, because we need all of those we can get to eat the mosquitoes. And crickets, of course. They're good luck. And bees and butterflies—"

"Pollinators," Will filled in. "What about ghost crabs? Do you ever, you know, *cook* them?"

"Uch." I laughed. "Believe me, those things aren't for eating."

Will started to laugh with me, but before he could, he whooped and jumped to the side, kicking his right leg around frantically.

"I think one just crawled over my foot!" he yelled.

I burst out laughing.

"Who can't handle the crabs now?" I asked.

"Oooh," Will said, shuddering. "You win. I was trying to be all macho, but those things are skeeving me out!"

"I've got to go ghost-crabbing, Anna," I said in a deep voice. "It's *so* Dune Island."

This was me embracing the just-friends thing. Because you don't mock boys that you're angling to kiss, right?

Will uttered a faux growl and turned his flashlight on himself, making a gruesome face in the shadows.

I just laughed again, then pointed at his feet.

"There goes another one," I announced.

"Where, where?" Will yelled, running with pumping knees into the water.

"Oh, it must have just been your toes, wiggling around," I said.

"Oh, really," Will said.

"Yes, really," I replied, trying not to giggle. "It was an honest mistake."

"Like this?"

And suddenly Will jumped back onto the sand, grabbed me around the waist, and plunked me into the water.

I was just wearing cutoffs and a striped tank top, so I didn't care about getting wet.

I also couldn't remember *what* I'd always found so unlikable about boys scooping me up and dunking me into the ocean. Will's arms around me had felt as different from Landon Smith's as a hammock feels from a desk chair.

Will stepped back and pointed at my splashed clothes.

"Oh, it was an honest mistake!" he teased. "I'm sorry."

Then he splashed me some more.

I started to laugh, but it got caught in my throat when I looked at Will's smile in the moonlight. I still felt wonderful, but no longer in a giggly way. I wanted Will's arms around me again. I wanted to know what his lips felt like. I just plain wanted. Him.

Will's smile, too, faded and in midsplash he retreated, dropping his hand by his side.

Then, with a couple of quick strides, Will closed the open space between us and he *was* holding me. He pulled me tightly to him. I looked up into his eyes, feeling both surprised and . . . *finally.*

I didn't know how I could have doubted it. *This* was the place we'd been moving toward on all those walks and bike rides. Toward Will's warm, firm arms around my shoulders. Toward my hand on Will's back, feeling his muscles shifting under his clean-smelling T-shirt.

Toward this kiss.

This soft, sweet, so-worth-the-wait kiss.

July

$\mathcal{F}$irst off, the kissing.

Kissing Will felt like so many things. Like the time I swan dived off the lighthouse catwalk and felt, for just an instant, like I might swoop into the sky instead of plunging into the water.

It felt like a sun-warmed beach towel snuggled around you after the first chilly swim in April.

It felt both zingy and cozy; breathless and . . . like breathing. Like I could do it all day.

As June gave way to July and the days *stretched* out, kissing Will seemed like the only thing worth doing.

Of course, I couldn't tell Will that; tell him that the day after our first kiss, I'd woken up thinking about his perfect jawline and imperfectly beautiful nose.

That after I'd gotten out of bed, I'd zoned out in front of the bathroom mirror for a good ten minutes, my fingertips resting on my lips. I'd stood in a trance, remembering how we'd kissed while the ocean bubbled around our knees and indignant ghost crabs skirted our ankles.

That while I made a batch of Raspberry Bellini sorbet that morning, the peaches had reminded me of his breath.

Yes, I was so smitten, I was thinking swoony thoughts about Will's *breath*.

When he'd called that afternoon during my shift at The Scoop, it had felt strange to hear his voice but not be able to touch his smooth, callused fingertips, or put my cheek against his shoulder.

I still wanted to talk to him, though. I headed back to the cooler, flashing my dad a *be back in five* signal and trying not to grin like a complete fool.

"So I realized something," Will said as the cooler door *whoosh*ed shut behind me, "about last night."

"Um, what's that?"

His serious tone made me nervous suddenly. After all this— was something wrong?

Nervousness was the one emotion I'd forgotten to feel in the blissed-out hours since our kiss. Now it caught me by such surprise that I stubbed my toe on a milk crate and had to sit down on the floor. I felt myself bracing for whatever Will had to say, but couldn't imagine what it would be.

"I never did," Will said, "catch a ghost crab."

Now I heard the laugh in his voice—and something more. A sweetness. An *I really like you, Anna Patrick* lilt.

"Yeah, you really fell down on the job, didn't you?" I flirted.

"Well, something got in the way," Will flirted back.

"Some*thing*?" I said.

"Some*one*," Will corrected. "A terrible distraction, really."

"Oh, yes," I said, trying *hard* not to giggle. "Terrible."

The throbbing in my toe had stopped completely. All the

blood had clearly rushed from my foot to my flaming, grinning face. The blood certainly *wasn't* flowing to my brain. This conversation was vapidly cute, the kind of banter that always made me roll my eyes when I saw *other* people engaging in it.

Well, how could I have known that flirting could be so *fun*?

I decided that I should read a really dark and existential book to counteract the cuteness suddenly flooding my soul. It'd be penance for my hypocrisy. I vowed to go to the library the next morning—and plunged right back into the flirtfest.

"So what are we going to do about this ghost crab problem?" I said. "Try, try again?"

I imagined us going back to the beach that night after sunset, and once again my mind flashed on me and Will tangled up together in the surf. A strand of my hair had blown against his cheek as we'd kissed, and he'd smoothed it back, gently looping it behind my ear. Then he'd let his fingers flutter down my neck before resting on my shoulder.

I shivered as I remembered it, and not from the chill in the cooler.

"How about we try again," Will posed, "*minus* the ghost crabs?"

"Don't worry," I said through my smile. "There are plenty of other things you can do to bulk up your Dune Island cred."

"Well, that's what I was thinking," Will said. "There's another Movie on the Beach tonight. I know it's dorky. But come on. They're showing *E.T.* How can you not like that little alien? He's all big-eyed and . . . lumpy."

"Lumpy." I laughed. "How can I resist?"

I was *so* grateful to be locked in the dark, damp cooler right then. Nobody could see me *glowing* at the thought of snuggling up with Will on a blanket. We'd lean back on our elbows as we ate candy, whispered jokes to each other about the movie, then tried to suppress our laughter as adults shushed us. Sitting nearby might be some girl of thirteen who had no idea (yet) what it meant to like a boy this much. She would roll her eyes because we were so disgustingly smitten.

"Anna?" Will said. "Are you there? Is the idea of going to a Movie on the Beach *that* bad?"

"No, no, it's not that," I said. "I was just wondering if they have any books by Sartre or Camus at the Dune Island library."

"Oh-kay," Will said, clearly confused.

"So, Will?" I said. I cradled the phone between my head and shoulder and ran my fingernail across the side of an ice cream tub, scraping a wavy trail through the frost. "What do you like at the movies—popcorn or Twizzlers?"

When I returned to the front, my arms covered with goose bumps, my mom was just walking in with Kat and Benjie for the evening shift. The kids immediately ran to the chalkboard tables and began scribbling. The Scoop was sleepy at the moment. No gaggles of summer people in sight.

I saw my mom's eyes flicker to my phone, and thus, mine did as well. Only then did I notice that I was clutching it like it was a staff of life. I stuffed it into the pocket of my cutoffs like it was something private and personal instead of just . . . a phone.

"Getting ready to go?" my mom said. She walked behind the counter, gave my dad a quick kiss on the cheek, then started neatening the stacks of cups and bowls.

"I think I'm gonna head to the Movie on the Beach," I said, trying not to cringe as I admitted it out loud.

"Oh," Mom said with forced casualness. "Are you going with Will?"

"Yeah," I said with just as much false breeziness.

My mom knew *just* what my friends and I thought of the cheesefest that was a Movie on the Beach. I was as much as coming out and telling her that I was going on a Date with a capital D.

"Well, I thought he was very sweet, when he was in here yesterday," Mom said. "Didn't you, honey?"

She looked pointedly at my dad.

"Oh, sure," my dad said jovially. "A very nice boy."

Oh my God. That made Will sound about as sexy as a puppy. A neutered one.

"You know, he kind of reminds me of your dad when we first met," my mom said, her smile going all dreamy.

Wow, she'd actually come up with an image that was even less sexy than a neutered puppy.

"You know, back when your dad had more of it," Mom went on, "his hair was kind of shaggy like Will's."

"Okay, no offense to Dad?" I said. "But I've seen old pictures of him. There is *no* resemblance between him and Will. Mom, he had a mustache."

"Eh, I was going through a phase," Dad said, waving his hand.

"Well, everyone thought *you* were a phase I was going through, remember?" Mom teased him. "There I was, all set to go to *law school . . .*"

When my mom talked about her near miss with the legal profession, she always made it sound like she'd caught the last lifeboat off the *Titanic*.

". . . and instead I find myself on Dune Island, Georgia, with this guy!"

"Yeah, yeah, just some guy," my dad scoffed. "That's all I was to you."

"Well, they all are," my mom said. She glanced in my direction. "Until one is more than just some guy."

"Yeah!" Kat piped up. She'd just meandered over from the kids area and was studying the day's ice cream flavors. "And that's the boy you *kiss*. Right, Anna?"

"No!" I sputtered. I felt myself turn bright red.

When I looked at my parents, standing side by side behind the ice cream case, they looked a little green. My mom quickly went back to fussing with all the ice cream paraphernalia, but I could tell when she accidentally plunked the sticky hot-fudge ladle into the ice cream scoop bin that the kissing comment had flummoxed her a bit.

"Well, anyway," she said brightly, "it just shows that you have to keep an open mind in life, right? I chucked the world of suits for a life on a crazy island. And you, Anna—"

She looked up from the counter to smile at me with the same happy/sad/freaked-out expression she always had when I did something for the first time, whether it was riding a bike or muddling through my first batch of ice cream.

"—you gave a 'shoobee' a chance," she said.

I shrugged and tried not to grin swoonily.

"You know, Mom, they're not all shoobees," I said.

"I know that," Mom said. "Like I said, he's a very nice boy. I'm glad we got to meet him, sweetie."

The whole exchange, so different from our usual recaps of Dune Island gossip or check-ins about school, made me feel sort of floaty as I went to the bathroom to freshen up for my date. I couldn't help feeling happy about their thumbs-up for Will.

And not just because it validated my sense that he was special and different. My parents were raising four sandy-footed, Southern-speaking (allegedly) Dune Islanders. But if they could see me with Will, perhaps they also had an inkling of the future Anna that I envisioned. The one who rode subways, had been on plenty of dates, and had a card to a library twenty times the size of Dune Island's.

Somehow that made getting ready for *this* date that much more exciting.

Will and I sat a bit apart from all the other moviegoers, in a pocket of sand surrounded by a narrow horseshoe of panic grass.

Since I'd come to the movie straight from The Scoop, I'd had nothing to bring but some Italian sodas and a bag of broken waffle cones, still warm.

Will provided the picnic blanket, a classic red-and-black plaid one. As we stretched it out between us, our eyes met, and Will smiled. His grin started out quiet and shy, then grew.

I wondered if he was feeling the same way I was. My emotions were so up and down, I felt like my head was on a seesaw.

First I thought, *I almost can't believe it happened. We actually kissed, after all that yearning. And then we went right back to being normal and hanging out. Which makes it kind of hard to imagine doing the kissing again.*

This quickly led to:

If I don't kiss Will again, and soon, my head might explode.

Followed by:

How do you go about kissing a second time? The first time was this grand fit of passion. But after that it's sort of premeditated, isn't it? Which sounds awkward. And probably not as exciting, right?

Then I was back to:

No, seriously, my head will explode.

I felt self-conscious crawling onto the blanket with Will. The sun had already set, leaving blue-gray dusk, a light in which everything looked a bit fuzzy and everyone seemed to be at loose ends, just waiting for something to begin.

For most of the folks here, that something was the movie.

For me, of course, it was that inevitable liplock. I wondered when the kissing would happen. Would Will sneak one in during the movie?

Or maybe he'd see me home and kiss me good night at the door, the way they always did on TV shows.

Whenever it was going to happen, I couldn't stop thinking

about the fact that it *would* happen. It was just *out* there, this destination, this sure thing. I didn't know whether to be excited or terrified.

The one thing I *did* know—I hoped Will would take the lead. Despite the perfection of the previous night's kissing, I was now feeling a little shy.

I arranged my snacks on the blanket and said, "Sorry, it's not much. I figured ice cream would get too melty."

"It's awesome," Will said. "I love waffle cones. I brought snacks too."

He reached into the backpack he'd brought with him and pulled out a familiar-looking white paper sack.

"Is that . . . ?"

"It's candy from Angelo's," Will said with a grin. "Didn't you say that was your favorite beachmart on the island?"

I was stunned. I peeked into the bag and saw a garish rainbow of gummies, a packet of Sugar Babies, and some Good & Plenty.

"I didn't know your favorites," Will said with a shrug, "so I got a range."

Clutching the bag in my lap, I gaped at Will.

I wanted to tell him that he'd somehow picked *all* my favorites. That he'd paid attention to me, and to the little things that delighted me, in a way that few people had ever done. That he'd looked into my soul—and seen high-fructose corn syrup.

But I couldn't seem to form any words that would express all that.

So I did the only thing that *could* demonstrate how I was feeling right then.

I threw my arms around Will's neck and I kissed him.

A big part of me didn't want to have another date like the one at the Movie on the Beach.

Don't get me wrong. The snuggling on the picnic blanket was great. The candy and kissing? Even better.

I even loved the movie, despite the fact that the holey screen made little Drew Barrymore look like she had chicken pox. Watching such a kiddie flick with Will made me feel somehow grown-up. I listened to the kids around us squealing when E.T. got left behind by his spaceship, and I could remember so vividly when that was me. Mermaid-kicking, cartwheeling, boys-are-gross me.

But those days also felt very far away. In the course of just a few weeks, I felt like I'd crossed a divide from childhood into . . . I didn't quite know what. A place that wasn't quite adulthood but was way more complicated than being a kid.

All of it made me feel 80 percent thrilled, 10 percent baffled, and 10 percent freaked-out, the way I'd feel if I woke up one morning to find myself several inches taller. (Not that *that* was ever going to happen. I was more sure of that with every day in my puny body.)

I even got into the goofy date-nightness of the Movie on the Beach. I looked at the couples around us—the other young people lounging on blankets with their ankles lazily intertwined; the parental types in fancy folding chairs, pouring each other plastic cups of wine. For the first time in my life, I felt like I had something in common with them. Like we shared a secret.

It was just . . . lovely, it really was.

But, after years of mocking the Movie on the Beachers, it also made me *cringe*.

I just wanted to be a tourist in the land of cheesy dates. I didn't want to move in.

So when we talked on the phone the next morning, I told Will, "I have to admit, I liked our little Movie on the Beach. . ."

"Wait a minute," Will squawked. "'*Little* Movie on the Beach'? *E.T.* terrified you!"

"No it didn't!" I sputtered.

"You're telling me you *didn't* grab me and spill all the Good & Plenty when the government agents swooped in to grab E.T.?"

"Well," I muttered, "guys in hazmat suits are always scary."

I shuddered at the memory of the cute little alien trapped in an isolation tank. Then I pressed on.

"Will, that doesn't make the whole Movie on the Beach scenario less corny."

"So what are you saying?" Will asked, a laugh in his throat.

I chose to ignore it as I declared, "No more dates out of a romantic comedy. No tandem bicycle rides, no milk shake with two straws, no mini-golf. I *refuse*."

"Mini-golf?!" Will exclaimed.

I couldn't see his face, but I could tell it was lighting up like the Statue of Liberty's torch.

And *that* was how I ended up at Putt Putt Dune Island! (exclamation point not mine), strolling the Astroturf with Will, clunking my neon pink ball into holes, and—despite my best efforts—loving every minute.

What made this even more implausible was that I was possibly the worst mini-golfer in the history of mini-golf. That's probably a pretty short history, but still . . .

"How is it," I asked Will when I failed for the third time to clear the puddle (excuse me, *water trap*) on the seventh green, "that you're so much better at this than I am? You've never played mini-golf in your life. I *lived* here when I was a little kid."

"Maybe it's an attitude thing," Will teased me. "Or maybe it's your stance. You keep ducking your head, afraid that someone will see you."

"No worries," I said with a laugh in my voice. "My crowd doesn't come here anymore. Not since *every* single kid in the third grade had his or her birthday party here. After that, putt putt was *so* over."

Will got that look on his face again. The one that was a cross between *who* is *this girl?* and *I* like *this girl.*

Before I knew it, he'd crossed our little putting green and wrapped me in a hug that took my breath away.

"So if we're basically all alone here," he said, burying his face in the crook of my neck, "I guess you won't mind a little PDA?"

Will smelled wonderful, like clean ocean water and a little bit of coconut. I found myself wondering if he was different here on Dune Island than he was back home. Surely he couldn't smell like this during a New York winter, could he? And would he have been this *demonstrative* if we were on a busy Manhattan street?

I contemplated asking Will this. But when he planted a soft, smiley kiss on my lips, all contemplating ceased. All that mattered was Will in this very instant. And in this instant, he was pretty—

"Amazing."

I startled. "Amazing" was exactly the word I'd been thinking, but the voice wasn't mine. It was sarcastic and exasperated and *loud*, coming from behind the windmill at the next hole.

And if I didn't know better, I'd have been sure that voice belonged to . . .

I pulled away from Will and said, "It can't be."

I stalked over to the windmill, peeked around it, and saw—Caroline! Her fists were planted on her hips and she was staring, no, *glaring*, at Sam.

"Um, hi?" I blurted.

Caroline saw me and Will and threw up her hands.

"Oh, that's just *great*," she sputtered. She scooped her neon yellow golf ball off the green and tossed it over her shoulder.

Sam spun around.

"What are you doing here?" he demanded.

"What are *you* doing here?" I retorted.

Caroline pointed at Sam—just as I pointed at Will.

I coughed, trying not to laugh.

Will covered his mouth with his fist, clearly working hard to keep a straight face.

And this was the part where all four of us were supposed to

crack up, right? We'd been caught in the act of the goofiest dating ritual of all time.

But the tension between Caroline and Sam quashed it.

"Okay, okay," I said. "What happened, y'all? Did Sam start doing the Caroline voice again?"

I rasped my way through a bad imitation of *Sam's* bad imitation of Caroline's voice.

At which point Will really *did* crack up.

But Caroline just looked down at the Astroturf and bit her lip.

I stopped my little comedy routine with a lurchy feeling in my stomach. Something really *was* wrong.

"Caroline?" I said, reaching out for her arm.

She sidestepped me.

"Whatever," she said. She acted as if she was shrugging it off—whatever *it* was. But I could tell she was upset. She had those two pink spots that always flame up on the apples of her cheeks when she's trying to keep her emotions in check.

Then she waved one hand back and forth in front of her face, the same irritated flutter she'd use to shoo a horsefly.

"I'm just . . ." she said. She took a deep breath and started over. "I used to be the putt putt champ!"

"I know, right?" I said with a little laugh. "Is it that we're too tall now for these little clubs?"

"Anna," Sam said, the defeated S-shape of his torso straightening a bit. "I don't think you're too tall for much of anything."

"Yeah, yeah," I said with a grin. "Heard it all before, Jolly Green."

Sam always laughed smugly when I called him a giant, but this time he just gave me a weak smile. Caroline wandered away, idly swinging her putter around her ankles. The leaf-green tape on its handle was frayed and faded after years of being clutched by sweaty kid hands.

"This was supposed to be . . ." Sam trailed off. "I don't know what. But whatever I thought, it's not happening. We should just go to The Swamp or something."

I didn't know if he was talking to Caroline alone or if he wanted me and Will to join them. I glanced at Will, who gave me a little smile and a shrug.

"I think it's kind of fun," Will said apologetically.

"Well, we set the bar pretty low," I allowed. "Seeing as you dragged me here kicking and screaming."

"You know you love it like you love curly fries," Will said.

"See?" I said indignantly. "I tell you my dirty secrets and you just throw them back in my face."

As Will laughed, I realized I'd turned toward him—and away from Sam and Caroline. For a moment I'd even forgotten they were there. Feeling strangely guilty, I spun around to discuss plan B with them.

But they'd already headed for the cinder-block building—painted the same swimming pool blue as Will's golf ball—to turn in their clubs.

"Do you want to go with them?" Will asked. "Seems like there's something going on there. Maybe . . ."

I bit my lip as I regarded the foot or so of space between my friends as they walked through the course. Sam refrained from leapfrogging the giant red mushroom at the eleventh green or jumping the stepping-stones that crossed the "rushing river" at the eighteenth hole. This was definitely out of character for him. Then again, Sam was a boyfriend now. Maybe maturity, even while playing mini-golf, came with the territory?

I didn't know, probably because the ways of boyfriends and girlfriends were as mysterious to me as math. It wasn't as if I'd learned much yet from being with Will. And besides, he wasn't my boyfriend. At least, I didn't think he was.

Wait a minute, *was* he?

Bubbles of happiness at the idea began to fizz up in my brain, but I tried to shake them away and focus on what was going on with Sam and Caroline. I couldn't imagine their issue was anything that couldn't be solved by a little loud music and chili-laced grub at The Swamp.

So I said to Will, "Oh, they're fine. Sam and Caroline bicker. They always have. I think they had a little hiatus when they first started going out and now . . ."

"The honeymoon's over?" Will said. "Well, we won't let that happen to us, will we?"

He said it casually, before dropping his golf ball on the faux grass and nudging it toward the tee with his putter. I was glad he wasn't looking at me, because I was suddenly feeling almost dizzy.

I couldn't imagine anything more boyfriendy than what Will had just said.

I also truly believed it. Will and I were our own little island,

and nobody else's rules applied to us, not even Sam and Caroline's.

I suppose this was just another version of me being a loner, like Caroline always said.

The only difference was, this time I wasn't *alone* alone. I was with Will, who seemed to fit me like my favorite T-shirt but also felt more like a wonderful surprise with each day that I knew him.

*E*very year my parents throw a big Fourth of July barbecue. I mean *big*. Every bar, restaurant, and sno-cone stand on Dune Island is run by skeleton crews that night because everybody *else* is in my backyard.

The day starts at sunrise, when a bunch of other dads show up in their grubbiest clothes and help my dad dig a pit somewhere between the vegetable garden and Benjie's sandbox. They fill it with smoldering hickory wood and—a pig. Snout and all. Twelve hours later, he or she is the main course. (I try to avoid learning whether the pig *is* a he or she, and my siblings and I definitely don't name the pig, ever since our great Wilbur boycott of a few years ago.)

Also on the menu are bourbon-boiled peanuts, ambrosia salad, cheese straws, dog head biscuits, boiled shrimp, pickled okra, and basically every other super-Southern morsel that my Midwestern parents find fascinating. If you could put grits on a stick, they'd serve that, too.

The one thing they don't serve is ice cream. Oh, it's there of course. We roll an entire eight-tub freezer out of The Scoop and transplant it onto the screened porch. My mom always makes up a special one-day-only flavor for the party. But it's a rule that nobody in our family is allowed to scoop. It's our holiday. The guests make a big deal of putting on aprons and paper soda-jerk hats. Then they take turns dipping gargantuan scoops and making lopsided cones and sundaes that shed gobs of marshmallow and fudge across the grass.

When everybody's good and full and sticky, we all head to the field out back. It's a big, shaggy mess of wildflowers and scratchy grass that's separated from our (slightly) more groomed yard by a thicket of blueberry bushes. The field is tree free, which makes it the perfect viewing spot for the Beach Club fireworks, about half a mile due east.

Inevitably, when the fireworks finish, someone starts singing patriotic songs and somebody *else* tells them to shut up. Then the parents make more spiked Arnold Palmers, the kids twirl with sparklers and gobble fizzy candy, and everybody stays up way past midnight.

I hadn't thought twice about inviting Will to the barbecue. I'd even told him to bring his mom and Owen. (I mean, our *mailman* comes to the Fourth of July barbecue.)

It was only after the three of them arrived that night at seven o'clock—and stopped cold in our red dirt driveway to gape at Figgy Pudding—that I saw the party from an outsider's eyes.

Oh yeah, I realized, *this must look kind of weird.*

My family (and the rest of Dune Island, for that matter) are so used to our Fourth of July tree, otherwise known as Figgy

Pudding, that even Sophie isn't embarrassed by it. It's just part of our summer landscape, along with sea turtle nests, sunburned tourists, and the constant *slap-slap-slap* of flip-flops.

Figgy Pudding became Dune Island's tackiest icon when I was still a baby. One of my parents decided that since the Fourth of July in a beach town is like Christmas everywhere else, it required a tree. But not some tasteful fir swagged with garlands and earnest ornaments. They chose the sprawling fig in the center of our front yard.

From then on, instead of bringing covered dishes to the barbecue, guests have brought strange things to drape on Figgy's branches. The ornaments are different every year, but platform shoes and feather boas are always popular, as are stuffed animals and Slinkys. People make scary fairies out of twigs and feathers. They also hang kooky cooking utensils and, of course, ice cream scoops.

After everyone has looped their decorations around the tree's branches—plucking handfuls of sticky, purple figs while they're at it—the poor tree looks like a huge, bedraggled drag queen on the morning after Mardi Gras. Enterprising tourists have even been known to come out and snap pictures of it.

We keep Figgy in her finery until the first rain turns everything to muck. Then Sophie and I climb the branches and throw down the decapitated fairies, sogged-up feather boas, and musty shoes, returning the tree to her natural state.

Benjie always cries about the dismantling of poor Figgy Pudding, but I've never thought much about it. I've always known she'd be back the following year.

And now Will and his family were meeting Figgy for the first time. Even though she was only halfway to her full gaudy glory when they arrived, she was still kind of a shock to the system.

As usual the decorations were pink, white, and blue (but heavy on the pink). Figgy was bedecked with lawn flamingos, pinwheels, and even a pink bicycle, its wheels straddling the point where the trunk split into two thick branches. There were many shoes and feather boas, of course, somebody's collection of troll dolls, and a shocking pink stuffed boa constrictor twining around the trunk. The Garden of Eden gone wild—that was my front yard.

Once they got past Figgy Pudding, I realized, Will and his family were going to see the pig, the tipsy adults making *jokes* about the pig, the not-completely-ironic pastel mini-marshmallows in the ambrosia salad, and half a dozen other possibly mortifying things.

For a moment I considered saving face by shrugging off the party as an obligation I didn't really like; a parental eccentricity.

But then I looked at Will—who was grinning like mad at the tree, while his mom shook her head in amazement—and reconsidered.

Will liked my (allegedly) Southern accent. He fed my gummy habit without judgment. He didn't think it was weird that some-times I'd rather spend my time alone with an ice cream churn than with my friends on the South Shore.

And unless I'd been very misguided, he'd like our wacky barbecue, too.

Even though I'd never really stopped to think about it, *I*

loved our Fourth of July party. It was one of my favorite nights of the year. On the Fourth of July, I felt like we were one big, crazy, happy family—me and the Dune Islanders.

And I wanted Will to be a part of it too.

So I swallowed my self-consciousness and smiled at Will's mom. She was pretty in a mom-ish kind of way—thin, with an upturned nose and freckles. She wore her hair in a slightly frizzy blond bob, and she had the same pointy chin as Will and Owen.

"Ms. Dempsey?" I asked. (Will had told me she'd gone back to her maiden name after the divorce.) "Can I get you an Arnold Palmer?"

*W*ill didn't like the party.

He loved it.

He loved the fact that Ellie Dunlap, Dune Island's mayor, was singing old standards with a karaoke machine on the back porch.

He loved that there were kids (and grown-ups, too) swooping on our swing, which hangs from a high branch in an ancient water oak.

He was nuts about the food, especially, as a matter of fact, the boiled peanuts.

He loved it all so much that I worried (just a little bit) that *I* was being overshadowed. I mean, how could I—even in the cute navy-and-white-striped halter dress I'd fished out of Sophie's closet—compete with the *feeling* of this party? With food that made your mouth sing, in a yard strung with so many white lights that the stars were superfluous, while on the porch a town leader in white braids and overalls sang, *"If you don't like them peaches, don't shake my tree . . ."*

But then Mayor Dunlap started a new tune. The song was clearly very old. It made me think of women wearing silk stockings with seams up the backs. Mayor Dunlap's clear, pretty soprano was both lilting and melancholy, making the couples dancing on the patio sink into one another and sway more slowly. As for me, I recognized the sweet yearning—and reward—in the lyrics.

"I wished on the moon, for something I never knew," Mayor Dunlap sang.

And Will asked me to dance.

"Seriously?" I asked. I was sprawled on the porch steps, one arm propped on the banister, the other dunked into a bowl of butter mints. I did *not* look, I was sure, like the kind of girl you asked for a waltz.

"Anna," Will said, standing over me with one hand extended. "Don't make me lose my nerve."

I laughed with a whoosh of relief.

"Okay, so this *isn't* something you routinely do in New York?" I said.

"Trust me," Will said, looking at the other dancing couples. Most of them were senior citizens. "I *never* do this."

"So it's okay if I step on your toes?"

"Considering you're barefoot?" Will said with a grin. "Not a problem. In fact . . ."

Will kicked off his own flip-flops, stashing them next to the stairs.

"Now we're even," he said.

"I *do* wear shoes, you know . . . ," I said as I took his hand and got up.

"Oh, I saw them," Will said with a nod and a sly smile. "You had 'em on for about five minutes before you ditched them."

He was right. As we walked to the patio, I tried to remember where those cream-colored espadrilles even *were*. But then Will put his arms around my waist and began to sway me in a gentle circle to the music. And suddenly I could barely remember my middle name.

My hands were on Will's shoulders. And I wasn't stepping on his feet, because he was leading me, with a soft, gentle pressure, in a loop around the patio.

I felt like I should say something. Something that poked fun at the two of us; that made this dance a lark instead of a love song.

But swaying in Will's arms didn't feel jokey. It felt serious in the most wonderful way. Will pulled back a little bit and looked down at me. Our eyes met for a long moment, much longer than would have been comfortable with anyone else.

I knew he wanted to kiss me as much as I wanted to kiss him. That if we weren't out here in front of our parents, the mayor, and the mailman, we'd be kissing.

Instead, I lightly laid my cheek against Will's shoulder. His arms tightened around me, and I closed my eyes as we danced on.

The lyrics in Mayor Dunlap's antique song might have been corny, but suddenly they made perfect sense to me.

"I looked for every loveliness. It all came true. I wished on the moon . . . for you."

Mayor Dunlap's pretty voice trailed off. The crowd clapped and cheered while she pulled at the seams of her overall legs and did a mock curtsy.

I didn't really want to let go of Will, but I had to, especially when the mayor announced, "That's it for me, folks. I've got to get over to the pit before that pig is completely gone. But stick around for a couple minutes and we'll have something *completely* different for y'all."

During the lull between acts, Will and I wandered over to the drinks table. The lingering swooniness of our dance made me want something special, so I made a spritzer of limeade, sparkling water, and a handful of raspberries. Will was reaching for the iced tea pitcher when his mother walked over arm in arm with our neighbor Mrs. Sumner. Mr. Sumner trailed behind them, looking bemused.

"Will!" Ms. Dempsey gushed. "I want you to meet Marlene Tifton and Bobby Sumner! Well, she's Marlene Sumner now. I knew the two of them when I was fourteen years old, if you can believe it."

"Well, *I* can't believe Sissy's back for the summer!" Mrs. Sumner gushed, giving Ms. Dempsey a squeeze.

"*Sissy?*" Will said to his mother.

"Oh, you know your uncle Roy was always the star when we were down here," she explained. "So for a while I was just known as his little sister."

"Sissy means sister," I said, translating Southernese for Will.

"Good thing she wasn't a little brother. Then she would have been Bubba."

"Bubba means *brother*?" Will gaped.

"What else would it mean, son?" Mr. Sumner said in his loud, booming voice.

"I think this is why I teach so much Faulkner in my lit classes," Ms. Dempsey said with a laugh.

"Oh, I know I sound like a redneck," Mrs. Sumner said with a shrug. "But, Sissy, I just can't call you by your real name. *Lizzy*. It sounds so *formal*."

The three of them guffawed like teenagers, then drifted toward the barbecue pit.

"Your mom seems happy," I said to Will with a grin.

"Yeah," he agreed, gazing after her with raised eyebrows. "Huh!"

Before he could say anything else, a twangy crash rang out from the back porch. I grinned. I'd almost forgotten about the next act. They were shuffling onto the porch, lugging their instruments and equipment with them. I led Will back to the patio.

"I think you'll like this band," I told him. "They're called Undertoad."

"Cool name," Will said.

As Undertoad's four guys set up their stuff, every Dune Island High kid at the barbecue (especially Sophie and her posse of girlfriends) crowded around the steps and cheered. I saw Owen in the crowd too, slurping lemonade and chatting with some kids as if they'd known one another forever.

I nudged Will and pointed at the lead singer.

"See anyone you know?" I asked.

His eyes went wide.

"You didn't tell me Sam was in a band," Will said.

"Don't worry," I said with an elbow in his ribs. "You don't have to pretend to like them. They're actually good."

"How did you know what I was thinking?" Will said, shaking his head at me.

I shrugged and laughed. The fact that I'd successfully read Will's mind exhilarated me like a shot of espresso.

Apparently, the feeling was mutual. Will and I grinned at each other so hard you could probably see little cartoon birdies tweeting around our heads. Our own personal Disney movie was mercifully interrupted when Sam cleared his throat into the mic.

"Uh, hi, y'all," he said. "We'll be right with you. Just give us a chance to plug in."

As the guys started messing around with their equipment, Caroline came up, sipping peach cider from a mason jar.

"The pig's so cute this year," she said with a shudder. "I can't stand it."

"Cute . . . and tasty!" Will said, his grin turning devilish.

"So you're a carnivore just like Sam, huh?" Caroline asked.

"I think it kind of comes with the gender," I said sympathetically.

"Then what's your excuse?" Caroline said to me. "Didn't I see you gnawing on a big, juicy rib earlier?"

"I was *not* gnawing," I protested, giving Will a shifty glance. "I was . . . nibbling."

"Oh yeah," she replied. "You always drip barbecue sauce down your chin when you 'nibble.'"

I gasped in horror until Caroline leaned across me and said to Will, "I'm kidding, of course. Our Anna is the picture of manners and decorum."

"Well, let's not go too far," I said while Will cracked up.

But before the quipping could continue, Sam hunched over his battered black guitar and started tuning it.

Twang, twang, twaaaaang.

The endless string-plucking, combined with a squeal of feedback from the bass player's mic, made for some awkward squirming in the audience.

Some of the guys started hooting, "Sam-MEH!" Sam waved them off.

I laughed, but Caroline just huffed and shifted from foot to foot, taking agitated slurps of her cider.

"I *told* him to tune up during the mayor's boring set," she muttered.

"I liked that music," I protested, taking a tiny sidestep closer to Will.

"You *did*?" Caroline squawked. She pursed her lips and shot me a cynical squint. Her eyes swung from my red cheeks to Will. When I followed her glance, I saw that *he* was gazing at me.

And when I looked back at Caroline, I saw a quick succession of emotions flash across her round, oh-so-readable face—recognition, amusement, and a*maze*ment. Then she glanced at Sam and I saw one more emotion flash across her face—wistfulness.

Which was puzzling to me. Were Caroline and Sam already such a fusty, old couple that it made her nostalgic to look at shiny, new Will-and-me?

Before I had a moment to think about this, a swell of music jolted all thoughts from my head. Undertoad had launched into one of their edgy, throbbing anthems of angst. Most of Undertoad's songs were self-mocking meditations on being awkward, adolescent, and loveless. I realized now that Sam had probably written many of them while he was pining for Caroline.

She surely knew that too, because her twisty mouth softened as she watched Sam thrash at his guitar strings, his brow crunched up with the effort of singing:

"Then there was your voice

"Like a windup tin toy

"Like the sweetest nails on a chalkboard

"That I ever heard."

I threw back my head and laughed.

"I've heard Sam play this song a hundred times," I yelled in Caroline's ear over the peppery drumbeats. "How did we never realize it was about you?!"

Caroline gave a wan smile and shrugged.

"The guy knows how to make a romantic gesture, that's for sure," she yelled back at me. But instead of affectionate, her voice was hard, even a little bitter.

I'd been shimmying my hips, dancing to the music, but at that comment, I stopped.

"Caroline?" I said, turning toward her. "What's *wrong*?"

She shrugged again and waved me off.

"Nothing," she said. "I'm just being moody. At least that's what *Sam* says."

For the first time since they'd gotten together, Sam's name didn't lilt in her voice, like its own little song. Instead, it sounded off-key. And frankly, a little pissed off.

"C'mon," I said, hooking my arm through Caroline's. I began to pull her away. "Let's talk."

Even as I said it, I felt a pang at the prospect of leaving Will's side. My left arm felt a little cold after being pressed up against his right one.

But then Caroline shook her head and planted her feet.

"No," she said. "It's nothing. Besides, Sam'll unravel if he doesn't see me listening to the whole set. Prepping for this party was, like, all he did this week."

She glanced at Will's arm, which was making its way around my waist again, and her mouth got a little twisty. But she didn't say anything. She just returned her gaze to Sam and the band.

I craned my neck to try to meet her eyes, but Caroline was dancing vaguely, staring at the porch/stage. Had she detected my reluctance? That was the problem with friends who knew you as intimately as anyone in your family did. They could read your every gesture. It was a blessing and a curse.

I wondered if that was part of Will's appeal. His mystery. All the things I still *didn't* know about him—but wanted to find out.

Of course, I realized as I looked at Caroline's stony profile, you never knew *anybody* completely.

Not even yourself.

But at that moment, I was feeling anything but introspective. My world was simple. I was all about dancing on the smooth, flagstone patio in my bare feet. And feeling Undertoad's music thrum through my whole body. And hanging out with my boyfriend and my best friend.

Even the sight of my mom—absentmindedly hugging Kat to her waist as she chatted with Mayor Dunlap in the side yard—warmed me from the inside out tonight.

I closed my eyes and lifted my arms over my head as I danced, enjoying the small symphony of all these sensations.

Then I stumbled into Will. (Dancing with your eyes closed is not as easy as it looks.) He put his arm around my shoulders to steady me—and kept it there. I cuddled into the crook beneath his arm, feeling happily incredulous.

Was this really me? Was I half of a joined-at-the-hip couple?

Happy couples had always felt to me like the shoobees' glamorous vacation homes. They were all around me yet untouchable. But now there I was—on the inside of this mysterious phenomenon. Somehow it had been as easy as turning a doorknob.

Undertoad's set was six songs long. I could tell by Will's raised eyebrows and the intent way he was taking in the show that he was impressed by the music.

And when Sam brusquely introduced the final song by saying, "This is for Caroline," I could tell Will was impressed with *Sam*. I turned to Caroline to get her reaction and was surprised to see that she'd slipped away.

She must be at the front of the crowd, I thought with a smile.

Whatever tension was simmering between my friends, I was sure it would be smoothed over by Sam's dedication.

I melted back into Will for the last song. He moved me in front of him and wrapped his arms around me, compelling me to lean back against him. It felt as good as floating on my back in the ocean.

I could have stood that way for a *long* time, but too quickly Sam ground out the last chord. And then a voice in the crowd shouted out, "It's almost time, y'all!"

For fireworks of course. I glanced up at the sky, surprised to see that it had gone completely dark already. Beyond the shimmer of the white lights strung over the yard, the night looked like black satin.

"Whoops!" I gasped. I grabbed Will's hand (since it was still conveniently located on my shoulder). "We haven't gotten our ice cream yet!"

"I can't do it," Will mock groaned. "I'm so full."

"Will," I scoffed as I dragged him around the house to the ice cream case on the screened porch. "This is a Patrick party. You *can't* skip the ice cream."

My mom had gone simple this year and made a frothy but impossibly rich peach cinnamon custard. It was velvety, but with a sneaky, peachy punch. I reminded myself to compliment my mom on the flavor later. It was as elegant as Figgy Pudding was, well, *not*.

Once Will and I had loaded up two cups with ice cream, I ducked into the house and emerged with a beach blanket.

We hurried with all the other guests to the field behind

the house. People laughed as they tripped through the weedy yard.

We tiptoed around the pig pit, where orange-black embers still glowed in a bed of salt-and-pepper ash. Then we circled around the blueberry bushes. I grabbed a few early berries from one of them and plunked them on top of Will's ice cream.

"Blueberry and peach go perfectly together," I said.

Will grinned and took a big bite as I led him to a spot in the center of the field. All around us were the shadowy shapes of other couples cuddled up together, kids spinning under the stars, and the up-pointed feet of people who'd already flopped on their backs to watch the show. There was an electric murmur in the air.

I lowered myself to my knees on our blanket. My hand was on my ice cream spoon, but I didn't really feel like eating any more of it. For the first time that night, Will and I were invisible to all the other party guests. We could be together without all those eyes on us.

I could barely see Will's face in the darkness of the field. (That's what made it so perfect for fireworks-gazing.) I put my dessert down at the edge of the blanket and turned, just slightly, toward him.

He must have been waiting for this moment too, because suddenly I felt his palms—cool and slightly damp from his ice cream cup—on my cheeks. He leaned in and I closed my eyes. I couldn't wait to feel his lips on mine.

But then—I didn't. Confused and a little embarrassed, I

opened my eyes. Will was staring at me, looking serious. I felt a confused catch in my throat.

"Anna," he said, his voice a rumbly whisper. "This is the best night *ever*."

I laughed, because of course I'd been thinking that ever since the first boiled peanut. Then Will silenced my laugh with an incredible, romantic kiss.

After a few minutes of kissing, things started to feel serious again. Will's hands warmed up on the bare skin above the back of my halter dress. He pulled me closer and closer to him. With each kiss, I felt more and more like I was melting into him, like I never wanted to stop.

I gently pushed Will away for a moment so I could catch my breath. And that was when, off in the direction of the beach, we heard a dull thud.

Then *everyone* was catching their breath, waiting, waiting for—

Boom!

Our group cheered as the first firecracker exploded over the water. It was far away from us, but still dazzling, a bright blue starburst tendrilling out in every direction.

Will gave me one more quick kiss before we settled onto our backs to watch. I turned on my side and rested my head on Will's upper arm. The soles of my bare feet just touched the tops of his.

I'd watched this exact same firework display from this exact spot my entire life. Every few years the Beach Club boosters added a few new dazzlers to the mix—twisty sizzlers, explosions in the shapes of hearts, or double pows from one rocket. Mostly, though, the show felt very familiar.

But watching it with Will made every firework feel new—louder and more vivid and definitely more exciting. I let the big bangs and colored lights envelop me. I succumbed to each one the way you melt into your favorite song played really, really loud.

The fireworks started coming faster and bigger. It crossed my mind, for a fleeting moment, that this show might feel piddly and small-town to Will. I'd seen Times Square on TV on New Year's Eve. I could only imagine how vast and sparkly the Fourth of July fireworks over Manhattan were.

But as the show got more intense, Will squeezed my arm. He even hooted along with some of the other party guests at some particularly big *pow*s. So I squashed the insecurity as easily as I would a slow-moving mosquito.

Will wasn't *in* New York. He was here with me. And he was making it clear that there was nowhere else he wanted to be. I was as confident of that as I was of the annual rise and fall of Figgy Pudding.

Until something happened that changed everything.

A few blankets in front of us, a cell phone bleeped, then flickered open in someone's shadowy hand. I blinked as I realized that the face reflected in the phone's silvery glow was Will's brother, Owen.

"Hey, baby!" he said. Clearly his girlfriend was calling. "Aw, I miss you, too. Happy Fourth of July. So you're with the whole crowd? Ash and Ethan too? And Josh. *And* Mo? I'm jealous! Although, I gotta say, this is quite the scene here. You should visit!"

He paused and chortled at something his girlfriend said.

"Well, you won't have to wait long," he said into the phone. "I'll be back in, what? Eight weeks? That's nothing! Oh, I think the finale's about to start. Better go, babe."

Another pause, then Owen said, "The fireworks? Naw, they're nothing like that. But they're cute!"

Clearly I'd been right. Our fireworks were "cute." Great.

Owen snapped the phone closed and settled back onto his elbows, probably letting the brief phone chat drift from his mind as easily as firecracker smoke dissipating into the breeze.

But I felt a chill wash over me, as startling and painful as an ice cream headache.

If Owen was heading back home in eight weeks, so was Will.

Of course, I'd always known this. Will was a summer guy; an out of towner, if not quite a shoobee. His Dune Island stopwatch had begun ticking the moment he'd arrived.

But somehow I'd forgotten this. Because in June, as the days are just starting to stretch themselves out and the tomato plants are still crisp-leafed and runty, the idea of September seems like just that. An idea, as remote and hazy as a dream.

But now we were just a week shy of mid-July. Suddenly the summer felt to me like one of those log flume rides at an amusement park. You skim along a pleasantly lazy channel, until you land on a conveyer belt inching you upward. With every crank of the belt you grow more breathless, more excited, and then—you thunder downward, and with a cold splash of water to the face, it's all over.

I felt myself stiffen. Just a moment ago I'd been so pleasantly aware of all the points where my body and Will's were joined. Our feet were tangled up, my knees touched the side of his leg, my arm was slung across his chest, and my cheek rested on his shoulder.

But now I was painfully conscious of all the points where we were separated. The night air—damp and coolly redolent of pollen and grass—seemed to whoosh between us, making unpleasant prickles on the backs of my legs and neck.

I continued to stare at the fireworks, but now I found myself focusing less on the sizzles and lights, and more on the clouds of gunpowder that lingered in the air afterward, black and acrid.

Like a little kid, I wished that the fireworks could go on forever; that this *summer* could go on forever.

Involuntarily, my fingers tightened on Will's soft T-shirt.

Will felt it and turned to me. And then we were kissing again, without hesitation, without a thought. Our kisses became urgent, with me squeezing Will's arm, him clasping me tightly around the small of my back. We weren't so much ignoring the fireworks as channeling them.

Only when the finale pummeled us with an endless stream of booms and pops did we drag ourselves from each other and watch the end of the show. We sat up and Will shifted behind me. He held me and rested his chin on my head as he cheered on the last of the show.

When it ended, there was a moment of silence. A hovering. An intake of breath. I found myself closing my eyes and wishing that we could all just remain suspended in this moment of happiness and satisfaction; in this moment when all was perfect.

But of course I was wishing for the impossible. In the next

instant everyone started hooting, pounding their hands together, and getting stiffly to their feet. They shook grass from their blankets and began picking their way across the meadow, back to the party.

Back to real life.

My ice cream, barely touched, had melted. Will suggested getting a fresh helping and I nodded numbly. I let him hook my fingertips in his and lead me around the blueberry bushes. This time it was Will who swiped some berries from the branches. As he handed a couple to me, one squished in my palm, a glistening, black-violet blotch.

"It's overripe," I observed dully. "Already."

Will gave me a small, confused smile. He opened his mouth as if he was about to say something, then reconsidered.

"You need a pick-me-up," he declared a moment later. "What do you think of an iced tea float with peach ice cream?"

Despite myself, I felt my eyebrows rise.

"That actually sounds pretty good," I said.

"See?" Will said. "Your crazy flavor combos are making an impression on me."

He stopped walking and pulled me into an enveloping, breathtaking hug.

"Your *everything*," Will murmured into the top of my head, "is making an impression on me."

Later, much later, Will and I ducked under Figgy Pudding to say good-bye. Owen and Ms. Dempsey had already started walking home. Will had brought his bike, so he'd told them he'd catch up to them in a few minutes.

We hid under a branch that was heavy with sticky-smelling figs. While Will put the cup of lemonade he'd been sipping on the ground, I leaned against the trunk, my back cushioned by the neon pink boa constrictor. Will kissed me good-bye, a delicious lemon and sugar kiss. Then we kissed again. And again and again.

It was I who pulled away first. I looked down at my hands, trying not to bite my lip in disappointment. The end of this evening somehow felt like the end of *everything*.

When I looked up at Will, though, it was clear that he wasn't thinking anything like this. He was only surfing the swells of those kisses, not to mention the crazy crowd, the weirdness of Figgy Pudding, and the exotic party food.

Will pulled something out of his back pocket—a handful of plastic spoons and a long twist tie that he must have found on a bag of paper plates at the food table. He grabbed his Styrofoam cup from the mulchy ground and slugged down the last of his lemonade.

And then he started poking the spoon handles through the Styrofoam, just below the lip of the cup.

"What are you doing?" I asked.

"Hold on," Will said. "This'll just take a minute."

He placed each spoon about an inch from the last, so their handles crisscrossed inside the cup and their bowls protruded outside of it. The spoon bowls all faced the same direction, reminding me of the curvy wings of a pinwheel.

Next Will knotted one end of the twist tie and poked it through the bottom of the cup. Finally he dangled the sad little sculpture in front of his mouth and blew.

It spun.

"It's the best I could do on short notice," Will said.

"That's a whirligig," I pointed out, laughing despite myself. "Are you *sure* you aren't Southern? You're, like, one step away from catching ghosts with a glass-bottle tree."

"A what?" Will said.

I waved off his question with a weary smile.

We crept around the tree until we found the perfect branch on which to hang Will's ornament. Then I watched him swing his leg over Zelig and roll down the dirt drive. The *tick-tick-tick-tick*s of his coasting bicycle gears were quickly drowned out by the whirring of the cicadas. A moment after that, Will was swallowed up by the night.

Every time I left the house for the next few days—until a raging thunderstorm put an end to Figgy Pudding for another year—I stopped by the branch where Will had perched his whirligig.

I would reach out with a fingertip and graze the plastic, wishing it was Will's hand that I was touching instead. I'd pause and close my eyes for a moment of languid sensation that existed only in my mind, in my memory.

And then I would remember that too soon, *all* I'd have left of Will were memories.

My hand would drop to my side, a dead weight. I'd stalk toward my bike with hunched shoulders and ride away fast. As I sped along I'd hope that my ragged breath would drown out all these thoughts about Will leaving. I tried to push them below the surface, because I knew that they could easily muck everything up, like a broken well silently spewing oil from the ocean floor.

But like an ugly oil spill, I feared my obsession about summer's end was going to be almost impossible to contain.

When I called Caroline on the fifth of July and told her to meet me at the beach, I told myself that I was doing it for *her*, because I knew she needed to talk.

The fact that I had an iced tea float hangover and was suddenly feeling very much like an about-to-be-ditched Allison Porchnik? Oh, that had *nothing* to do with it.

And that's how two girls in already-beginning-to-fade wraps—one blue and one orange—ended up scouring the aisle of Angelo's for their breakfast.

If we weren't already feeling bitter, our food choices were definitely going to get us there. Caroline grabbed a cellophane tube of shell-on sunflower seeds, the kind that taste like bark and lodge in your throat like salty moth wings. I went for beef jerky.

"It's like everlasting breakfast sausage," I tried to joke, even though my own crack made my throat close up.

Then Caroline chose vanilla wafers, which always made my mouth feel like it had been coated with a partially hydrogenated film. I got some of those cheese and cracker sets where the tiny

tub of cheese is made out of wax or plastic or some combination
of the two.

And finally, because this was breakfast, after all, we chose
some minimuffins, but instead of getting blueberry or apple spice
like two sane people might, we went with banana nut, which
is universally known as the worst muffin flavor ever invented.
(And yes, I *am* considering bran.)

It was a feel-bad brunch, and we dug into the plastic grocery
sack before we even made it to the beach.

"So where's Will?" Caroline asked as Angelo's door swung
shut behind us. She popped a sunflower seed into her mouth
and chased it with a slurp of bottled iced tea.

"I don't know," I said, just a touch defensively.

Caroline gave me a sidelong glance as we crossed the parking lot and stepped onto the beach. Sand was sort of like truth
serum to us. Caroline, Sam, and I had always had our most honest talks here.

"So it didn't go well last night?" Caroline asked as we walked
down the beach.

"Um, actually." I sighed. "I'm pretty sure it was the best
night of my life."

"Oh," Caroline said. She nodded as she took another sip of
tea. "I can see why you're miserable."

"I'm *not* miserable," I said. I gnawed for a moment on my beef
jerky, which was literally as tough as leather. When I couldn't get
a bite off, I grabbed Caroline's iced tea instead and took a slurp.

"I'm just . . . pensive," I declared.

"You're overanalyzing," Caroline said, correcting me.

"I am not," I scoffed.

"Oh, yes you are!" Caroline said with a grin. "You're doing that thing where you imagine that you're a character in a Woody Allen movie."

I narrowed my eyes at my friend.

"You know," I said, "I think it is possible for someone to know a person *too* well."

"You love it," Caroline said.

And she was right. I sort of *did* love it. I think I'd forgotten for a while how much I needed Caroline to be my mirror in harsh light. I could always count on her to matter-of-factly point out my every blemish, literal and figurative—and love me just the same.

"Anyway, we're not here to talk about me," I said as we continued to tromp along. "What's going on with Sam?"

Caroline ducked her head quickly. She pretended to be fixated on tearing open the muffin bag so I wouldn't see her cheeks flush.

I knew not to press. Instead I walked ahead of her and chose a spot on the sand. I tossed my book and our bag of breakfast onto the ground, stretched out my wrap, and laid down on it, using one forearm to block out the sun.

"Why don't you get a pair of sunglasses ever?" Caroline asked as she sat next to me. There was a hint of annoyance in her voice.

"Too much to keep track of," I said without moving my hand. "I'd only lose them."

There was another long pause until Caroline said, "Sam told

me that before we got together, he used to dream about us having this perfect, romantic date."

"Really?" I said. I uncovered my eyes now and looked at her.
"That's sweet, if . . . kind of girly."

"I know, right?" Caroline said. "I mean, a perfect date. What
is that? A candlelit dinner with a violin player?"

"Can you imagine?" I said, trying not to cringe at the memory of my equally cheesy picnic with the champagne flutes
under the Beach Club pool deck. "So what was the dream?"

"Oh, he's kind of vague about it," Caroline said. "It hasn't
happened yet."

She glowered at the waves.

"He's probably off somewhere right now," she said, "plotting
this evening of devastating romance instead of just being here
with me. Being normal. Being fun."

"So Sam wanting to sweep you off your feet is a bad thing?"
I asked.

"Noooo," Caroline said, sounding confused. "I guess I'm still
getting used to the way things are now. I mean, you know how
little things about Sam used to annoy me?"

"Like the way he consciously tries to work surfer terms into
his vocabulary," I offered, "and loves raw onions and snorts when
he laughs?"

"Oh, don't let me stop you," Caroline said.

"Hey, I'm just quoting *you*," I said. "I think all those things
are endearing. Well, except the onions. Gross."

"That's the thing," Caroline said. "After we got together,
that's how *I* felt. Suddenly I liked all these things about Sam

that I *hadn't* liked before. Like it was his flaws that made me love him, in a weird way."

"That's so romantic." I sighed.

"Shut up," Caroline said, giving me a little swat on the arm.

I propped myself up on my elbows and looked at her.

"No, I'm serious," I said. "A perfect person is easy to love. But when somebody likes all your *im*perfections, well, that's when you know they really mean it."

"Well, try telling Sam that!" Caroline said. She grabbed a muffin from our breakfast bag but forgot to take a bite out of it. "I almost feel like now that we're together, he doesn't want me to see the real him. Only the dashing, romantic version of him. We never just hang out anymore, watching TV or sitting around on the beach being bored. Everything's a Date. That's why we ended up at the stupid putt putt golf place that night."

"Maybe he thinks since you're not just friends anymore," I said, searching for an explanation, "you shouldn't act like you did when you were?"

"Maybe," Caroline said. "Or maybe he was just friends with me so he could make me fall for him. Now that I have, he can spend his 'friend' time with *other* people, like the guys from Undertoad. Then when he feels like making out, or having someone to go to parties and dances with, he's got me. It's the perfect balance. For *him*."

Caroline's lip trembled just a little bit as she added, "But I miss being able to just bum around with my friend."

"I think Sam's just being careful," I said, trying to keep my voice optimistic. But deep down? I was as bewildered as

Caroline. "He doesn't want to mess things up. He wants you to make it for the long haul."

"Well, *that's* depressing on so many levels," Caroline said. "My God, Anna. We're sixteen. Who's thinking about the long haul?"

This made me bite my lip. I felt both bereft and ridiculous about *my* current angst.

On the other hand, I told myself, was it unreasonable to wish for more than eight weeks with Will? Eight weeks wasn't even a *little* haul.

Caroline finally noticed the squashed muffin in her hand. She began to pick the nuts out of it and throw them over her shoulder. A couple of seagulls immediately swooped down. They squawked and pecked at each other as they scrounged for the tiny bits of food.

I looked away from the bickering birds and squinted out at the waves. The sun hit the water at an angle that seemed to shoot the light directly into my eyes, making them almost hurt.

Everything just felt too intense this morning—the sun, the taste of all this processed food, the stupid seagulls, Caroline's anguish. . . . Most of all, my feelings about Will were as raw as an exposed nerve.

My impulse, as always, was to jump to my feet and run for the ocean, for that head-clearing plunge into the cold murk.

I got to my feet.

"Come on," I said to Caroline.

Without hesitation she threw the rest of her muffin at the gulls and jumped up. Joylessly we sprinted toward the surf, high-stepped over the frothy shallow bit, and dove together under the first big wave. When she came up for air, Caroline's fine blond hair was plastered to her scalp, satin smooth.

We swam past the breakers until the waves softened into lazy undulations. The water was calm and sleepy this morning, as if it, too, was drained after the holiday.

Caroline and I faced each other. We let our legs go slack, planting our toes in the sand and fluttering our hands to keep our balance. Then we let the waves rock us from side to side. I felt a fish flick against my calf. I sank down until my chin rested on the water's surface.

Caroline gazed at me, her face calm now. We were both deep in thought.

"It's kind of scary being in love," I said after a while. "The stakes are high, you know?" I paused again. Then, even though I was sort of scared to hear Caroline's answer, I whispered, "What are you going to do?"

Caroline lifted her legs and rolled onto her back. She floated on the bobbing water and gazed up at the almost cloudless sky.

"Maybe Sam's right and I'm just being moody," she said. "Maybe I should just get over myself."

How many times had I heard Caroline say those words to me?

"Get over yourself," she'd say when I complained about Dune Island's dinkiness or mandatory pep rallies or the fact that I had to share a room with my sister. She'd gotten this saying from her track coach, who shouted it across the field approximately 150 times per practice.

It was, I realized now, the perfect motto for Caroline. She was a jock. She had complete faith in her own power, whether she was pushing for another ten laps or telling herself not to read too much into the changes in Sam.

So maybe I could get over myself too, I thought. Caroline bobbed about on the water's surface as if a sudden easing in her mind had made her body feather-light as well. *Maybe I could just* force *myself to think, 'Yay! Eight more weeks!' instead of 'Only eight more weeks.' You know, half full versus half empty.*

This was a tactic that would have worked like a charm for Caroline.

But deep down I knew I had a different interpretation of "half full." It was halfway to *gone*. My time with Will was draining away fast, and when it was over, all I'd be left with was a big, old empty.

That's what I was feeling, I realized. *Pre*-empty. And after the unadulterated fullness of the past few weeks, it was depressing indeed.

Will showed up at The Scoop the next night at exactly nine o'clock. I was working alone because it was my mom's book club night and my dad was home with the kids. Will gave me a casual wave over the heads of the customers who'd arrived just before him. Then he went over to one of the chalkboard tables in the kids section to wait for me.

By this time of year, the summer people knew as well as the locals that The Scoop closed at nine. So around 8:50, every ice cream addict on the island (or so it seemed) would rush their dinner checks or snatch their picnic blankets off the beach. Then, boisterous and giggly, they'd all pile into our shop. At this time of night, they tended to buy extravagant desserts. They wanted towering sundaes, chili-spiced chocolate shakes, or crepes filled with piped Nutella and hazelnut gelato.

They lingered in the booths, groaning over the ice creamy goodness.

They had all the time in the world.

Some nights this annoyed me to death. I wanted to shout at them, *Go away already! Don't you know that Gabriel Garcia Márquez is waiting at home for me, not to mention my lime-green bathtub?*

Other times I lingered along with them. I'd make myself what I called a sampler platter—tiny divots of my favorite ice creams lined up neatly in a banana split dish. Then I'd sit a booth or two away from the customers; close enough to eavesdrop without seeming to hover. I'd close my eyes while the ice cream melted on my tongue and feel the work-induced throbbing in my feet ebb.

But tonight, Will was here. Which meant I didn't want ice cream and I didn't want gossip—I wanted him. I wanted to scooch into a booth next to him and give him a flirty kiss hello. I wanted to make him taste my latest flavor (Root Beer Float), then cut my chore list in half so we could go for a walk on the beach.

I couldn't allow myself to do any of those things, though. Because everything that brought me closer to Will was also another step toward certain heartbreak.

Has Will not even considered this? I wondered as I dished up the last order.

From the way he was smiling at me, his face as open as a window, it didn't seem he had. Or maybe he just didn't care about what was going to happen eight short weeks from then.

I was hoping the last-minute customers would provide a buffer between us for a while, but as soon as I rang up the last order, they all drifted out to the boardwalk to perch around the extra-long picnic table out front.

I tossed my scoop into the sink and trudged to the door to flip the OPEN sign to CLOSED.

"Wow, you work hard here," Will said, still sitting at the chalkboard table. "Your love for ice cream must run way deep if you can still eat it after scooping all night."

"Well . . . ," I said, shrugging and giving him what was probably a pained smile.

I went to the little closet where we kept the cleaning supplies and grabbed a spray bottle of bleach water and a rag.

I didn't start with the tables farthest from the kids section just to avoid Will. I *always* started there. I shot him a couple of awkward smiles as I started spritzing and wiping down the tables.

Will just looked at me for a moment. He rolled a piece of green chalk between his thumb and forefinger, then said, "I called you yesterday."

"I know." I sighed. "I'm sorry. Caroline needed some girl time, and then I was so tired after being up so late the night before . . ."

I trailed off, not wanting to allude to the barbecue.

"I called you this morning, too," Will said.

I didn't know what to say to that one, so I just focused extra hard on my work, making careful, straight swipes across each tabletop with my rag.

Suddenly I heard a clatter from the supply closet. When I looked up, Will was emerging from it with a broom and dustpan.

"You don't have to do that," I said, my voice trembling a little.

Will just shrugged and started sweeping, following just behind me to catch the crumbs I was wiping off the tables. I skipped the chalkboard tables, because Kat and Benjie were in charge of those. They got upset if anybody destroyed the artwork before they got a chance to see it.

After that Will silently helped me put the lids on the ice cream tubs, set the lights on dim, and carry the final load of sticky spoons, bowls, and coffee mugs to the industrial dishwasher in the back.

But when I started updating the grocery list, Will finally said, "You're not really going to the store after you close up shop, are you?"

"No," I said wanly. "It's just, whoever closes is supposed to make a note of all the things we ran out of that day."

"I have a feeling you never, ever skip a day of school," Will said. He grinned and leaned against a stainless steel counter, crossing his legs at the ankle.

I didn't laugh or joke back like I was supposed to. I just nodded, confirming that, yes, I was a total rule-following nerd.

"I also have a feeling that you're avoiding me," Will said. Now he crossed his arms over his chest.

I could have denied it. I could have tap-danced my way out of it.

But already Will and I were beyond that. There was no option but to be honest with him.

So I nodded again.

"Okay, that's weird, because the Fourth of July?" Will said. "It was one of the best nights of my life."

"Mine too!" I burst out, finally looking up at him. It was only then that I realized I'd been avoiding his eyes ever since he'd arrived. Now that I allowed myself to look at him directly, I had to stifle a quiet gasp.

After not seeing him for a couple of days, Will looked so good I wanted to throw my arms around him. His hair was getting longer. It hung in his eyes, looking painfully cute. After all these days in the sun, he had a deep tan, which made his brown eyes look kind of sparkly. He was wearing another one of his T-shirts that hung just so off his broad shoulders. I wanted to touch it, to touch *him*.

But that, I thought to myself, would hurt.

In that moment of hesitation, it also occurred to me what *I* must look like after four straight hours of working. My hands smelled like bleach after cleaning the tables, and my hair was coming out of its sloppy bun. I could feel a few tendrils grazing my cheeks. I reached up nervously to smooth them behind my ears.

"Anna, stop," Will said, apparently reading my mind. "You're beautiful."

I slumped against the dishwasher so that Will and I faced each other from opposite sides of the kitchen.

"Don't say that," I whispered.

"Why *not*?" Will said. I could hear an edge in his voice, a kernel of exasperation.

"Because, this just keeps getting better," I said. I was gripping the counter above the dishwasher as if I needed its support to be able to say all these things. "That's only going to make it hurt more when you leave."

"Leave?" Will shook his head in confusion.

"Leave!" I said. I was the exasperated one now. "At the end of the summer, remember? When you go back to your kuh-nishes and the Brooklyn Bridge and . . ."

I trailed off when I remembered that Will didn't exactly have a life of glamour and happiness waiting for him back in New York. I waved a hand in front of my face as if it could erase what I'd just said.

"Just," I revised, "when you leave *here*."

"Oh." Will cocked his head to the side. "Huh."

"So you hadn't thought of that at all?" I said.

"I guess not," Will said. "I mean, yeah, I knew it was out there. August twenty-ninth. That's the date on our return plane tickets. But, Anna—that's ages away."

"It'll fly by," I said glumly. "It already has."

"So that's a reason to ruin the time we *do* have?" Will said.

"Who's ruining anything?" I said. I pushed myself away from the counter and stalked over to the tall shelving unit where we kept the paper products. I yanked down a stack of napkins and pushed my way through the swinging door into the ice cream parlor. After the bright lights of the kitchen, the shop felt dark and shadowy. I stumbled a bit as I headed to a table in the kids section and began to push napkins into the spring-loaded dispensers.

I could feel Will behind me, staring at the back of my head, but I didn't turn around.

"Just don't think about that," Will urged me. "Think about now. Think about the other night!"

"I don't know if I can do that," I grumbled.

"You probably never pull all-nighters because you forgot to study for a test, do you?" Will said.

I whipped around and glared at him. My eyes had adjusted to the dusky light and he looked annoyingly handsome.

"I guess I'm just not as cool as you," I said. "I can't just live in the present."

"Well, you don't really have a choice, do you?" Will said with maddening logic. "I mean today is today. You're *in* it, Anna. And you can be in it with me, say, walking to that dumb place down the boardwalk and getting some curly fries. Or you could just stay here and make that grocery list for a shopping trip that's not going to happen for a week."

I bit my lip and looked away from him. I just . . . I just needed a minute to think. I went to the table where Will had been sitting when he'd first come in that evening. I started to stuff a wad of napkins into the dispenser. But then a doodle on the chalkboard tabletop caught my eye.

It was a tree.

A big, messy, sprawling tree covered with familiar-looking five-pointed leaves—not to mention a pink bicycle, a bunch of pinwheels, and a snake twined around its trunk.

Also on Figgy Pudding's trunk? One of those old-timey hearts with initials inside: *AP + WC*.

"Aw . . . ," Will said as he saw me staring at the chalk drawing. "I'm an idiot. I'll just . . ."

He grabbed a napkin out of the dispenser and wadded it up, clearly intending to smudge out the heart, the whole thing.

"No!" I cried, grabbing his wrist before he could get near the drawing.

It was the first time we'd touched that night.

We looked at each other, wide-eyed. An instant later we were tangled up together, kissing so hard that I couldn't breathe. Clearly Will couldn't either because when we pulled apart, we both gasped. This made us laugh until we'd exhausted what little breath we had left. Then we were kissing some more, and giggling at the same time. It was kind of messy—but wonderfully so.

At some point during all the making out, I sat on the chalkboard table and wrapped my ankles around the back of Will's knees. Later we'd discover that my backside had smudged Will's drawing, ruining it completely.

"It was only gonna get erased tomorrow," Will said with another big chuckle.

At that moment it was easy for me to shrug it off too. It didn't matter that I couldn't save the drawing; stash it in my vanity drawer to keep forever. It had been a moment. One of countless wonderful moments I'd had—and would have—with Will.

That was, if I let myself have them.

As Will and I locked up The Scoop and headed giddily down the boardwalk together, I told myself that I could. I could handle being with Will now, even if I had to say good-bye to him later. It was worth it.

But did that mean I could forget about that looming good-bye? About August 29?

Not really. Not, in fact, for a minute.

After that, I didn't want to waste another minute of my time left with Will. But—we barely saw each other for an entire week. What thwarted us? The most unromantic obstacle you can imagine—the *weather*.

Every day Dune Island was pummeled by tropical thunderstorms. The rain, lightning, and thunder would start rolling in around ten o'clock. It would linger on and off through the day, like a grumpy guest constantly dozing off, then snorting himself awake right in the middle of your house. The storms held us hostage.

And during the brief windows between storms? The sun would come out baring fangs. The heat was wet and claustrophobic. Just breathing became a chore. You couldn't see all the spores and mold and motes floating through the air, but you knew they were there, and they made everyone feel cranky.

Steam rose off Highway 80.

The boardwalk developed a disgusting sliminess that never had a chance to dry out.

My bedsheets became so damp and sticky, I seriously considered sleeping in the bathtub. Figgy Pudding's decorations, of course, were ruined, and we pretty much had to forget about making waffle cones at The Scoop. They were too floppy to hold anything. My dad came up with the idea of passing out waffle cone rain checks and got a write-up in the *Dune Island Intelligencer* for it. Sophie was so embarrassed, she went into hiding for an entire day.

Me? I was sort of grateful for the diversion, even if it was an incredibly silly one. Because the rain had also seriously dampened my opportunities to be with Will.

We couldn't go anywhere outside because my parents wouldn't let me drive their car during the storms. And *I* wouldn't let either of us ride our bikes to see each other.

"Anna, you spend half your life in the ocean," Will said on the phone one dark, thunderous morning. He was trying to coax me into meeting him for coffee on the boardwalk. "You're not willing to get a little wet for me?"

"Please, you think it's the water I'm worried about?" I said. "It's the lightning."

"Oh, come on, nobody really gets struck by lightning, do they?"

"Are you near a computer right now?" I asked. Cradling my phone between my ear and shoulder, I headed to the kitchen and grabbed my dad's laptop. Within a few seconds I'd sent Will a link to an article about the hundreds of coastal Georgians sizzled by strikes every year.

"Oh my God!" Will said as he scanned the article on his end.

"Yup," I said. "Lightning strikes and tractor accidents—*very* common cause of death and disfigurement around here."

"Talk about Southern gothic," Will said.

I closed the laptop. It was too wet and noisy to go out to the screened porch, so I wandered into the living room. Kat and Benjie were sitting on the floor with bowls of Cheerios in their laps and a board game between them. My mom was curled up on the couch with some knitting. It felt like one of those boring national holidays where there's nothing to celebrate and nothing to do.

"Speaking of gothic," I said, settling into the lumpy chair near the window, "did you hear about the new horror movie that's out? Sounds amazing. I heard it turned a reviewer's hair white. Needless to say, he gave it a thumbs-down."

"Why am I not surprised that you're not the romantic-comedy type?" Will snorted.

"A movie!"

That was my mom. I glanced over at her. She'd dropped her knitting into her lap and she was grinning at me.

"That's the perfect thing to do today," she said. "We could go to the first matinee. Your dad doesn't need me at The Scoop until four."

"Movie, movie!" Kat and Benjie shrieked, which of course, summoned a *thump thump thump* to the staircase. Sophie poked her head over the banister.

"Are we going to the movies?" she asked. "Can I ask Emily?"

"Sure," Mom said, getting to her feet and smoothing her hair. "That's why we got the minivan. Anna, tell Will we can be at his house in twenty minutes. I'll go get the movie·section."

"Um," I squeaked, "but I didn't . . . um, Mom?"

Over the phone I heard Owen's voice saying, "Wait a minute, are you going to a movie?"

And then a female voice called, "Take your brother. He's driving me crazy."

Before we knew it, Will and I were going on a date to a Cineplex in Savannah—with almost everyone in our families. I didn't know whether to laugh or cry.

But Will laughed—so I did too. In fact, Will seemed goofily charmed by the whole thing—scrunching into my mother's van, running through the rain to the theater, waiting in line at the concession stand while Kat and Benjie debated popcorn versus candy.

Then we all split up to go to different theaters. Will and I went to the horror flick, my mom and the kids picked something G-rated, and Sophie and Emily chose a chick flick. Owen was on the fence, but at the last minute, he said to the girls, "Ah, what the heck. I'll go with you."

"Seriously, Owen?" I squawked while Sophie and Emily dissolved into delighted giggles.

I looked at Will in surprise.

"Does your brother really like chick flicks?"

"Let me ask you something," Will said as Owen sauntered

toward the theater with the girls. "Who among us has the most snacks?"

Sophie and Emily had a giant tub of popcorn to share and a box of candy each, plus Cokes. I pointed at them.

"Not for long," Will said.

"Your brother is literally going to take candy from children?" I said.

"Shamelessly," Will said. "He's the best food-filcher you've ever seen."

I laughed as Will and I walked into our own theater. When the doors closed behind us, Will looked around with exaggerated paranoia.

"Are they all gone?" he asked. "Are we alone?"

"At last!" I said with mock drama.

He grabbed my hand. We hurried down the aisle, sank low into a couple of seats, and finally, *finally* kissed each other hello.

"This is so much better than coffee," Will murmured as the lights went dark and the previews started.

"Yeah, because there's candy." I cackled, rattling the box of overpriced gummy bears that I'd bought at the concession stand.

"Yeah," Will said sarcastically, before he started kissing me again. "That's exactly why. The candy."

I laughed. Then I forgot about all the family members in the building and snuggled up with Will. With the air-conditioning blasting, I actually felt chilly for the first time in ages, and Will's warm arm against mine felt good. Over the sinister music of the movie trailers, you could just barely hear the soft patter of the rain on the roof. It was the coziest sound.

Instead of clasping my hand, Will rested his arm on mine and traced the inside of my wrist with his thumb. For some reason, this made my upper lip tingle. And not in a bad way.

I was just resting my head on Will's shoulder and getting up the nerve to breathe something romantic into his ear when I heard someone tumble into the seat right behind us.

Will and I peered over our shoulders.

"Owen?!" Will said through gritted teeth.

"Dude, I couldn't take the chick flick," Owen said. "There was a shopping montage in the very first scene! Hey, did you guys get any popcorn?"

Will's thumb left my wrist.

My head left his shoulder.

And let's just say, after that, I didn't miss one minute of the movie. (But at least it *was* horrifically good.)

For the rest of the Monsoon—as Will and I came to call that rain-ruined week—we saw each other only during damp, snatched moments at The Scoop.

So at night, we talked on the phone. And talked and talked and talked.

"You were in my dream last night," Will said during one of our epic conversations. I was on the screened porch during a lull in the rain. I lay on the hammock at an angle with one big toe on the sandy floorboards, pushing the swing back and forth.

"Will, that is the cheesiest line," I said with a laugh.

"No, it's true," he said. "And believe me, it wasn't that romantic. We were in a supermarket; this *endless* grocery store.

We kept going up and down the aisles like we were searching for the exit, but there never was one. It was actually kind of boring."

"Okay, that doesn't seem good," I said with a frown.

"Well, I know I was happy to be with *you*," Will said. "I was just ready to get out of that stupid store."

"Hmm," I said. "What was in our cart? No melons or whoopie pies, I hope. Because that would just be too ridiculously Freudian."

"Or, from what you've told me, Woody Allenian," Will said, laughing.

Another late night, I lay on my bed with the phone between my ear and the pillow. I watched the raindrops spatter my skylight. They made me think of these little water balloons Caroline and I made one night when we were eight. She was sleeping over while our parents went out for dinner together, leaving us with a sitter. We filled about a hundred balloons and nested them in a box, like a giant, jiggly litter of baby animals. Then we waited on the balcony. We waited for *four hours*. Finally my parents came home and we pelted them with every balloon in our box, after which Caroline wasn't allowed to sleep over for a long, long time.

I told Will this story because I knew it would make him laugh.

And because that was what we did during these meandering conversations. We told each other our silly stories and ancient memories and random thoughts. They were our ways of revealing ourselves to each other, even if we didn't always realize it. Sometimes these talks felt more intense, more intimate, than kissing.

"So you were always scary stubborn," Will said about the four-hour wait with the balloons.

"Just like *you've* always had issues with crustaceans," I retorted. One of Will's silly stories had been about him crying when his parents boiled a batch of lobsters during a long-ago vacation in Maine.

"Yeah, I was scarred by the murder of my little friends," Will admitted. "I don't know what I was thinking asking you to go ghost-crabbing that night."

"Oh, *I* know what you were thinking!" I burst out with a laugh.

Will laughed too.

"Yeah, I guess I was," he said, speaking in a shorthand that we both understood. "I guess I was."

And then we got quiet for a moment. I listened to the distant creaking of Will's front-porch rocker. He could probably hear the soft *slap-slap-slap* of the rain on my skylight. And both of our minds swooped back to that night with the ghost crabs, the night of our first kiss.

"I wish I could see you right now," Will said, his voice low and a little husky.

I wanted to see him too. Desperately.

It was the desperation that made a small part of me *not* want to see Will too.

Mostly, being Will's girlfriend made me feel the same way I did after acing a test in school: a little light-headed, a little proud, and somehow utterly relaxed while also buzzing with excitement.

But given that Will was a boy, and not an English midterm, my emotions were more complicated than that.

The more I was with Will, even on the phone, the more I *wanted* to be with him. I was starting to feel like I could never get enough of him.

I'd be reading a novel, washing my face, or making Benjie a peanut butter and jelly sandwich and suddenly I'd remember a certain kiss. Or a moment when Will's fingertips had grazed the side of my neck. Or the feeling of his warm hand resting for a moment on top of my head before skimming down my hair. I'd literally relive the sensation, my eyes fluttering shut, my body giving a little shudder. My mind was like a luxurious landmine. At any unpredictable moment, I might be overwhelmed by a memory, by a feeling, by Will.

I loved being so consumed by Will. Adored it. But I kind of hated it too, because I felt like a huge part of myself had been wrested from my control. I mean, sometimes you just want to make a peanut butter sandwich without being overcome by your own passion, you know?

The fact of August 29 only made it all worse. That's what turned my desire for Will into desperation. I hated to hang up the phone each night, even after we'd talked so much we were dry-mouthed and half asleep.

I'd watch the weather radar online to try to pinpoint the one lightning-free hour when I could safely dash to Will's house for a fifteen-minute make-out session, then dash back without being electrocuted.

My ice cream–making skills were off. One batch was bitter

with too much vanilla. Another ice cream emerged from the churn as a masterpiece, one of the most subtly delicious flavors I'd ever invented. Only then did I realize that I'd forgotten to write down any of the ingredients I'd used and had no idea how to re-create it.

Every time I even glanced at a calendar, I had to fight off tears.

Basically, I felt completely out of control. And as Will had already figured out, I didn't like being out of control. Since *he* was both the cause and the cure for this feeling, however, I was flummoxed as to what to do about it.

When the rain sputtered out for the last time on Saturday afternoon and Sam hatched the idea for a double date, it seemed like the perfect way to reunite with Will. I could be with him all night, but with my friends there to diffuse the intensity, the *need*, I was feeling.

Maybe I'll get used to being with Will again and I'll get a grip, I'd told myself as I got ready. I carefully chose my favorite pair of holey jeans and a fluttery, cream-colored off-the-shoulder top. I dusted my face with shimmery powder and swept my hair into a loose topknot with a couple of chopsticks. I looked cool, breezy, and probably a little too wholesome for our destination—The Swamp.

"So this is the famous Swamp," Will said when we arrived. "If possible, it's even . . . swampier than I expected."

"The name don't lie, my friend," Sam said, clapping Will on the shoulder.

"Oh, please, the whole island's a swamp after all that rain," Caroline complained, grabbing a tea-stained cardboard menu off the bar and fanning herself with it. "You know it's bad when *my* hair is frizzing."

I would have laughed, but I was too high-strung. I felt about as vulnerable as an oyster in high season.

We picked a round table near the wall of screens that divided the dining room from the deck. Like the rest of The Swamp, the table looked like it was one hard wallop away from splintering into little pieces. It was fork gouged and wobbly, and its putty-colored paint was peeling. On the table was a roll of paper towels (no holder), a sticky jar of jalapeño vinegar, and about eight different kinds of hot sauce.

The Swamp walls were darkly paneled. Every surface that didn't hold a dart board was covered with artwork made by Arnold Eber Senior, who was the father of Arnold Eber Junior, who owned The Swamp. Mr. Eber Senior was an outsider artist who pretty much made the same thing over and over again—life-sized preachers cut out of old sheet metal and painted with metallic car enamel. The preachers wore candy-colored suits and had black pompadours, as well as voice balloons coming out of their mouths that said *You'll burn in hell, sinner!* in about fifty different ways.

"Isn't this a bar?" Will asked, glancing at the neon Pabst Blue Ribbon sign by the door. There were also foamy pitchers on just about every table except ours. "How can anybody take a sip of alcohol with those guys *staring* at them?"

"Well, *you* don't have to worry about that, sweetheart," said a high, scratchy voice above our heads. Our waitress had just tossed a bunch of neon-colored wristbands onto our table. Stamped on each band in blocky letters was the word UNDERAGE.

"Hi, Helen," Sam, Caroline, and I singsonged together.

"Put 'em on, kids," she said, sounding bored. She fluffed up her white-blond bangs with her frosty pink fingernails. No matter how tan and leathery Helen got in the face, she would always have the hair and nails of a teenager.

"Helen," Caroline protested, "we know you wouldn't serve us, any more than we would ask to be served. Don't make us wear the nerdy bracelets."

"Don't make me call your mother, little girl," Helen said, scowling. "Now put 'em on."

We put 'em on.

"Back in a minute for your orders," Helen said, swishing away in her very tight white jeans.

I watched Will take in the other Swamp customers. The Swamp attracted a very specific clientele, which didn't include people like my parents, my teachers, or any other professional types. This place was for fishermen and oil-rig guys, truckers, off-the-gridders, and curmudgeons. *And* high school kids, because it was the only bar on the island that would let us in— with our blazing wristbands, of course.

It was definitely a slice of the "real" Dune Island.

And once again I was noticing that only because I was looking at it through Will's eyes. Sam and Caroline were oblivious. They were fixated on the clouds of bugs swarming just outside the screening.

"Look at all those mosquitoes," Caroline said, pressing her nose to the screen. "They're as big as birds!"

"Yeah, you know you want it!" Sam called out to the mosquitoes, pressing his bare arm up to the screen. "But you can't have it, skeeters!"

"Don't you think you're tempting fate, teasing them like that?" Will asked with a laugh.

"Whatever, I like to live dangerously," Sam replied, grabbing Caroline around the waist and giving her a squeeze.

Caroline laughed, but it was a little forced. I reached across the table, plucked the menu out of her hand, and slid it over to Will.

"Ooh, they have boiled peanuts," Will said when he'd given the short menu a read. "My new favorite food."

He grinned at me, and I swooped back to us kissing on the wool blanket on the Fourth of July, the salty, briny taste of boiled peanuts still on his lips.

And then I *had* to look away so I didn't pounce on Will. I glanced at Caroline, whose lip was curled.

"Trust me, you don't want Swamp boiled peanuts," she told Will. "They smell like old-man sweat."

"Caroline!" I said. "Gross."

"Sorry, but they do. They do, don't they, Sam?" Caroline said.

"I like 'em," Sam said with a shrug. "But if they skeeve you out, babe, we'll skip 'em. And no crawfish."

"Wow," I said. "Sam forsaking crawfish?"

Caroline squirmed in her seat, and I started to get what she'd been talking about when we were at the beach. It was sweet of

Sam to be so considerate, but it was also so *different*. He wasn't acting like the happy-go-lucky, unapologetic crawdad-eater that Caroline had fallen for.

The truth was, I didn't really want to suck the head of a mudbug in front of Will either, so I didn't make a bigger issue of it.

Which left us in awkward silence, until Helen stalked over with a bucket of jalapeño-studded hush puppies. She thunked it on the table along with four red plastic tumblers of sweet iced tea.

"Um, I didn't order any tea?" Will started to say, but Helen wasn't hearing it. She spun on the heel of her pink Keds sneaker and bustled away.

"Sorry about that," Sam said to Will. "Like I said, the name don't lie. I guess we're just used to, you know, the rudeness."

"And the dirt," I said with a grin.

"And the old-man sweat," Caroline chimed in, giggling.

"And don't even think about going in the men's room," Sam said.

"Will," I said, "we can just drink our tea and go back to the boardwalk if you want. I guess when you think about it, The Swamp *is* kind of gross."

"No way," Will said, folding his hands behind his head and leaning back in his chair. "I love this place!"

But as he said it, he was looking at me, as if he was saying, I love *you*.

It made my heart dance around in my chest, but it also made my neck go prickly and sweaty.

"Music," I announced. I held out my hand. "Who's got change?"

"I do," Will said, standing up to go with me to the jukebox by the front door.

"Great," I said just a little wanly.

The jukebox was not an antique and it wasn't charming. It was pure truck-stop-issue tackiness, with rainbow-colored lights skimming up and down the front and a digital CD selecter.

The songs ranged from new country to gospel to old country, along with a whole lot of Elvis. I'd always assumed that was the request of Mr. Eber Senior, who painted Elvis hair on every one of his tin preachers.

"It's two songs for a dollar," I told Will, flipping through the titles in the jukebox. "Fast or slow?"

"Slow," Will said, slipping his arm around my waist. I couldn't help myself, I leaned into him. Perhaps because I'd been trying to resist Will, pressing up against him seemed to feel twice as good as usual.

Still, I didn't meet Will's eyes as I made my choices. Only one of them was slow. The other was a swively Elvis number.

Only as we were walking back to the table did I remember that Elvis is famous for being so sexy, he'd made teenage girls scream and faint.

Maybe that wasn't *the best choice after all*, I thought, groaning to myself.

When we got back to our table, it was Sam who was hot and bothered—but not in a good way. He was standing up and glaring at Caroline, whose arms were crossed over her chest.

"What *is* it lately, Caroline?" Sam was saying. His face, usually as placid as water, was pale with confusion and anger. "I just want to have a nice night out with you and you're not in the mood? I haven't seen you all week!"

"Well, whose fault is that?" Caroline retorted.

"What, you think I control the weather?!" Sam said. "Well, if tonight isn't *convenient* for you, maybe you'd be happier if I just left."

Caroline shook her head and said, "No, I wouldn't. It's just . . ."

She trailed off and shrugged helplessly.

"Well . . ." Now it was Sam who was searching for words. He spotted me—Will and I had taken a few steps away from the table as if that would give Sam and Caroline some privacy—and gave me a beseeching look.

I gave him a sympathetic grimace, but the last thing I could do was chime in on a fight between my two best friends. Talk about a minefield.

"I need some air," Sam muttered.

"It's a screened porch," Caroline pointed out.

Sam took a deep, frustrated breath, then slammed through the screen door that led to the big deck. Shooting off one corner of the deck was a narrow bridge that led to another, small, circular deck. Sam kept it together while he wove around the crowded tables on the deck, but when he hit the bridge, he broke into a loopy run.

"He's going to see the gators," Caroline said, hanging her head. "Well, I guess this wasn't the dream date either."

"Caroline," I said. "Why don't I go talk to him?"

Caroline shrugged and nodded.

"Do you mind?" I asked Will.

I saw his shoulders deflate just a bit, but he waved me out.

"Yeah, yeah," he said. "Go."

Now I felt torn between all *three* of the people I was with. But I headed outside after Sam. Before I hit the bridge, I stopped at the cart where the waitresses kept the water pitchers and grabbed a handful of dryer sheets out of a box. They were supposed to ward off mosquitoes if you didn't have any bug spray handy. I tucked one into my jeans pocket and one into a strap on my sandal. I took the other two out to Sam.

He was sitting at the edge of the deck, dangling his legs over the swamp. He dipped his hand into a plastic garbage can filled with fishy smelling pellets and tossed some to the alligators arrayed in the swamp beneath his feet. There were so many, they looked like a very uncomfortable area rug, all prehistoric crags and sleepy, reptilian eyeballs.

"Maybe you should pull your feet up," I said to Sam. "You don't want the gators to think they're a snack, too."

"Aw, these guys are so domesticated, they don't even remember that they're carnivores," Sam said sadly. He threw another handful of chow at the alligators, who growled and snapped at one another as they lunged for the little tidbits.

I sank down next to Sam and handed him some dryer sheets.

"Thanks," he said. "I forgot to get these. And Will was right. The mosquitoes are getting their revenge on me."

He slapped at a few of them as he tucked the dryer sheets into his pockets.

"Okay, so what is it?" he said, looking me in the eye. "How am I screwing things up with Caroline?"

"Why are you so sure you are?" I said.

"Aw, come on, Anna," Sam said, looking miserable. "I was bound to. I mean, I waited all that time to tell her how I felt because I was scared it would screw everything up. That *I* would screw everything up. Now I guess I went and did it, hard as I've tried not to."

"Sam," I said, "why *are* you? Trying so hard, I mean."

Sam looked at me like I was a little challenged.

"Anna! Because she's *Caroline*. She deserves it."

"Yeah, and you're *you*," I retorted. "Remember? The guy that Caroline fell for? Why do you feel like you have to be different from before, just because you guys are, you know . . ."

"Makin' hay?" Sam drawled with a mischievous grin.

"Oh, my God," I laughed. "You are so *country*."

Sam laughed too, briefly. But then he sobered up again.

"The thing is, things *are* different now," he said. "They can't not be. And if we can't make it work as a couple, that's it. Friendship's over. Maybe it'll ruin my friendship with you, too."

"It won't!" I said fiercely.

"Yeah, well, it's easy to say that now," Sam said sadly. He stared down at the rumbling gators. "I never should have told her."

"No!" I insisted. "You shouldn't regret going for it, Sam. It was so brave of you. Maybe that's what you need to be now that you're together."

"Brave?" Sam said, looking confused.

"Confident," I said. "You're worthy of Caroline. Don't forget it."

"Huh," Sam said, giving me a sheepish glance. This was pretty touchy-feely for us. I guess he was right about everything being different now. And not just with him and Caroline.

"Sounds like you're saying I just need to get over myself," Sam said.

"Yeah," I said. "Like Caroline always says." Now we grinned at each other. We had shorthand too, me and Sam.

After a thoughtful moment, I cocked my head.

"You know what else might be going on with Caroline?" I said. "I think she's mad at you because you've softened her up."

"Caroline?" Sam said. "Never."

"No, you have," I said. "She's gaga over you, and I think she doesn't like to feel that vulnerable."

"You guys are peas in a pod in that area," Sam said, flinging another handful of gator chow into the water.

"Um, what?" I said with a barky little laugh.

"Well, you're doing the same thing Caroline is," Sam said. "In a way. Anybody can see it, Anna. On the Fourth of July, you didn't know anybody was at that barbecue except Will. But now there's, like, this wall between you."

"Sam," I said, half outraged, half impressed. "Have you been watching chick flicks or something? You seem to know what you're talking about."

"I know *you*," Sam said. "I know you think too much. I know you like to hold this whole island at arm's length. And now you've found someone you *don't* want to hold at arm's length and it scares the hell out of you."

Whoa. It looked like Caroline wasn't the only one who could turn that mirror of truth on me.

"Sam," I said. It came out as something close to a moan. "I have less than seven weeks left with Will."

"Yeah, and . . . ?" Sam said.

"The harder I fall for him, the harder it's going to be when he leaves," I said, hating how needy that made me sound. "And *then* what do I do?"

"You do what you would have done anyway," Sam said. "You go to school. You make amazing ice cream. You crush Landon Smith's soul when he asks you to the junior prom and you turn him down. You just . . . deal."

"I deal," I said, rolling my eyes. "You make it sound so easy."

"It isn't, but you do it anyway," Sam stated with a shrug. He slapped at a mosquito on his leg.

"I don't think these dryer sheets really work," he said. "It's one of those urban myths."

I laughed.

Then we were quiet for another minute or two. We tossed nuggets to the alligators, zoning out to the swishing of their tails until we got to our feet and started back across the bridge. But before we reached the main deck, Sam stopped and turned to me.

"You know, *you're* brave too, Anna," he told me. "And strong. You can take it. Will leaving, I mean."

Suddenly I had that same choky feeling I got every time I glimpsed a calendar. It didn't exactly make me feel strong.

But Sam had been right about everything else. I *had* been

trying to push Will away to protect myself. And *that* was definitely weak.

So I decided to get over myself. For real this time. I pushed ahead of Sam and stalked right back into The Swamp. When I saw that Will was sitting alone at our table, I plunked down next to him. Then I planted a big kiss on his lips.

"Wow," he said. His smile was immediate and wide. "You smell like clean laundry. I *love* the smell of laundry."

This time, I didn't look away when he said it. Instead, I kissed him again.

"Now, none of *that*, children," Helen said as she skimmed by with steaming buckets of food dangling from both arms. Will and I broke apart, bright red, but grinning.

"So," Will said, raising his eyebrows at me, "good talk with Sam?"

I glanced around to make sure Helen wasn't looking. Then I gave Will one more kiss, sweet and lingering.

"Yeah," I said, gazing happily into his eyes. "Good talk."

The dinner invitation from Will's mom had been casual enough. It came a few days after our night at The Swamp, when I'd stopped by to pick up Will for a morning swim.

"We're going to get some fish for the grill tonight," Ms. Dempsey had said. "Why don't you join us?"

Since it happened to be my night off from The Scoop, I said yes without thinking twice about it.

But now that I was knocking on Will's cottage door at

six p.m., I felt a nervous thrill. Like our first kiss and our first fight, the first dinner with Will's family seemed like a sort of milestone. I gulped when Will swung the door open, his hair still wet from the shower. His T-shirt stuck to his skin in places where he hadn't dried off before throwing on his clothes.

He looked so irresistible, I wanted to throw my arms around him and bury my nose in his shampoo-scented neck. But we were in his doorway, with his mother bustling around the kitchen behind him. There was also the minor obstruction of all the things I was carrying.

"Anna?" Will said, grinning at me. "Are you in there?"

I plopped the rather large bunch of flowers I was holding into Will's arms.

"It's just a few hydrangeas," I said, fluffing up the pompoms of tiny blue-and-purple blooms. "I snipped them on my way out of the house. They're gonna start shriveling up in the heat soon anyway."

"A *few*?" Will said, pretending to stagger under the weight of the (not *that* huge, I swear) bouquet.

I followed Will into the kitchen. The big, open living/dining room was classic rental cottage. Everything was the color of ocean, sky, and sand. Every available surface was covered with sand dollars, starfish, driftwood seagull sculptures, and glossy wood plaques that said things like *Our memories of the ocean will linger on long after our footprints in the sand are gone.*

"Oh, Anna!" Ms. Dempsey said when she saw the hydrangeas. "Those are beautiful! Where did you get them?"

"Just, you know, from my front yard," I said.

Ms. Dempsey clapped a hand on her forehead.

"Of course, I remember noticing those amazing bushes at your house on the Fourth," she said. "You know, you live in New York long enough, you forget that flowers don't all come from the deli wrapped in plastic."

While Ms. Dempsey left in search of a flower vase, I plunked my other packages—a soft cooler and a grease-stained white paper sack—on the Formica counter. Will unzipped the cooler.

"Anna," he burst out. "There are *four* pints of ice cream in here!"

"Well, *I* can't exactly show up at a dinner party without ice cream, can I?" I said with a shrug.

"And what's that?!" Will asked, pointing at the paper bag.

"Um, just some fried pies," I said. "Well, a dozen. To go with the ice cream. What? Too much?"

Will wrapped his arms around me with that delighted/bewildered expression that I'd come to recognize.

"Yes," he said very softly, planting a sweet, smiley kiss on my lips. "Too much."

"You really are a Yankee," I whispered, grinning up at him. "This is nothing. Most people would have brought a casserole, too."

An instant after we parted, there was a shriek from the kitchen doorway.

I spun to stare at Ms. Dempsey, my heart flapping around my chest like an injured bird.

She just saw me kissing her son, I thought. *And now she's going*

*to sit me down and give me a lecture about respect and boundaries,
from which I will never recover.*

Ms. Dempsey's scream brought Owen running from the
long, narrow hallway that led to the bedrooms. He was holding a
book and wearing chunky black glasses that made him look like
a nerdy hipster. I glanced at the book cover. David Foster Wal-
lace. I raised my eyebrows, impressed, but Owen didn't notice.
He was looking a little freaked-out.

"What happened?" he burst out.

"Are those . . . Hubley's fried pies?" Ms. Dempsey asked me
breathlessly.

Hubley's logo—a grinning peach flashing a thumbs-up—was
stamped in blurry purple ink on the side of the bag. Hubley's
was a bare-bones bakery on Highway 80. They made cakes and
cookies, but nobody paid any attention to those. You went to
Hubley's for one thing and one thing only—half-moon-shaped,
white-glazed fried pies.

"Those *are* Hubley's," I told Ms. Dempsey, the bird in my
chest starting to calm down. "Have you had them?"

"Not for twenty years!" Ms. Dempsey sighed. She peeked
into the bag and breathed in the pies' burned-sugar scent.
"Mmmm. You won't believe this, but when I talk to my com-
position students about recalling sensual imagery, I use Hubley's
fried pies as my example. I tell them about the glaze that piles
up in the crimps of the crust and the almost-too-much nutmeg
that makes your mouth tingle . . ."

Owen pulled off his glasses and rolled his eyes.

"Uh-oh," he said to Will. "Nostalgia alert."

"I just can't believe I forgot to make a pilgrimage to Hubley's myself," Ms. Dempsey said to us, shaking her head. "It's literally in my lesson plan."

"I got peach," I told her, "cherry, and sweet—"

"Sweet potato!" Ms. Dempsey interrupted, almost jumping for joy. Between that and the jeans and stylishly frayed T-shirt she was wearing, Ms. Dempsey looked about twenty years old. "That was the best one."

"Well, you can't leave Hubley's without the sweet potato pies," I said. "It's like a law."

"You know, I think that joint was actually in the guide book," Owen said, peeking into the bag.

"Anna, you are a sweetheart for bringing over all this stuff!" Ms. Dempsey said. "I'm going to eat big pile of them, even though it would give my yoga teacher back home a heart attack if she knew."

She took another whiff from the bag.

"Of course," she reconsidered, "they might not be as good as I remember."

She seemed to get a little pensive then, no doubt drifting into a memory.

"Mom," Owen piped up, "have one now. Call it an appetizer. I'll split it with you. We can save the rest for dessert."

Will crossed his arms over his chest and leaned against the counter, watching Owen break a pie in two and hand half to his mom. Will's face darkened, even looked a little sullen, and I remembered what he'd said about Owen's anti–Valentine's Day.

"I never would have thought of it."

But clearly he wished that he had.

My attention shifted to Ms. Dempsey when she took her first bite of the shiny glazed pie.

"Oh my God. It's exactly the same."

"So they were always that greasy?" I asked. "Even I can't eat too many of those in one sitting. And Will will tell you, I can *eat*."

I shot Will a conspiratorial grin, but he seemed to have trouble returning it. That melancholy that I'd seen around his mouth and eyes when we'd first met—and which I'd barely detected since—was making his face seem long and pale.

Owen didn't seem to notice. He was too busy bonding with his mom over the revelation that was a Hubley's sweet potato pie.

"Yummm," he groaned. Then he glanced at his mom. "Maybe we should split another one?"

Ms. Dempsey giggled like a kid.

"Well, while they're fresh," she said, digging into the bag. "Anna, Will? Don't you want some?"

"I'm going to wait until after dinner and have it with the Bananas Foster ice cream I brought over," I said. Now I had a conspiratorial grin for *her*. Clearly Will had gotten his taste for salt from his dad.

The thought jolted me. Will's dad. Will had barely told me anything about him—yet even I could feel his absence here. It created a halo of sadness around even this goofily delicious little moment.

"Okay!" Ms. Dempsey announced, popping the last bit

of her pie into her mouth and dusting off her hands. "I'm quitting until after dinner. And I'm doing an hour of vinyasa tomorrow."

"Yeah, heard that before," Owen said, pretending to yawn. He wandered over to the fridge and started pulling out paper-wrapped packages of fish. "I'll man the fire."

Over his shoulder he added, "Hey, Will. As long as we're getting all nostalgic, you should show Anna *the room*."

"The room?" I said.

"It's my room," Ms. Dempsey said. She went to the counter, which was piled with salad ingredients and unshucked ears of corn. "It's the only one the owners didn't strip bare of all character, then stuff with seashells and driftwood."

"This place *is* a bit of a theme park, isn't it?" I had to admit, eyeing a scary-looking coral collection on top of the microwave.

"But they left one room in all its old, fugly glory," Owen said. "That's how *I* ended up with the master bedroom."

He pumped his fist in the air and hooted before he started ripping open the packets of fish.

"C'mon," Will said, lightly hooking my fingers with his. "I'll show you."

"Wait, I don't think I made the bed today!" Ms. Dempsey gasped. "Anna, what will you think of me?"

"You're on vacation," I told her. "You're not supposed to make the bed!"

"Will, I like this girl," Ms. Dempsey said as she tossed the lettuce into a salad spinner.

I felt giddy as Will led me down the hall. His step seemed

to lighten too. We were clearly approaching the cottage's star attraction.

"Whoa!" I exclaimed as we walked through the door. "I think I went blind for a second there."

There was a lot of wallpaper. Zigzaggy orange and brown, seventies-glorious wallpaper. And a big, yellow faux-fur rug. Clustered on one wall was a collection of framed needlepoints of owls, mushrooms, twiggy-looking girls in short A-line dresses, and other blasts from the past. The curtains had little orange pompoms dangling from the hems, and the disheveled bed-spread was orange velvet.

"I know, right?" Will said. "It's like a shrine. I lie awake sometimes wondering why the owners kept the room this way."

"Why on earth?" I said.

"Anyway, my mom laughed for five minutes straight when she first saw it," Will said. "Which was definitely better than her bursting into tears. So we like The Room."

"And *Owen* got the master bedroom," I teased. "Did you guys fight for it or something?"

"Nah," Will said. He picked an ancient troll doll up off the low dresser and spun it between his two palms so its bright orange hair stood on end. "Soon he's going to be living in a cinder-block dorm with a roommate. I figured I'd throw him a bone."

"NYU, huh?" I said.

"The honors program," Will said, looking both proud and a little gloomy. "Full scholarship. You wouldn't know it to look at him, but Owen's kind of a genius. Someday he's gonna cure cancer or something."

"Right now it seems like he's trying to cure your mom," I said.

Will's mouth formed a grim line. For the first time I noticed that only one side of the queen-sized bed was unmade. The sheets and quilt were all over the place, and the bedside table was littered with books. The other side of the bed was still tucked, the nightstand bare.

"Do you miss your dad?" I asked Will quietly.

He shook his head angrily.

"Nope," he said. "I guess maybe I miss the past when, you know, everyone was together, but . . ."

"It must be a lot of pressure," I said. We both leaned against the edge of the dresser, our upper arms pressed together. Will was still fussing with that dumb troll. "Being the only one left with your mom after Owen leaves?"

"I guess," Will said, looking down.

"You know, you don't have to make up some ingenious scheme, or cure cancer, to cheer her up, right?" I said. "You just need to be *you*."

"Well . . ." Will gave me a heavy-lidded glance before returning his gaze to his mom's smashed pillow. "Thanks but it's not that simple."

"I know," I said. I leaned my head on his shoulder. "I know."

I guess this was another milestone—Will showing me how he really felt about what had happened to his family. I realized that the more Will and I revealed to each other about our quirks, our passions, and our wounds, the more complicated our relationship would become. We were getting more serious. The knowledge filled me with a surge of happiness . . . and a twinge of trepidation.

The rest of the month slipped by in a watercolor wash of swimming, snacking, strolling, and of course, kissing and talking, talking and kissing. As every day got hotter, we moved more slowly, like the lizards that dozed the days away under flat rocks.

Will took to showing up at my house early in the mornings to help me and Sophie fish prickly cucumbers off our vines and fill bulging grocery sacks with teardrop tomatoes. The tomatoes were ripening so fast now, we pretty much had to eat them as fast as we picked them.

Kat and Benjie were in charge of picking the blueberries, but Will and I helped them with the tall branches. We worked side by side, munching a piece of toast or a Belgian waffle with one hand while we gathered fistfuls of fruit with the other. We tossed the warm berries into a basket that rested on the ground between us, and somehow our picking rhythm always had us reaching down at the same time, our fingers grazing one another and our eyes meeting through the leafy branches.

By the time we finished picking, even though it was barely nine 'o clock, we'd be sweaty and spent. We'd stumble onto the screened porch, turn the ceiling fans to turboblast, and flop onto the hammock.

Or we'd coast our bikes to the beach and swim under the pier. Our laughter and chatter echoed in the dank cave of wooden planks and logs. When we couldn't take any more slimy seaweed twining around our ankles, we braced ourselves and swam back into the relentless sunshine.

We couldn't get enough shaved ice.

During all our lazy hours together, I memorized every detail of Will's face. The little crescent that appeared at the right corner of his mouth when he smiled, for instance, was deeper than the one on the left. Fanning from his eyes were white needles of untanned skin that had been sheltered from the sun by his squint. (Will didn't wear sunglasses either.) And he had just a hint of love handles around his muscled waist.

Someone else might call these flaws, but I liked these little detours on Will's body even more than the perfect parts of him. Maybe because they felt like my secrets, so obscure that nobody except Will's girlfriend could possibly notice them.

Will usually spent the afternoons with his mom and Owen while I worked, but just about every night, he came to The Scoop in time to flip the OPEN sign to CLOSED, then help me wash ice cream scoops, stuff napkin dispensers, and maybe even whip up a batch of custard to be churned the next day.

We often worked silently, side by side, intent on finishing as quickly as possible so we could get to the boardwalk or the beach; so we could just be together and talk—or not talk.

Sometimes it felt like our breathing slowed to match the waves.

The length and the sameness of the days were comforting to me. Each day felt endless, as if one just blended into the next. I couldn't have counted all the kisses, the embraces, the times we dozed off together on the hammock with iced tea glasses leaving sweaty rings on the floorboards beneath us.

I tried to lose track of the days of the week. I denied the fact that the sun was setting a few minutes earlier each day. I ignored anything that would mark time.

But there was one Dune Island milestone I *had* to show Will, even if it forced me to face the fact that July was coming to an end. And that was the hatching of the sea turtle eggs.

On the thirty-first, the Dune Island LISTSERV went crazy. That night, we were all assured, was going to be *the night*— birthday for hundreds of tiny loggerhead turtles.

When I told Will about this during that morning's meandering swim, he grinned.

"You mean the POTATOhead reign of terror is actually going to end?"

POTATO was the *really* bad acronym for the group called Protectors of Turtles and Their Offspring. In June the sea turtles had dug their nests in the dunes. Ever since, the turtles' protectors (or POTATOheads, as Will called them) had been camping out next to every nest.

The POTATOheads huddled in front of their little pup tents until around midnight, making sure no people stepped on the nests and no animals made off with the eggs. Then they grumpily went to sleep with their tent flaps open and their ears cocked for intruders.

They took their POTATO duties *very* seriously, and Will mocked them every chance he got.

"Will," I scolded him after the reign of terror crack. "You know loggerhead turtles are extremely endangered."

"I know, I know," Will said, lifting his shoulders from the water in a shrug. "I mean, it's great what these folks are doing. But do they have to be so *grim* about it? This one lady took my flashlight the other night and literally slammed it against a rock until it broke."

"Well, lights can confuse the baby turtles," I said. "If they're blinded by our cameras or flashlights, they can't find the horizon and crawl their way to the ocean."

"I'm just saying," Will said, "she could have just asked me to turn it off."

"Maybe the POTATOheads are just looking for a little excitement," I said. I dribbled a fistful of salt water on top of my head, which felt like it was sizzling in the sun. "In case you haven't noticed, Dune Island gets a little boring around this time of year."

Will dove under the surface, then came up with his arms around me. Water streamed down his face, but his eyes were wide open and smiling.

"No, I hadn't noticed," he said, before kissing me deeply. Which made me seriously consider just bagging the whole turtle-watching thing in favor of spending the evening making out.

But Will loved Dune Island rituals, and this one was the Dune-iest of them all.

When I was a kid, my family and I had tried to watch the turtles hatch many times. Every year the effort had been a bust. We'd stay until midnight, see not even a single hatchling, and then my parents would drag their sleepy kids home. It seemed the baby turtles always emerged right after we left. Or the very next night. But never for us.

To tell the truth, I expected that to happen again this year. But I decided not to tell Will and squelch his anticipation.

That night after sunset, Will and I joined a few dozen turtle-watchers at a rarely used beach entrance off Highway 80. A narrow, creaky bridge vaulted us over the dune grass into the turtles' protected area. Waiting at the end of the gangplank (at least, that's what it felt like) was a POTATOhead.

And not just any POTATOhead. It was Ms. Humphreys, who'd been my seventh-grade science teacher. Ms. Humphreys could make any middle-school kid's insides shrivel up with a single glare. She was terrifyingly tall with a long, fuzzy steel-gray braid and a hawkish nose. She was the only teacher who'd *ever* given me detention.

Will grabbed my hand and squeezed.

"That's the one who broke my flashlight," he said. "The brute strength on that woman. It's formidable!"

I tried not to snort.

I gave her a shy glance and suddenly realized that her hooked nose was less birdlike than it was turtleish. Her eyes had a reptilian coldness about them as well.

Well, now I know where the passion comes from, I thought, then immediately bit my lip and squeezed Will's hand to keep from laughing.

Ms. Humphreys glared at us, her small, dark eyes glittering in the moonlight.

"No talking," she ordered our group in a loud, hissing whisper. "You could scare the offspring. No cameras, flash or no flash. No flash*lights*. No trash. No food. You may drink beverages, but no alcohol. Note the orange flags marking the placement of the nests."

Ms. Humphreys pointed with a knobby finger at dull orange flags attached to thin metal rods. They demarcated a wide swath of sand.

"Stay outside those flags!" Ms. Humphreys threatened. "Lastly, be patient, people. It's likely that the offspring have already hatched and are, as we stand here, digging their way out of their nests. They may emerge tonight, but they may not. It's their business, not ours."

Ms. Humphreys stepped aside.

But we were all too intimidated to do anything but gape at her. The only sound was the distant roar of the waves and the nervous rustling of everyone's Windbreakers. Until Ms. Humphreys finally growled, "I said no talking, yet now you are making me use my *voice* to tell you to *move it, people?*"

We all jumped, then hurried down the steps, fanning out on both sides of the large, flag-marked area. In the dunes behind us, several nests were surrounded by bright orange posts and *lots* of threatening signage.

Everybody went to stake out a spot along the line of flags. Some people paced the sand excitedly. Others sank gingerly onto blankets, sitting ramrod straight. Will and I hadn't brought a blanket so we simply plunked down in the sand and cuddled up together.

Then we all stared at the nests, willing the little hatchlings to come out and start creeping toward the sea. The waiting sand almost seemed to glow in the moonlight.

But of course, nothing happened.

"I think we might be here for a loooong time," I breathed into Will's ear.

"With absolutely nothing to do," Will said. "Except . . ."

Well, I thought as Will leaned in to kiss me, *I guess we're going to spend the evening making out after all.*

The almost-full moon was a good notch higher when Will and I came up for air. Shyly, I glanced at the silhouettes around us, wondering if anyone had noticed what Will and I had been up to.

But most people seemed absorbed in their own little worlds. The individuals stared needily at the turtle nests. The couples whispered or maybe did a little making out themselves. I was relieved to realize that it was hard to tell what anybody looked like or what they were doing.

It was a strange feeling, being here to experience this profound moment with, but *not* with, all these people. The anonymity of them somehow made me feel closer to Will, the one I *could* see. And touch. And taste . . .

With that thought I was ready to resume the kissing, but Will was distracted. He was staring at the moon over the ocean. In its glow he looked a little nervous, his lips pressed together, his jaw tight.

"Will?" I whispered. I touched his shoulder and felt a lurch of nerves myself.

Don't, I pleaded in my head. *Don't say anything to mess this up.*

I'd been doing a pretty good job of living in the lazy, luxurious present with Will. Basically I was in big, fat denial—and loving it the way I loved an endless morning in the ocean or a giant bowl of ice cream.

But I knew my ability to maintain this willful state of delight was precarious. So I'd been trying to keep things between me and Will breezy and blissful. No heavy conversations. No allusions to our future (or lack thereof). I just wanted to *be*. With him.

But now I was sure Will was working up the courage to say something. And it didn't seem like it was going to be breezy.

Will got to his feet and searched for something in his pocket. Whatever it was seemed to be caught. After a brief struggle he finally extricated it, turning his pocket inside out as he did.

I stood up too as Will quickly stuffed his pocket back inside his pants. He was wearing, I realized, the same roughed-up khakis that he'd had on the first night I'd seen him at the bonfire. I found myself staring down at his pant legs. For some reason I didn't want to lift my eyes and look at him.

But finally he whispered, "Anna," and I had to.

He still looked nervous, but also happy. And a little sheepish.

"I got you something," he whispered, thrusting the thing that he'd pulled from his pocket at me.

"Like, a present?" I whispered back. I don't know what I'd expected, but it *hadn't* been a present. The idea of Will and me giving each other gifts had never occurred to me. Maybe because I knew we'd never have a Christmas together. And Will's birthday was in May, while mine was in October.

"Yeah, like a present," Will said.

I could barely see what Will was holding out toward me. Only when I took it could I tell that it was a square velvet sack, about the size of my palm, with something round inside.

I stared at Will.

"It's no big deal," Will started to say, forgetting to whisper. A chorus of *shush*es pelted us from all sides and Will ducked his head.

"It's just something I saw in one of those little boutiques on the boardwalk," he whispered very, very quietly, "and it made me think of you."

I continued to stare at him like a turtle in a flashlight beam.

Will's gaze dropped to his feet and he shook his head, muttering to himself. I had a feeling this moment was not going at all how he'd wanted it to.

I opened the cinched top of the little velvet bag and pulled out a bracelet—a silver bangle that was somehow both chunky and delicate. It was shaped like a flat ribbon with three half twists in it. It immediately made me think of a high diver gracefully turning through the air before skimming into the water.

"It's a Möbius strip," Will explained, still whispering. "It's kind of an optical illusion."

Will put my fingertip on one thin edge of the silver ribbon, then guided it around the twisty circle. The metal felt slick and cool. As my finger traveled along the edge of the bangle, Will kept turning it and turning it.

"See, it only has one side and one edge," Will whispered.

"You can follow along it forever and it never ends. Cool, huh?"

"I . . . love it," I whispered. I slipped the bangle onto my wrist, enjoying the weight of it. Then I put a hand on each of Will's shoulders, stood on my tiptoes so that we were almost eye to eye, and repeated myself. "I love it."

Will kissed me softly. When we sat back in the sand, we didn't talk or kiss. We just gazed toward the loggerhead nests. I think Will was a bit drained. Maybe he'd been nervous all night about giving me the gift.

As for me, I was stunned.

Suddenly everything felt different. Solid. As solid as this pretty band of silver.

I wrapped my hand around the bracelet. It was a memento of Will, one that I *could* keep in my vanity drawer forever if I didn't intend to wear it every day. But I very much *did* intend to wear it every day. It immediately felt like a part of me.

Like Will was a part of me.

And *that* was heavy indeed. It made me feel ecstatic and shaky all at once.

But before I could even begin to process it, I heard a gasp.

Somebody on the other side of the orange flags stood up. She began bouncing on her toes and pointing urgently toward the dunes.

We all scrambled to our feet and stared into the dune grass, which seemed to be jostling and rustling. Collectively, we held our breath. Literally. I could *feel* the people around me inhale and then stop. Frozen. Waiting.

And then—there they were. At first I just saw one or two little black discs creep out of the grass. They were tinier than I'd expected, maybe the size of my thumb.

As these first hatchlings started inching their way forward, a sudden flood of them followed. They almost looked like a wave of ants spilling out of a mound but, of course, a lot cuter. There were *hundreds* of them. The turtles' legs moved stiffly and rhythmically. They began to parade with surprising swiftness toward the water.

I clapped my hand over my mouth (and clocked my chin with my new bangle) to smother a cheer.

I could tell other people were having trouble containing their excitement too. Will perhaps most of all. He threw his arm around my shoulders and jumped up and down.

"This is the most amazing thing I've ever seen," he hissed, trying to be quiet.

A few of the hatchlings seemed to be confused and headed toward the orange flags instead of the sea. A turtle watcher leaned over the barrier and gently nudged them in the right direction with his fingertips.

But most of the little turtles knew exactly where to go. Their flat, winglike legs churned so hard they almost hopped down the sand.

Tears sprang to my eyes. I wanted to cheer for the little turtles, but since I couldn't, I just clasped my hands beneath my chin and grinned as I watched them.

I think every person on that beach—maybe even Ms. Humphreys, too—was feeling one simple emotion at that moment: joy.

The turtles started to reach the water. The breakers crashed into them, sending them tumbling backward and skidding sideways. Most of them immediately regained their bearings and kept on creeping.

And then the waves began to sweep them out to sea.

"They're making it!" I said to Will, pointing at the disappearing turtles.

Will was grinning back at me when I heard the first squawk. Seagulls.

The sound was familiar. I heard gulls every day at the beach. Or rather, I *didn't* hear them. They were just white noise, like the waves and the soft whoosh of the breeze. I never gave them a thought.

But these gulls hovering over the beach—their wings arched out to the sides and their bills aimed downward—weren't wallflowers anymore. They were predators. Greedy, *mean* sea rats, getting ready to strike.

"Oh no," I muttered. Then the first seagull made its dive.

It must have been the easiest hunt of their lives. Each gull swooped down, plucked up a turtle, then flapped away, squawking in triumph.

People started making noise.

Men took off their T-shirts and flapped them in the air, trying to slap the birds away, but the gulls just dodged them and flew to the middle of the turtle pack. The only way to get at them would be to hop the orange flags and risk crushing the turtles under our feet.

I wanted to scream as I watched one gull snatch up a

hatchling by its leg. The rest of its body dangled, limp, from the gull's hooked beak.

I found myself looking back at Ms. Humphreys, who still stood at the foot of the bridge. Her back was straight. She seemed stoic. In fact it looked like she was gazing at the surf, not at the diving seabirds. She was focusing on the hatchlings that got away, rather than the ones that died.

Maybe this was why Ms. Humphreys was so harsh. Every summer she guarded those little eggs with all the viciousness of a mama bear (since mama turtles obviously weren't the most protective types) only to see scads of them gobbled up before they'd even had a chance to begin their journeys.

And as anybody who's gone to school on Dune Island knows, the carnage doesn't end on the beach. Big, toothy fish, crabs, and countless other predators nab more of the hatchlings once they hit the water. Only a tiny fraction of the turtles survive.

Those who do could live for decades. Still, as I watched the gulls feast, the odds against the sea turtles seemed devastating.

I started shaking.

The bangle bracelet suddenly felt intrusive and unfamiliar around my left wrist. I wrapped my right hand around it, squeezing it until it pressed into my skin, probably leaving a mark.

I started crying.

No, I sobbed. In big, loud, embarrassing heaves.

I turned and stumbled away from the hatchling run, heading north. I wanted to put my fingers in my ears to block out the horrible squawks of the gulls, but that seemed even more childish than running away.

So I just ran until all I could hear were the waves and, a moment later, the huffing and puffing of Will running after me.

Immediately he wrapped his arms around me. He held me while I gasped and sniffled.

But I didn't melt into him the way I usually did. I couldn't.

"I'm sorry, I'm sorry," Will said. "But think of how many of the turtles made it to the water. They *made* it, Anna. And it was awesome."

This only made me stiffen more.

Will pulled back and looked at me in confusion.

"Anna?"

"What!" I blurted. Then I cringed. I'd sounded so impatient, even hostile.

"Sorry," I muttered.

Oh great, now I sounded sulky.

"Is this . . . ?" Will began. "Are you . . . ?"

He searched for the right thing to say, because he clearly had no idea what was wrong with me. I wasn't sure I knew myself. All I knew was I was suddenly hurting so much, my body almost ached with it.

I spun away from Will to face the ocean. I imagined turtles paddling their way through the dark shallows right in front of me. I could picture their tiny bodies buffeted by the water, but doggedly swimming along. Evolution had wired them for this. But it hadn't taught them how quickly, and brutally, everything could end for them.

This thought made me start crying *again*.

"Oh, Anna," Will moaned. "Stop. Please stop."

I shook my head angrily.

"I am *not* a crier," I declared.

I heard Will stifle a laugh. I should have laughed too. It had been a ridiculous thing to say under the circumstances.

But instead I whirled around and glared at him. It was dark on the beach, and my tears were blurring my vision, but Will *still* looked beautiful to me.

I wanted to look at him forever. But since I couldn't do that, suddenly I didn't want to look at him at all.

Or perhaps, ever again.

Every once in a while, my sisters and brother and I spend an obsessive day building a sand fort. We pack and smooth the sand until it looks as sturdy as cement. By day's end, part of me fantasizes that *this* fort will somehow last. It always seems impossible that something so strong, so solid, can just be washed away by the tide in less than an hour.

I realized now that I'd done same thing with Will. I'd built a happy little fortress of denial around us, filling it with blueberry picking, ice cream, and kisses. I'd convinced myself that August 29 would never *really* arrive.

But of course it would.

And when I forced myself to finally acknowledge this, it hurt like a sudden, startling muscle cramp. Like a flash of heat.

And who wouldn't try to protect themselves from that, right?

"Will," I said, shaking my head slowly and for too long. "I can't do this."

"We won't go back," Will agreed, glancing over his shoulder

at the loggerhead run. "Let's just go get some coffee or some-thing. And we can talk."

"No!" I said. "I'm saying I can't do *this*. Us."

Will looked at me incredulously. And then his face shifted, subtly, to stone.

"If *I* can do this," he asked in a low almost-growl, "why can't you?"

"You don't know how badly it's going to hurt when you leave," I said. "Do you even care?"

"It'll hurt me, too," Will said. "Believe me."

"But the difference between you and me is"—I clutched at my middle with both hands, the way you do when you have a bad stomachache—"it's hurting me *now*."

"I don't get it," Will said. I saw his eyes flicker to the shiny bangle on my wrist. "Anna, I'm having the most amazing summer—because of you."

"And then your summer *ends*," I flung back, "and you go back to New York, to your old life where there's not a glimmer of me. But me? I'm still gonna be here bumping into you, the memory of you, *everywhere I go*."

"I know that," Will said. He took a step closer to me. "And it's not fair. But, Anna, we talked about this already. Why ruin what we have now just because we can't have it later?"

"Because that *does* ruin it for me," I said, backing away from Will.

"Well, if you ask me, *you're* ruining it," Will said. He crossed his arms over his chest and glared.

"You're a shoobee, Will," I said.

It was the first time I'd said that word to him, though certainly by then he'd probably heard it around the island. He probably also knew it wasn't complimentary. I saw shock register on his face, but I couldn't stop myself.

"You leave at the end of the summer," I said. "Maybe you go home and tell your guy friends about the townie you had a fling with. The one who couldn't pronounce 'knish.' The one who couldn't keep it casual like *you* could."

Will just shook his head in disbelief.

"Why are you doing this?" he asked.

"Because we're not the same, Will," I said. "That's why you don't understand how I'm feeling. And that's—"

I gasped, on the verge of tears again.

"And that's why we shouldn't be together," I declared.

Will stared at me.

And then he closed his mouth so hard, I could hear his teeth click. He shook his head angrily.

"You know," he said, "I get it now. You hate Valentine's Day and you love Independence Day."

"What does *that* mean?" I sputtered.

"You don't want to be with *anyone*, Anna," Will said. "Even me. Maybe *especially* me. Maybe you've just been looking for a way out."

Will stopped and swallowed. He stared at the ground, breathing hard. I stood there, my hands fisted at my sides, waiting for him to speak. I was still crackling with indignation but I also felt confused. *How* had this fight happened? It felt like it had come out of nowhere. And I couldn't make it stop.

When Will looked up again, his eyes were defeated.

"Well," he said quietly, "you got it. You got your way out."

He turned abruptly and stalked away with swift, sure strides.

As I watched him go in stunned silence, it occurred to me that Will was walking without stumbling. He had spent his first two months on the island struggling to get his bearings in the sand, always sinking in too deep or losing his balance in a hole. But now he was skimming over the beach like a local.

Like me.

Not that it changed the reality. He *wasn't* a local. And *I* was stuck here on Dune Island.

And that was that.

I watched Will until he was swallowed up by the darkness. Even if I had wanted to call out to him, I don't think I could have. My throat felt so choked, I was surprised I could breathe.

Will had gone back to taking my breath away.

This thought made me laugh. A dry, humorless laugh.

And then, instinctively, I turned to the ocean. I stared at the waves and cried—for a *long* time.

When I couldn't cry any more, I sat at the very edge of the surf and gazed at the water some more. Only the roar of the surf, pushing, pulling, and thrashing, could drown out my thoughts about Will. About everything.

At some point I jolted out of this trance and looked around, blinking. The moon had shifted in the sky. The turtle watchers had gone home. I was all alone.

And that's exactly how I felt—alone, which was perhaps even more shocking than what had happened between me and

Will. Never in my life had I felt lonely at the beach. Even on a weekday in winter when *nobody* was around, the sea and sand had always felt like a haven. Like home.

And now, I didn't want to be here.

Which meant I'd lost more than Will—I'd lost a part of myself.

And the part that remained was already roiling with regret.

August

$\mathcal{M}$y mom always says August in south Georgia is like February in Wisconsin. The weather is so beastly and unrelenting, it's like a cruel joke.

The ice cream is always runny, no matter how long it hibernates in the deep freeze. Our back field turns brown and crackly, littered with grasshopper husks and lost blueberries, as dry and hard as pebbles. The cicadas sound tired, their chirps thin and grating. Or maybe they're just drowned out by the grind of the air-conditioning units, which blast constantly, or so it always seems.

In August we all retreat indoors. We can't even stand the screened porch, where the ceiling fans just waft hot air at you, which is about as refreshing as being under a hair dryer.

My parents spend the month puttering (when they're not at The Scoop). My dad does the taxes on the dining room table and my mom pulls out her to-do list. Then she grabs any kid within reach and assigns him or her random, awful tasks like scrubbing the bathroom grout with an electric toothbrush or spray painting all the chipped air-conditioning vents.

Every year Sophie and I have to choose between two evils—mom and her chore chart or the furnace blast that was the world outside.

This August, I decided, I would stay in.

I wandered around the house for the first couple of days, clutching Judy Blume books under my arm. In chick flicks, brokenhearted women always seem to devour pints and pints of ice cream. That, of course, was normal behavior for me so I devoured Judy Blume instead.

I kept telling myself that, yes, I felt lonely and awful now. But if I'd let the relationship go on longer—and get that much more serious—the ending would only have been worse.

I was doing the right thing, I insisted in my head. I was looking out for myself.

I was being a realist.

I was being the strong one.

And did any of these things I told myself help? Not even a little bit.

By the end of day three (or was it four?), I couldn't stand my own wallowing any more. If I couldn't get happy, I decided, at least I could get distracted. So, I went to my mom, who was decked out in rubber gloves, scouring something in the kitchen sink. Dinner was over, Sophie was working with my dad at The Scoop, and Benjie and Kat were running around the backyard with dryer sheets hanging out of their pockets, snatching fireflies out of the air.

"Okay, what have you got for me?" I asked my mom, going over to the bulletin board where she'd tacked her to-do list. She'd been jotting on the long sheet of yellow legal paper for months.

The list was a little crinkled, with a tea stain on the corner and about four different colors of ink. I skimmed through it. I spotted *sand and stain porch table* and *organize photos, past 2 yrs*. I shuddered.

But if I read one more page of *Deenie*, I was going to throw myself off my bedroom balcony, so I stood my ground.

My mom turned around and leaned back against the sink.

"Oh, honey," she said. "You don't have to do anything. I know . . ."

I watched her face as she paused and searched her parental database for the proper words.

". . . I know you're going through a hard time right now."

Tears sprang to my eyes. I was grateful that neither of my parents had pried into what had happened the other night. They'd gotten the gist—that Will was no longer in the picture. And though I'd spied them exchanging lots of meaningful glances and gestures, they hadn't interrogated me about it. Even Sophie had been sympathetic in her own way. She'd offered to do my laundry, adding, "I'll even iron stuff so you don't have to look all wrinkled, the way you usually do."

The problem was, all this familial sensitivity hammered home how wretched my situation was. Which only made me feel more pathetic. It had gotten so bad that I had to fight off tears every time my mother even *looked* at me.

I hadn't been lying when I'd told Will that I wasn't a crier. I hated crying, especially in front of people. It was humiliating and soul baring and just . . . messy. So the fact that I was now a blubbering mess was making me *really* cranky.

I guess that was why, in response to my mother's completely

nice comment, I snarled, "*Mom*, could you please just be *normal* and give me one of the dumb chores already?"

Acting like such a jerk, of course, made me feel even worse. And trust me, *that* was a feat.

I don't *think* Mom was getting revenge for my smart mouth when she gave me shower curtain duty, but I couldn't be sure.

In case you're wondering, shower curtain duty means taking down the vinyl curtains from all three of our claw-foot tubs (and remember, a free-standing bathtub requires *two* shower curtains), laying them out flat, scrubbing off all the black mildew and pink mold that's accumulated at the seams, then hanging them back up.

It was a yucky, tedious, *hard* job and it suited me perfectly.

I was actually a little hopeful, as I unhooked the curtains from my parents' tub on the second floor, that the tedium would help me. Sam had once confided to me that he'd done some meditating after his parents' divorce and that it had really helped him just wash all the churning thoughts from his mind, even if it was only for the twenty minutes a day that he was able to sit still and focus.

What was more meditative, I thought, than scouring a giant sheet of funky plastic, inch by inch?

I got some soapy rags and headed outside, laying the curtains out on the patio.

I knelt before the yucky bottom edge of the curtain, took a deep, cleansing breath, and started to scrub.

Fifteen minutes later, I was ready to go back to my Judy

Blumes. If I'd done any meditating at all it had gone like this:

Okay, breathe in, breathe out. Focus on the task at hand and only the task at hand. . . .

Ugh, not only is this mold disgusting, it's not coming off. Why can't we just buy new shower curtains when they get all funky like this?

Okay, that's not very green. Something tells me meditators frown on disposable culture.

Maybe some bleach will help.

(Five minutes later.)

Okay, breathe in, breathe out, breathe—agh! Bleach is searing lungs!

(Suddenly, bleach smell reminds me of cleaning Scoop tables with Will.)

Don't think about Will, think about scrubbing. It's like a metaphor. I cleanse the curtain, I cleanse my mind of unwanted thoughts. Like thoughts about the last kiss I had with Will. I think I could still sort of taste it—until breathing in this bleach probably killed some of my taste buds!

Whatever, just breathe, darnit. Breathe in, breathe out—

Hey! I wonder if you could put these things in the washing machine!

And that pretty much was the end of my meditation—and my help with the to-do list. (For the record, the washing machine didn't work so well, either.)

So now on top of feeling tragic about Will and guilty about sassing my mom, I also felt like a failure at both my hideous chore *and* my meditation.

I climbed up to the screened porch and slumped onto the swing. Through the open front door, I could hear my mom rallying Kat and Benji for a bath.

"Hey, where are the shower curtains?!" Kat asked cheerfully, making me feel like even more of a loser. The air on the porch felt like warm, soggy wool on my skin and my hands smelled of bleach. Yet after a few minutes, the cricket chirps and the *creak, creak, creak* of the swing's chains began to make me feel a little less wretched.

I glanced through the window into the kitchen. The room was quiet, empty, and lit only by the small light over the stove. I'd always loved our kitchen at this time of night, when the cooking smells from dinner still hovered in the air but the counters and appliances were shiny clean, like blank canvases, lying in wait for inspiration.

Of course, tonight I had none. I hadn't had a vision, or a taste, for any ice cream for days. Which just . . . sucked. Usually I could *always* find comfort in ice cream. I loved zoning out to the I-could-do-it-in-my-sleep process of making the custard— heating the milk, tempering the egg yolks, whisking the cream. Then coming up with a new flavor always felt a little bit like magic; like having a muse whisper in my ear.

Now the muse was so very absent that I was worried it would never come back. I would live the rest of my days in this radio silence, never again to come up with a Pineapple Ginger Ale or Buttertoe.

Just as an exercise, I consciously tried to think of some new flavor. Something, anything, that I'd never heard of before. I actually squeezed my eyes shut and pressed my fingertips to my temples, but—nope. Nothing.

I was starting to feel a little panicky when I remembered something. I had a notebook—just a cheap, pocket-size one from the drugstore—in which I'd once jotted ice cream ideas for future reference. I'd started the list last summer, but when I'd gotten better at creating flavors on the fly, I'd forgotten all about it.

Where was it?

I dashed upstairs to my room and searched my dresser drawers, peeked into purses and tote bags, and even looked under the bed. I'd almost lost hope when I thought to look in the dusty old jewelry box on top of my dresser. Since I had almost no jewelry to speak of, I often tossed other random items inside.

I creaked open the wooden box and there, among some Mardi Gras beads and barrettes, was the notebook. I sighed with relief. My present self was clearly hopeless, but the past one just might come through.

I flipped through the pages hungrily, looking for an idea that made me feel zingy inside.

Once again, nothing. I simply felt tired and so lonely that I physically ached. And bitter. Oh, was I bitter.

But that was one reason I'd always loved making ice cream. It was such a sweet, simple antidote—if a temporary one—to all of life's bitterness. It was a little vacation that lasted until you popped the last bite of your sugar cone into your mouth.

After losing Will, I was finding it hard to care about much of anything, but deep down I knew I still cared about this. I didn't want to lose this.

So I decided to choose a recipe at random. I closed the note-book and reopened it, landing on a page with the heading *Greek Holiday*. The title, I remembered vaguely, had been inspired by an Audrey Hepburn movie my mom had rented.

I skimmed the ingredients: *honey, orange zest, a little almond oil, maybe some crushed pistachios.*

If I wasn't exactly moved, I wasn't repelled either. I might have even been a tiny bit intrigued. It wasn't a bad idea, if I could pull it off. We had all the ingredients. I could make up the cus-tard now, chill it overnight, and churn it up tomorrow.

With nothing else to do (believe me, *nothing*), I went down-stairs to start separating the eggs.

*B*y the next day, I'd really settled into my new routine. Open eyes around ten, lie in bed staring through skylight until the sun rises high enough to blind me, then roll reluctantly out of bed for a day of reading and weeping.

The wrench in this day's plan, though, was Caroline. She arrived at nine, hauled me out of bed, and stuck a slice of toast in my hand. Then she barely gave me a chance to brush my teeth before she brutally kidnapped me.

When I stumbled outside with her, I blinked at the stuff piled in a trailer attached to Caroline's bike. In addition to a metal tackle box, a plastic cooler, and a bulging backpack, I saw . . .

"What are those?" I said, my voice full of apprehension.

"Fishing poles," Caroline said with a grin. "My dad's and my brother's."

"We don't fish," I pointed out dully.

"We do now," Caroline said with a grin. "I hear it's meditative."

I shook my head.

"Oh, no," I protested. "I tried meditating yesterday and almost asphyxiated from all the bleach."

"Okay, I'm not going to even ask you to explain that one," Caroline said. She fetched Allison Porchnik from beneath the screened porch and wheeled her over. "Hop on."

Within a few minutes we were sitting at the very end of the pier that jutted off the North Peninsula. I had to admit, after being such a shut-in, hovering out there over the gently lapping waves was blissful, even in the sweltering August heat.

I closed my eyes to soak in the sun for a moment while Caroline began unloading all her equipment.

"What are we going to use to catch these alleged fish?" I asked. "Did you dig for worms or something?"

"Oh my God, Anna. I don't even *eat* fish and I know that saltwater fish don't like worms," Caroline blustered. "They eat *other* fish."

She flipped open the cooler to reveal a plastic bag filled with raw fish chunks.

"Ugh," I said, putting a hand on my stomach. Caroline looked a little green too, but her stubbornness beat out her many food aversions.

"Come on," she said. "We're doing this."

We actually started laughing as we picked up the disgusting

fish chunks and awkwardly threaded them onto the hooks.

"How is it that we're expert ghost crabbers and clam diggers," I asked, "but we've never been fishing?"

Caroline shrugged and grinned as we got to our feet to clumsily cast our lines into the ocean.

I sat back down and propped my fishing pole on the rail of the pier.

"Okay, what do we do now?" I asked.

"I guess we just sit here and wait for a nibble," Caroline said. "Pretty lousy excuse for a sport, huh? *That's* why we've never been fishing."

"Mmm," I said. Now that we were past the giddy novelty of this expedition, I was quickly swinging back to my previous state—tragic and dreary. I drew my knees up beneath my chin, wrapping my arms around my shins. I sighed a shaky, on-the-verge-of-tears sigh.

"It's seriously annoying how much I've cried in the past few days," I complained. "I mean, I'm not—"

"—a crier. I know," Caroline finished for me. "But sometimes you've just got to cry until you're done."

That did it. I buried my face in my knees and wept. Caroline's sympathetic hand on my back only made me cry harder.

"If I'd known how awful it would be to say good-bye to him," I sobbed, "I never would have gone out with him in the first place."

"No, no," Caroline insisted softly. "You won't always feel that way. You know that saying, 'Tis better to have loved and lost . . .'"

I wiped my nose on the back of my hand and wailed, "I always thought that saying was a load of crap."

Caroline gave a quick snort before slapping a hand over her mouth.

"It's not funny," I said, looking at her through what felt like a river of tears. "You're lucky you never have to know what this feels like—"

Suddenly I stopped my soggy rant. I wasn't the only one with boy troubles, I remembered. I hadn't even asked Caroline what had been happening with Sam lately.

Between sniffles and hiccups, I said, "So are things still weird with you guys?"

Caroline allowed a small smile.

"Actually, the other night," she said, "we had our first good, meaty talk in ages. Maybe because we were just sitting on the beach eating huge, sloppy, sno-cones instead of doing the whole Dinner at Eight thing."

"That's good," I said, nodding as I blew my nose in my orange wrap.

Caroline smiled a little wider, then fiddled with the handle of her fishing pole.

"Sam finally came out and told me how much pressure he's been feeling to make this relationship perfect," she said. "So I told *him* that perfect is not only an illusion, it's just no damn fun."

"Good answer." I actually laughed a little. "So . . . what now?"

"I don't know," Caroline said. "I guess we just wait and see. I'm hoping this is sort of like growing out a short haircut. You know if you can just stick it out, you'll be rewarded with long, lustrous locks. Or you could freak out and chop it all off. I'm trying for the long and pretty hair."

"Somehow I actually understood that metaphor," I said. I smiled, if wanly, rubbed the last bit of moisture out of my eyes, then grabbed my sports bottle and held it out toward Caroline.

"Here's to long, lustrous locks," I said.

She grinned and bumped her sports bottle against mine, making a plastic *thunk*. We both took big swigs of iced tea.

Zzzzzzzzzzz.

I looked around.

"What's that sound?" I wondered.

ZZZZZZZZZZ!

Caroline gasped, jumped to her feet, and pointed at my pole.

"Fish!" she shrieked.

"Oh my God!" I cried. I'd forgotten all about our propped-up poles. Whatever it was at the end of my line was pulling so hard, it was threatening to take the pole with it. I grabbed it just in time and scrambled to my feet.

"What do I do?" I yelled.

"Turn the handle thingie!" Caroline said. She was gasping with laughter now. "Reel it in."

I started to crank the handle backward. The fish was really tugging.

"It's big!" I cried. "Help me hold this pole. I'm freaking out here."

Caroline grabbed the pole and I reeled. I reeled and reeled and reeled, but the fish didn't seem to be coming any closer. I peered into the water and didn't see a thing.

"You want some help with that? You're about two reels away from breaking your line."

Caroline and I peeked over our shoulders.

"Sam!" Caroline squeaked.

"Sam," I huffed. "Take this thing, please!"

Somehow, Caroline and I maneuvered the pole into Sam's hands. With some mysterious rhythm, he began pulling at the pole, letting the line zing out, then reeling it back in. At the same time, he chatted with us as if this was the most normal situation in the world.

"Hey, baby," he said to Caroline. "So is this spontaneous enough for you? It doesn't get any less formal than this, am I right?"

Caroline grinned and gave Sam a kiss on the cheek.

"You're right," she said.

They didn't make a big deal out of the fact that, instead of orchestrating some big date night, Sam had moseyed down to the beach just like old times. That he seemed more comfortable in his skin than he had in a long time. And that Caroline was looking at him the way she had when they'd first gotten together.

I think maybe they got over themselves, I told myself.

Sam finally pulled a thrashing, foot-long fish out of the water.

"Redfish!" he announced, exchanging a gleeful smile with Caroline. "Good one!"

I felt myself choke up again, this time from sentimentality. A dull glow of happiness for my friends was bumping up against my own shadowy sadness.

Perhaps it had made a small dent.

But despite Sam and Caroline's sweet efforts, the emptiness I felt in the wake of Will remained.

When I got home, I quickly retreated to my new normal—me brooding on the screened porch while my brother and sister played a noisy prebedtime game of hide-and-seek upstairs.

My parents had given me several nights off from work, but I decided that I would head back the next day. Even if the idea of being out among people (read, *couples*) kind of made me want to walk straight into a riptide, anything would be better than another night stewing alone at home.

Of course, I still had *this* night to get through. A few *ping-ping-ping*s of rain on the porch's tin roof, along with a distant rumble of thunder, were encouraging. A big ol' storm would suit my mood.

The rain's gentle patter quickly became an onslaught.

I got off the porch swing and pressed myself against the screen to catch a whiff of it. The rain smelled dark and acrid as it steamed up the clay and gravel in our driveway. In a few more minutes, I knew, it would start smelling green, as the parched trees and grasses began soaking up the water and coming back to life. When everything had been completely saturated, the night would smell blue. Clean. Renewed.

I wanted to enjoy it. Or *anything* for that matter. But I felt as flat as a pancake.

When I decided to go ahead and freeze the ice cream I'd mixed the night before, it was only because it would kill a half hour. I found myself wondering if the rest of the summer was going to be like this—incrementally trying to fill the Will-free hours.

I went back inside and got the Greek Holiday mix out of the fridge, then pulled the ice cream churn from the pantry. But just as I was plugging it in—*zap!*

The power went out.

I heard a screech from my siblings upstairs, followed by my mother laughing to calm their nerves. Then there was that eerie silence that happens only during a power-out. No humming appliances, no thrumming air conditioner, no ticking oven timer, no nothing.

"Seriously?" I sighed.

It seemed a perfect excuse to just give up and go to bed.

Instead, I glared stubbornly at the plastic container of luscious-looking custard. Then I went back to the pantry. I grabbed the flashlight from the hook on the door, then dug our manual ice cream churn, along with a box of rock salt, out of a dusty corner.

After all, why snuggle up in my nice comfy bed when I could engage in the self-flagellation that was *hand churning* ice cream?

I pulled some ice out of the dark freezer, then brought the whole business outside. I set up the churn on the front steps, where I could get a prime view of the rain from under the eaves.

Then I started cranking.

I almost didn't notice that I'd started crying again. I suppose that was my new normal too. Through my tears I watched the rain puddle in the dirt and splash my outstretched feet. It made

Figgy Pudding's tired leaves do little shimmies; made them shine like they had on the Fourth of Jul—

I closed my eyes, leaned my forehead on my knees, and stopped cranking.

Now I'd gone and done it.

I'd gone back to *that* night.

So many of my dates with Will had seemed charmed, even the completely dorky ones like that putt putt golf outing.

But the Fourth of July had been more than charmed. It had been magic.

That was the night I'd fallen in love with Will.

I'd realized this—that I loved Will—a while ago, but I'd never put it so bluntly into words, even in my own mind.

But now, as I stared at the fig tree and remembered the way we'd leaned against its trunk, kissing and kissing and never wanting the night to end, suddenly the words were there.

I almost said them out loud: *I am in love with Will Cooper.*

Caroline had been right. There'd been no earth-shaking sign of it. No before and after. It was just a feeling that suffused my entire body, the way a hot bath warms you from the inside out on a chilly night.

"What did I *do*?" I murmured. "Why did I let him go?"

I'd told myself so many times since that horrible night of the turtle hatching that I'd done the smart thing, pushing Will away before he could leave me. That I was taking care of myself.

But if that was true, why was I so *broken*? So pathetic?

My tears were angry now. I stamped my foot on the rain-slick steps, spattering myself with water and sand. I went back to cranking the stupid ice cream. I wanted to crank until I got blisters on my palms.

In truth, I wanted to scream my frustration out into the rain, but I knew that would only bring my mother running down the stairs to see what was wrong. So instead I cranked harder, almost glad to feel tender welts begin to rise up at the base of my fingers. As I cranked, I stared out at Figgy Pudding, awash in blissful, painful memory.

And that's when everything stopped—the scenes running through my head, my hand on the ice cream churn, and I'm pretty sure, for an instant, my heartbeat.

Because just beyond the fig tree, at the end of the driveway, a figure had appeared—on a chunky red bike named Zelig.

Will rode toward me, his hair rain-plastered, his T-shirt drenched, and his face looking both hopeful and tortured. His eyes looked about as puffy as mine felt.

I don't remember running down the stairs to the driveway. In hindsight, I'm surprised I didn't fall on the slippery steps and break an ankle.

But somehow, in an instant, there I was. With Will. Rain pelted down on me, soaking me almost immediately. I barely noticed it, much less cared.

Will stumbled off his bike and let it fall to the ground without bothering to kickstand it. Then he stood before me, his arms hanging limp at his sides.

For a long moment we just stared at each other. Looking at his face, I felt like I was getting my first bite of food after starving for days.

"I missed you," Will said. His voice sounded raspy and he was still breathing hard from his bike ride.

I couldn't talk at all, so I just nodded hard.

I reached out to touch his arm, then pulled my hand back again. I'd just been telling myself that I'd been right to end things with Will. Completely miserable, but right.

So now I didn't know what to do.

Will, however, seemed to have arrived with a plan.

"Anna, I've thought and thought about this," he said. "And being apart now *isn't* better than seeing this through the summer. Because *this* is a breakup."

Hearing Will use that term—"breakup"—made tears spring to my eyes again. Over the past few days, I hadn't ever used that expression because it had seemed so melodramatic and ugly.

But Will was right. Melodramatic and ugly was exactly what this was.

"If we stayed together," Will said, "we would have to say good-bye at the end of the summer, yes. But we'd be saying good-bye to something amazing, Anna. Something happy.

"But this?"

Will held his hands out, his palms turned upward.

"This feels awful."

"You're right," I said through the lump in my throat. "Terrible."

"And do you know why?" Will said.

I shook my head, confused.

"Because, Anna . . ."

I saw a flicker of fear in Will's eyes. He looked downward for a moment, the same way he had the other night after the turtle watch. He was considering his next words very carefully.

When he looked up, he took a swift step toward me. He put a hand on each of my cheeks and gently lifted my face so that we were gazing into each other's eyes.

"I love you," he said. He almost yelled it. "And I know that sounds crazy. That's what you say at the beginning of something, not when it's almost reached its end. But—I don't care. I just want to be with you. Maybe it'll only be for these next few weeks. Maybe it'll be forever. We can't know what'll happen, Anna. All I know is *I love you* and . . . we should be together. We just have to be together. We *need* to be together."

I began to sob. I lifted my hands and put them over Will's, which were still cupping my face. His skin was warm beneath the chill of the rain.

And then I was kissing Will; crying and kissing him all at the same time. He wrapped his arms around me and lifted me off the ground. All the hurt and confusion and regret of the past few days flowed off us along with the rain.

When we pulled apart, I turned my face toward the sky, gasping as cold droplets landed in my eyes and mouth and even my ears.

Then, suddenly, my crying turned into laughter. Incredulous, grateful laughter.

I was getting a second chance.

Will was right. Being with him now was worth braving the uncertain future.

This was worth it.

I blinked the rain away, gripped Will by the shoulders, and said, "I love you, too, Will."

Will grabbed me again, so hard it took my breath away, and buried his face in my neck. I felt his shoulders shake for just a moment before his lips were on mine again.

And these kisses weren't about cleansing away our hurt, or healing the rift between us. They were simply, and happily, about sealing the deal—Will and I were together again, for however long we had.

Like Will had said, that *was* an amazing and happy thing. I was finally and absolutely certain of it.

I just *knew*.

I wanted to do so many things with Will before he left. I wanted to walk through all twenty-four of Savannah's historic squares. I wanted to go back to The Swamp, play nothing but slow songs on the jukebox, and dance to them. I was going to teach Will how to eat crawdads, head sucking and all. I was going to invite him to family dinners and private picnics. Or maybe we'd just skip some meals altogether and proceed directly to making out (plus ice cream).

I could have made a to-do list as long as this one on my mom's tattered legal pad.

But I also wanted to do *nothing* with Will. I wanted our last days together to be luxurious, lazy, and most of all, long. I wished I could spend an entire day just drinking in his face, his salty, shampooey scent, the way he looked in those khakis, the way he looked at me. I wanted to memorize all of it, somehow store it away.

The morning after he'd shown up at my house in the rain, I had an idea for a memory to give Will—a part of the island I knew he hadn't seen yet. I wanted him to see it now—with me. And I wasn't going to let the chance slip by, even if it meant waking up at six a.m.

Out of politeness, I waited until six fifteen to call him.

"Hello?" he rasped, his voice cutely sleep clogged.

"Hi," I said. "It's me."

How I loved being able to say nothing more than that and know that it had probably made Will smile, even if he wasn't a morning person. (And he definitely wasn't.)

"You know not *all* of us have skylights above our beds waking us at dawn, right?" Will joked.

He was definitely smiling.

"Oh, I've been awake since before dawn," I said. "Look out your window."

From where I was standing—which happened to be on the deck of Will's cottage—I saw the slats of his window blinds wink open and shut.

Two minutes later, he burst through the door in a frayed green T-shirt, gray cotton shorts, and bare feet. His eyes were still puffy with sleep and his rained-on hair was going every which way, but he was grinning.

When he closed the door behind him and took me in—I was wearing a faded blue sundress dappled with white flowers, my also-rained-on hair ringleting down my back—his smile faded to something more reverent. He all but ran across the deck and wrapped his arms around me. Without a word, he kissed me—a long, hungry, amazing kiss.

A minty one.

"You stopped to brush your teeth before you came out," I noted, a hint of teasing in my voice. "Confident, aren't you?"

"I had a feeling I might get a kiss," Will admitted, his smile sly.

"Just one?" I asked.

It was an invitation and he took it. I have no idea how long we stood there kissing and holding each other tightly. I think both of us were still trying to get our brains around this new reality—that we got to be together again. We could kiss and touch and hold each other to our hearts' content.

At least for another few weeks.

When we finally broke apart, I handed Will the coffee I'd brought for him, lots of milk, no sugar. Then I picked up the canvas bag I'd brought and started down the bridge that led over the dune grass to the beach.

"I want to show you something," I told Will.

"Am I going to need shoes?"

I pointed at my flip-flops, which I'd kicked off the moment I'd arrived. "Do you have to ask?"

Will gave a little laugh, took a big slurp of coffee, then caught up to me so he could grab my hand.

When we reached the beach, I turned right.

"Wait a minute," Will said. "We're going south? Where you might actually be forced to commingle with shoobees?"

"Shut up," I said, veering into him. "I happen to have a new-found respect for shoobees. And besides, nobody's going to be there this early."

"Why are *we* going to be there this early?" Will broached.

"You'll see," I said.

We walked down to the lip of the shore where the sand was slanty but nicely packed for a long walk. I pulled a sports bottle of sweet tea out of my bag, and Will and I walked for a few minutes, silent other than our occasional slurps of caffeine. I watched Will's bare feet make shimmery dents in the wet sand. I drank in his presence, his warm, dry hand in mine, his matted hair breezing off his forehead, his beautiful shoulder just at my eye level.

I pulled him to a stop. I couldn't help it. I *had* to kiss him again before we walked on.

The next time we stopped, it was Will's fault.

"You're so pretty," he said, sounding a bit awestruck. "Can I just look at you for a minute?"

Suffice it to say, it took us a while to get to the spot I'd been aiming for. But finally we were there, a round patch of sand that jutted out into the ocean. Everyone called it the Knee, because as soon as you passed it, the island curved west, making it look a little like a bent leg.

I led Will out to cusp of the Knee and stopped. I pulled my wrap out of my bag and spread it on the sand for us to sit on.

"Wow, this thing has seen better days," Will said as we settled onto the faded orange fabric. He skimmed his fingers over a frayed, unraveling edge and poked his thumb through a sizable hole.

"Yeah, it was a good wrap," I said. "I'll be chucking it soon."

I ran my hand along the rough, wrinkled wrap until it landed on Will's hand.

"Actually, maybe this one I'll save," I said. "I can pull it out one day and remember . . ."

I didn't need to finish my sentence; list all the things I wanted to remember. There were too many anyway.

Will leaned over to kiss me, and we kept on kissing until his stomach growled loudly.

I pulled away, laughing, and reached for my bag.

"How are you hungry when you're usually asleep this time of day?" I wondered. I took out a container of biscuits with honey butter and another of sliced peaches, watermelon chunks, plums, berries . . . summer fruits that would be good for only a short while longer.

I couldn't help thinking that everything was on a countdown now, from the fruit to my wrap to Will. I was no longer letting this fact defeat me, but it still made me feel a tiny bit tragic—and glad that I'd started this, the first of our last days together, early.

I leaned my head on Will's shoulder while he munched the breakfast I'd brought. Both of us gazed out at the water until Will suddenly straightened up, pointing toward the horizon.

"Is that . . . ?" he said. "Anna, *look*."

Even before I spotted them, I knew what Will was seeing. Dolphins. Perhaps fifty of them in a tightly packed school. They leaped out of the water in rhythmic, silvery arcs, racing back and forth in a pattern that clearly made perfect sense to them, even if it was a mystery to me.

"This is fantastic," Will gasped. "I knew there were dolphins here. Owen said he saw them one day when I wasn't around. I always kind of kept an eye out for them, but never saw them myself."

"Well, the Knee at seven a.m. is kind of a sure thing," I said. "They're almost always here, having breakfast. They leap to corral the fish. Something about the water pattern out there brings 'em in droves, I guess."

Will shook his head in amazement and gave me a quick kiss.

"Thanks for the wake-up call," he whispered, before returning his gaze to the school of dolphins.

I watched with him. Dolphins had factored into my childhood fantasies almost as much as mermaids. Those leaps through the air looked so joyful. I didn't want to believe my parents when they told me dolphins leaped for practical reasons, to spot the fish or perhaps shake off barnacles.

Instead I told myself that they were reveling in their freedom, their strength, their ability to swim forever and never stop.

Now it occurred to me, though, that the dolphins never strayed very far. They came back to the Knee every morning, like clockwork. Who knew, maybe they liked their glimpses of people pointing at them excitedly.

Or maybe the dolphins just liked Dune Island itself. At the moment—and not only because it was full of wonders to show Will—I was in love with it, too.

* * *

A couple of nights later, I introduced Will to the Crash Pad behind Caroline's house. Sam was there too. The four of us sprawled on the enormous trampoline and counted stars through the halo of bushy crape myrtle branches.

In Savannah, I'd noticed, the crape myrtles were trimmed into orderly little shrubs—tasteful gateways to elegant mansions. Apparently, that was how those trees were *supposed* to look.

But Caroline lived in a lemon-yellow house as sprawling and janky as my own. The patio furniture was kelly green, there were planters filled with bright, plastic flowers, and the crape myrtles were wild and leggy. The trees were garish and overgrown, just like so much on this crazy, lush island. Being here with Will made me see it all with new eyes, as had happened so many times that summer.

Sam and Caroline seemed shiny and new too, or at least more comfortable with the blurry line between friendship and more-than-friendship. They teased each other, but bookended their jibes with kisses. They spoke in shorthand and private jokes.

From what each of them had told me, they were still adjusting to being SamAndCaroline. Maybe they always would be. (I was starting to get the sense that shifts and adjustments were a constant of couplehood.) But instead of freaking them out, their blips almost seemed to bring them closer together.

"I think I'm getting the hang of it," Caroline told me on the trampoline while the boys were in the house making us all smoothies. "I just kind of fold the maddening parts of being with Sam in with all the good stuff. You know, for better, for worse."

"Wait a minute," I blurted. I'd been lying on my back, but now I sat up. "That's what you say at *a wedding*, Caroline. Is there something you want to tell me?"

"God, no!" Caroline said with a laugh. But to tell the truth, she didn't sound *that* freaked out by the W-word. "I'm just saying, when you commit, you commit to the whole package, that's all. Even if it's not necessarily forever, you know?"

Sam and Will emerged from the house, each carrying two frosty glasses filled with something orange and delicious-looking. They'd even fished around Caroline's kitchen and found some paper umbrellas, no doubt a relic from one of the family's famous luaus.

Will saw me look over at him and grinned. He clinked his two glasses together and lifted one of them in my direction, as if sending me a toast.

I grinned and gave him a little wave, jangling the silver Möbius bracelet on my wrist.

I always thought romance novels were being ridiculous when they used phrases like "Her heart swelled." But being there with my best friends and Will, all of us so full-up with love that it was a wonder we could even think about food, I think I definitely felt some extra *thump-thump*s going on inside me.

With a bit of difficulty I tore my eyes from Will and looked at Caroline.

"Yeah," I replied. I could hear the gratitude and happiness in my own voice. "Yeah, I know."

The smoothies cooled us off a bit, but they also somehow made us more hungry. Lately, I'd been of two minds about food. I was either completely uninterested—*why eat when you can kiss?* Or I was ravenous and everything I ate tasted way more delicious than usual.

Tonight, I was in the latter camp. I wanted to get a shrimp po' boy and lick the remoulade from my fingers. I wanted a slaw dog with extra mustard. I wanted curly fries.

I didn't have to ask anyone twice. We all headed to Crabby's Crab Shack and emerged as they were closing up shop, clutching our overfull stomachs and smelling like deep-fried fish.

Caroline tested the air like she was feeling a piece of fabric, rubbing it between her fingertips.

"Is it possible that it's hotter now than when we went in that place?" she asked.

"Sno-cone?" Will proposed, pointing at the crowd milling in front of The Scoop a block down the boardwalk.

"You know I never go there on my night off," I said, shaking my head firmly. "Especially during the rush. They'll rope me in so fast . . ."

"I'd help," Will said, slipping his arm around my waist.

I knew he would, too. He'd gone back to coming to The Scoop each night at closing time, grinning at me as he flipped the OPEN sign. He'd wipe tables while I squeegeed the windows.

Or we'd stand side by side at the sink in the back, Will rinsing dishes and me loading them into the industrial washer. I'd nudge him with my hip or let my hand linger on his while he passed me scoops and sundae glasses. Then we almost always had to pause for kissing. One night, we just blew off the chores and raided the ice cream case, fixing ourselves a towering sundae for two and kissing between bites.

I'd always thought these post-closing chores were dowdy and domestic, especially when I saw my parents doing them together. But with Will, they were kind of sexy.

Of course, not when we were surrounded by my family and a bunch of customers, so I put my foot down.

"Y'all say hi to my folks," I said to Will, Sam, and Caroline, waving them toward The Scoop. "I'll wait for you out here."

Then I whispered loudly to Caroline, "Just don't let Will scoop any ice cream. The guy makes the most lopsided cones I've ever seen."

"Oh, nice," Will said, stalking toward me slowly with mock menace on his face.

"Uh-oh!" I giggled at Sam and Caroline. "I made it mad."

Will stiffened his fingers into claws and lunged at me.

"Aaaah!" I shrieked. I darted to one of the short staircases leading from the boardwalk to the beach, skipped down it, and started running.

Will laughed as he chased me toward the water. He didn't catch me until I'd hit the surf and turned to run along it, away from the boardwalk. He grabbed me around the waist and spun me around until I cried out, "Stop! I just ate!"

Will put me down and we clutched each other for a moment to keep from falling down in a dizzy, sweaty sprawl. I could feel the muscles in his chest move beneath the soft cotton of his shirt. His arms circled around the small of my back.

And since we were holding each other anyway . . .

Only after we'd been kissing for a good two or three minutes did I suddenly gasp, "Oh, no! I forgot about Sam and Caroline."

Completely mortified, I peeked over Will's shoulder to see if they were watching us from the boardwalk, and possibly sticking their fingers down their throats.

It would serve them right, I thought with a sly smile. *They nauseated me all spring with their kissy-kissy ways.*

As I searched the boardwalk for Caroline's pale ponytail and Sam's slouchy lope, my cell phone rang. I dug it out of my purse.

"Put it on speaker," Caroline said when I answered it.

"Where are you?" I yelled at the phone after I hit the speaker button.

"We're watching your dad shave ice," Caroline said. "You put the bug in our ears."

I covered the mouthpiece and whispered to Will, "I don't think they saw the PDA."

"And don't worry," Caroline added with a cackle. "I won't tell your dad about the hanky panky I just saw on the beach."

"Guess they did," Will said with a shrug.

When you're from New York City, I think you're much less mortified by people seeing your business. Nobody stays home in their tiny apartments, Will had told me, so people do all *kinds* of things right out in the open. Or at least in the backs of taxis.

Speaking of, Will was . . . peeling off his shirt? Then he hopped around on one leg while he pulled off one of his shoes.

"Uh, *what* are you doing?" I asked.

"*Oh*-kay, on that note," Caroline said, "good ni-ight."

"No, Caroline!" I screeched. "It's not what it sounds like—"

Click.

Will grinned, took off his other shoe, then unbuckled his belt.

"Okay, really," I said, getting a little nervous. I glanced over my shoulder to make sure nobody *else* was watching us from the boardwalk. "What *are* you doing?"

"Don't worry," Will said, tossing his belt on the sand next to his shoes. "This is as far as I go."

Holding up his khakis with one hand, he started to walk into the water.

"Will." I laughed. "No! I love those khakis."

"A little water's not going to hurt 'em," Will called over his shoulder. "Now, are you coming in or not?"

Had we been on the North Peninsula, I wouldn't have thought twice about following Will into the water in my cutoffs and tank top. But we were a shell's throw from the boardwalk, which was teeming with post-dinner people—both tourists I didn't know and school friends that I did.

I bit my lip. Letting other people see me cavort in the waves with my boyfriend felt kind of like going out in public with my underwear on outside my clothes. On the other hand, skulking around with Will felt even more wrong. If our breakup had taught me anything, it was to embrace the scary. You missed out on too much otherwise.

So with only one more furtive glance to see if we were surrounded (we weren't, but we certainly weren't alone either), I kicked off my flip-flops, carefully slipped my silver bangle inside one of Will's sneakers, and splashed into the water.

As I waded toward Will, he ducked underneath the surface. When he came up, he flicked his hair off his forehead and whooped.

"Oh, that feels *good*!" he said. "What am I gonna do when I don't have an ocean outside my door every day?"

"I can't tell you," I said as I swam toward him, skimming easily over the lazy nighttime waves. "I've never had that experience."

"Man, I can't imagine this being my everyday world," Will said. He shifted onto his back and blinked up at the stars. "It doesn't seem real."

"Right back at ya," I said. "New York is *my* idea of a vacation. A frantic, crazy, sensory-overloaded version of it, anyway. I mean, you ride in elevators and shoot through underground tunnels every day. Do you know how weird that is?"

Will went upright and looked over at me.

"Sometimes it feels like we're from two different countries." His voice wobbled a bit as he said it.

I swam closer still, until my hands were on his bare chest.

"At least we don't speak two different languages," I said softly.

"Oh, no," Will said, one side of his mouth rising a bit, "*y'all* don't think so?"

"Watch it," I growled, "or I'll feed you to the ghost crabs."

"Hey, that's what I can be for Halloween in my building this year," Will said, snapping his wet fingers. "The kids'll be *terrified*. Or really confused. I don't think anyone in New York knows what a ghost crab is."

I grimaced. Halloween? With its Indian corn and pumpkins and nip in the air? Now *that* was surreal. I could barely imagine it.

"At Halloween, it'll have been two months," I whispered.

I didn't have to say *two months we'll have been apart*. Will knew what I meant. He sank deeper into the water, resting his chin on its surface and looking up into my eyes.

"What'll it be like, do you think?" he wondered. "Two months isn't very long."

"It'll feel long," I said. Now my voice was wobbly. "But maybe after that, it will feel less so."

I wondered if *that* would be even worse.

Will pulled me into a sad, salty kiss.

"Forget the ocean," he said. "What am I going to do when I don't have *you* every day?"

I was going to cry. If I didn't kiss Will right then, I was going to cry. So I did kiss him—with a heat and urgency that felt different from before.

We were heading into the end and we both knew it. It was time to weather the bitter and embrace the sweet and suck the marrow out of all the time we had left.

* * *

A couple of nights later, it was Will who had a plan.

"Guess what we're doing tomorrow?" he said as we cleaned up at The Scoop. "I signed us up for something."

I cocked my head.

"You signed us up . . ."

I paused and pondered what was going on on the island the next day. Then I gasped.

"You did not!" I said, slapping at Will with my bleachy rag.

"I did," Will said. "We're entered in that sand castle competition you told me about."

"Will," I sputtered. "People take that competition very seriously. They, like, *train* for it. My sister's been practicing with her girlfriends for months. They're making a re-creation of the Sydney Opera House."

Will snorted.

"You're kidding, right?" he said. "Anna, I don't want to dis your sister, but she doesn't seem like the Sydney Opera House type. Have you guys been to Australia?"

"Oh, please," I said. "We haven't even been to California. But the Sydney Opera House is a big favorite with the sand castle competition. Someone does one almost every year. That and Hogwarts."

Will's eyes went wide and he put a hand on top of his head.

"Oh, man," he said with a laugh. "I didn't know. You'd think for something this hard-core, they would have had an entrance fee or something to keep out the dilettantes. I just went to the chamber of commerce and put our names on a clipboard."

"Oh, well," I said, waving him off. "It's all just for fun."

Then I narrowed my eyes and added, "Grueling, cutthroat, *punishing* fun."

"This is *not* good," Will said. "But wouldn't it be lame to be a no-show? Especially since we got slot number six in the line-up. I think that's pretty close to the main action."

I shook my head in confusion.

"Wait a minute," I said. "When did you sign us up for this thing?"

"Um, I guess it was in July," Will said. Suddenly, he looked a little sheepish. "July fifth, as a matter of fact."

I put a finger to my chin.

"I get it now," I said. "That's why you showed up at my house in the rain. You need a partner for the sand castle competition. You just *had* to get that blue ribbon, didn't you?"

"What can I say," Will said, leaning rakishly on his broom. "I'm a sportsman above all else."

I spritzed my bleachy water in his direction. But after wiping a few more tables, I stopped and turned to him.

"How did you know we'd even be together now?" I asked softly. "When you signed us up in July?"

Will shrugged.

"It just seemed impossible that we wouldn't be," he said.

He walked toward me, trailing the broom behind him.

"Call it a leap of faith," he said, alighting before me and planting a soft kiss on my lips.

I wrapped my arms around his shoulders.

"So you had faith in me?" I asked, half flirting, half serious.

"I had faith in *us*," Will said. "Still do."

Will's broom clattered to the floor as I kissed him. And that was all the talking we did for a long while.

"Will?" I asked the next morning, "have you built a sand castle? Like . . . ever?"

"Well . . . " Will pondered this question as he mucked about our little lot on the South Beach, piling sand, smoothing it, and piling it again.

"I remember one summer when I was a kid," he said, "we went to Long Island and my mom taught us how to make drip castles. You know, where you fill your fist with super-wet sand and just drip-drip-drip it until you have these pointy towers."

I gasped. I would have covered Will's mouth if my hand hadn't been breaded with sand.

"Whatever you do," I said in a low voice, "don't mention drip castles around these folks. It's the sign of a complete amateur."

"I *am* a complete amateur," Will declared without a hint of embarrassment.

I sighed and glanced at the banner hanging directly over our heads. It read FOURTEENTH ANNUAL DUNE ISLAND SAND CASTLE COMPETITION!

I cast shifty looks at the castle builders stationed on either side of us. They, of course, were well into their architectural feats. It was only ten in the morning and I already saw some flying buttresses and six-foot-tall turrets.

If I'd been really brave, I would have walked the whole gauntlet of sandy construction sites to check out the competition. We were placed in a straight line that extended for about half a mile. The castle builders seemed to fit three different profiles.

First there were the gray-haired curmudgeons who'd been doing this forever and worked alone (or perhaps with a couple of cowed grandkids as assistants). They grumbled and growled through their castle building, working as intently as scientists trying to cure cancer.

Then there were the teams, like my sister Sophie's team of six fourteen-year-old girls. They gave themselves cute titles and usually functioned as both competitors and cheerleaders. Whenever things got too quiet along the assembly line, they'd start jumping around in their bikinis, hooting and shouting things like, "Team Patty Cake *rocks*!"

Finally, there was the pathetic minority—tourists who'd joined as a lark and had *no* idea what they were getting into.

Somehow—after a lifetime of looking down my nose at summer people—there I was in the last category. I was a dismal dabbler. No better than a shoobee.

But I loved Will, and he'd made this sweet gesture for me, so I was embracing the humiliation. I'd instructed myself to smile (and smile *big*) when Dune Island High kids strolled by and snickered. I'd agreed when Sophie had begged me to deny that I knew her, much less shared a bedroom and DNA with her.

And I wore sunglasses and a big floppy hat along with my shorts and bikini top.

When Caroline and Sam had stopped by our construction

site a half hour earlier, Caroline had given my wardrobe selection a skeptical squint.

"What?" I said defensively as I adjusted my enormous hat. "It's for UVA protection!"

"Uh-huh," Caroline said. Then she gave my bare brown torso a pointed look. I had the sort of honey-colored complexion that never burned. By this time of the year, my whole body was always as brown as an almond. Between that and the thick layer of SPF 50 I was wearing today, I didn't *really* have to worry about burning.

Caroline shook her head and gave me an indulgent smile. Then she gripped me by my upper arms and looked me straight in the sunglasses.

"Anna," she said, "I love you. I support you. But we can't be seen hanging around with . . . this."

She gestured at the crude beginnings of our castle.

"So we'll see you after you're done, okay?" she said gently.

I nodded somberly.

"I understand," I said. "It's too late for me. Go save yourself."

Then we both laughed so hard that we fell to our knees in the sand, crushing a good portion of the moat around the castle.

"All right, all right," Sam said, helping Caroline to her feet and pointing her toward the lighthouse at the southern end of the island. Every year the chamber of commerce set up a carnival in the lighthouse parking lot to coincide with the sand castle competition. I could already see the distant swing ride, roller coaster, and carousel flinging people about.

"We're getting breakfast, then going to the carnival," Sam said. "See you there?"

"If we make it out alive," I called dramatically, whereupon Will pretended to give me a swat.

"You better curb the attitude, *Allison*," he said with a grin.

I laughed and smiled at the little laser-printed sign that had been planted in front of our building site. It read STARDUST MEMORIES, BY LEONARD ZELIG AND ALLISON PORCHNIK.

About *that*, I had no objections whatsoever.

Once Caroline and Sam had left, though, and Will and I had gotten to work in earnest, I did have a few complaints. A lot of them, actually. I'd always known sand castle building was hard, but not *this* hard.

"Why couldn't this be an ice cream competition?" I grumbled as I slapped sand around with little plan or purpose.

"Anna, don't take this the wrong way," Will said, "but I'm not the only amateur here."

"I know." I sighed. My experience making sand forts with my siblings had given me exactly *no* edge in this contest. So far all Will and I had done was dig our foundation and assembled a very tall mound of sand, ready for carving.

But since our castle was supposed to be a tall, skinny triangle, our curvy hill was of little use to us.

"Are you *sure* people are going to recognize this building?" I asked Will, peering at the already damp and runny photo printout he'd brought to the beach. "I mean, it's cool, but *I've* never heard of the Flatiron."

"It's the third most famous building in New York," Will said with a shrug. "I guess we could have done the Chrysler Building or the Empire State, but I figured those would be trickier."

"Ya *think?*" I said sarcastically.

I began rifling through our box of tools, which mostly consisted of spatulas and spreaders, buckets and shovels, plastic cutlery and a large spray bottle of sea water. I pulled out a long, floppy cake-frosting knife and tried to shave a section of sand off our mound to make one of the long, flat walls of the Flatiron.

The wall promptly caved in on itself, shedding a big chunk of sand that plopped right onto my foot.

"Okay, it might be time to think about forfeiting," I said, trying not to break out into funeral giggles, which is what Caroline and I call it whenever we laugh at completely inappropriate times. "Or at least taking a swim break."

"No, we can do this!" Will ordered. I could hear a laugh in his voice too. If not for the super-serious builders to the right and left of us, I think we would have kicked our castle attempt down that very minute and gone off for a sno-cone.

But even Will knew that giving up on the sand castle competition would invoke mockery at best, righteous scorn at worst. So . . . we stayed. Will grabbed our spray bottle and started moistening the collapsed wall of the castle.

"We let it get too dry," he said. "If we keep it wet enough, we can keep the shape together, then carve in all these details."

Will pointed at the curvy windows, crown molding, and elaborately decorated bricks of the building in our photo.

"And then we'll be done," Will said, "and we can go do something else. *Anything* else."

"That's all the motivation I need," I said, squelching the last of my giggles. "Let's go."

We got quiet as we heaped our wet sand into a passable Flat-iron shape, then got busy with forks, knives, toothpicks, and our ever-present spray bottle. Before long, we'd started carving all the building's beautiful details out of our giant, skinny triangle.

"I still can't imagine," I said as we worked, "growing up with a building like this right down the road. Hundreds of 'em."

Will chuckled.

"'Down the road,'" he said. "That's something you don't hear too many New Yorkers say."

"Oh, God," I groaned. "I'm a bumpkin."

"Bumpkins don't make ice cream flavors like Greek Holiday," Will said, making me hide my face with my hat brim so I could blush proudly. "Anyway, I like it. 'Down the road.'"

"Okay, enough of that," I admonished, returning my focus to the tricky columns at the curved point of the building.

"You're right, though," Will said. "Living in New York is amazing. I take it for granted sometimes, but then something always happens to make me remember that there's no other place like it."

"I want to go back some day," I said. "I always have."

It went without saying that now I had even more reason to want to go back to New York. But I *didn't* say it.

Just like we didn't talk about whether Will and his family might come back to Dune Island the following summer.

We'd silently agreed not to make our last days together all about clinging to fantasies about the future. We didn't propose spending school vacations together or applying to all the same colleges. Because those things might never materialize and we knew it.

It felt better just to be honest. Just to *be*.

Even if now we were being seriously bad sand castlers.

I did allow myself to ask Will one question as I started shaping window frames with a popsicle stick.

"Do you think you'll go to college in New York like Owen?"

"I used to be sure I would," Will said. "But after being away from the city this summer—I mean *really* away—and loving it so much, I wonder if I wouldn't want to do the same thing for college. Maybe go somewhere that's completely different."

"That's exactly what I want to do," I said. "I'm definitely leaving Dune Island, probably the South, too."

Usually when I talked about graduating from high school and leaving (and I've been known to talk about that a *lot*) I felt restless and itchy, defiant and even a tiny bit bitter. Those emotions were so familiar, they'd worn a groove into my life; a permanent sound track that I'd considered unalterable.

But as I told Will my plan, those familiar emotions weren't there.

Which wasn't to say I'd suddenly become a born-again Dune Islander. But now when I pictured myself leaving, I imagined myself as an adventurer, rather than a rebel.

Small towns, as everyone knows, don't like to lose their young people, so I'd always thought of it as a triumph/scandal when someone graduated from Dune Island High, then seemed to disappear forever to the nebulous Up North.

I used to wonder if I'd be one of those disappearing acts, except for brief visits home for holidays and special occasions. But after this summer, I was starting to think that that wasn't how it was going to go for me. Now I pictured my future self— the one who might or might not dart down subway steps with a chic handbag under her arm—coming home often. I saw my sweet, chaotic house as a haven in the world, instead of a shelter that was holding me back from it.

Maybe, like Will's mom, I'd bring my own family back to Dune Island someday and spend a summer exploring all my old haunts.

I didn't know if Will would be a part of that future, but I *did* know that he was partly responsible for my new vision of it. Just like Will, I'd taken my home for granted. And *he'd* been the something that had made me remember there was no other place like it. He'd made me realize that having the ocean outside my door was a gift, not a given.

He'd made me want to leave Dune Island—but not flee it.

After four hours of packing and carving, our Flatiron Building wasn't great. It wasn't even good. But it was finished.

"All that work!" Will huffed as he gave our castle a final spritz of water to make sure everything set. "And it's just going to be washed away by the tide tonight."

"You do know that those other folks probably put twice as much time into their castles, don't you?" I said. I'd just used a trowel to smooth Fifth Avenue out in front of our building.

"Yeah, but it only looks like they put in thrice as much time,"

Will scoffed. It took me a moment to process what he'd just said and then I laughed—wearily, but still.

I tossed my floppy hat and sunglasses into the toolbox along with all our other makeshift tools. Then we stashed the box behind our castle and I took a deep breath.

"Well," I said to Will with a wry smile, "let's go congratulate the winners."

"Now where's the optimistic Anna that I know and love?" Will asked, wrapping his arm around my sweaty, sandy waist and giving me a squeeze.

I turned to him with wide eyes.

"Do you even *know* me?" I blurted.

"Um, Anna," Will said, "I was being sarcastic."

"Oh," I said. We stumbled down the beach gaping at one unspeakably brilliant sand castle after another, including Sophie's opera house, which was huge and elegant.

I shook my head to clear it.

"I think all the manual labor—not to mention our impending disgrace—has left me a little impaired," I said.

"I've got something for that," Will said, pointing to the carnival.

"Oh yeah, the carnival," I said sleepily. "I'd almost forgotten."

"I think you forgot something else," Will said. "It's not *us* who are going to come in last place in the competition. It's Allison Porchnik and Zelig!"

I *had* forgotten that. I grinned at Will.

"Our poor bicycles," I said. "They must be horrified that we roped them into this *crazy* scheme."

"You're right!" Will cried. "I was a fool, Allison. It won't happen again."

I stopped clowning then.

Of *course* it wouldn't happen again.

Every time Will or I inadvertently said something like that, it shut us up quick. Then we had to glance away from each other and swallow hard until the moment passed.

"I'll make it up to you with cotton candy," Will whispered in my ear before planting a sweet kiss on my cheek.

"You better," I said. "*And* frozen lemonade."

With that, we forgot about sand castles entirely and went to the carnival.

We found Caroline and Sam quickly after we arrived and dragged them to all the rides—the bumper cars, the small roller coaster, and the spinning teacups.

My favorite ride was the giant wheel of swings that simply spun us around in long, lazy loops. We weren't whipped about or turned upside down. We just made swoop after swoop around a giant ring with flashing lights and chimey organ music. The swings made me feel windblown and free after my very grounded morning of castle building.

When our feet touched the ground after the swings came slowly to a stop, I clapped my hands like a little kid and cried, "Let's go again!"

So we did.

We ended up skipping the cotton candy in favor of corn dogs and blooming onions, which we ate while we played the silly carnival games.

Will and I both failed to lob Ping-Pong balls into a row of glass milk jugs, so we moved on to the contraption where you tried to ring a bell by pounding a pedestal with a giant hammer. A roly-poly guy was manning the game in front of a table piled with stuffed animals and plastic prizes. Among them, I recognized the hot pink boa constrictor that had been twined around Figgy Pudding on the Fourth of July.

I touched the garish plush lightly and pointed it out to Will.

"Do you remember that?" I asked.

"I'll never forget that," he whispered in my ear. "I'll never forget a bit of that night."

I leaned into him. Who knew if that was true. Who knew if that was even possible. But I wanted to believe, as much as Will did, that all these days and nights together *would* stay with us, etched like a tattoo into our memories.

Sam broke into our bubble by offering the heavy hammer to Will.

"Naw, you go first," Will said. "I'll watch your technique."

"Watch and learn, buddy," Sam said with a grin. He planted his feet and swung the hammer. It hit the end of the pedestal, which seesawed to send a little metal disc zinging up a cord toward the bell. The disc hovered for a moment *just* below the bell, then plummeted back down.

"Awww," Sam groaned.

Then it was Will's turn. He flexed his muscles at me, waggling his eyebrows.

"Sah-woon!" I joked in a high-pitched girly voice. Of course,

I *was* actually admiring the way Will's arms looked as he hoisted the hammer—all sinew and muscle and smooth, tan skin.

Will pretended to spit on his palms, then swung. Once again the metal disc seemed to slow down just before it hit the bell. But it *did* hit it.

Or rather, it just barely tapped it, making the weakest ding in the history of bells.

"Sorry!" the carnie yelled. "Try again!"

"Aw, that counted!" Sam yelled with a grin. "C'mon, dude. Throw the guy a bone. Or at least these giant sunglasses."

Sam plucked a pair of preposterous lime-green glasses off the table and put them on.

"Nope!" the carnie said, pulling the prize off Sam's face and shooing us away. "Move it along, kids."

"I was robbed," Will complained. "I guess you think me less of a man now, Anna?"

Caroline hooked her arm through mine and whispered in my ear, "Can you imagine being here with boys who actually *cared* about winning these things?"

"Yes, I can," I said with a shudder.

I grabbed Will's hand with my free one and squeezed it hard. I loved how different he was from so many competitive-about-everything guys.

I loved how much fun he was having at this dinky carnival and how much fun *I* was having because I was here with him.

I supposed I was just giddily in love. It was as simple as that.

Or so it felt right then, when Will was still so solidly here.

How many times had I wished I could freeze a moment with Will and just live in it, luxuriate in it, forever? It was a silly wish, but I couldn't help making it over and over. I wrapped my arm around Will's waist as we left the midway, feeling grateful for the wish, even if I couldn't have the actual phenomenon.

Very soon after that, the moment really did have to end because I had to go to work. The Scoop was always slammed on the day of the sand castle competition.

"I'll come by later," Will promised me. "After I have dinner with my mom and Owen and, of course, go to the sand castle judging."

"You're going?!" I laughed. "What, the big hammer thing didn't bruise your ego enough?"

"That thing was rigged," Will said, flexing his biceps at me again.

I laughed and because of all the people milling around us, gave him a quick kiss on the lips. But I wished it could have been much, much longer.

*L*ater that night, Will marched into The Scoop, dodged around the swarm of people peering into the ice cream cases, and slapped a muddy brown ribbon onto the counter.

"Our prize!" he announced proudly.

I stared at the rosette-free ribbon. In small gold letters it said PARTICIPANT.

"Participant!" I sputtered. "Not even honorable mention?"

"Would you rather it say 'last place'?" Will asked.

"Good point," I said with a laugh. I started to take the ribbon but Will snatched it away.

"I'm keeping this for posterity," he said. "It's much cooler than my childhood baseball trophies."

I thought of the little keepsake drawer in my bathroom and wondered if Will had one of his own.

Then suddenly my mind zipped into a distant future in which I was poking around in my vanity drawer for a walk down memory lane. I pictured myself pulling out the toothpick I'd saved from my first date with Will. I wondered if it would make me get dreamy and smiley, or if I'd be all tragic soul-searching.

Where will I be then? I wondered. Who *will I be?*

Not that I had time to get philosophical. I had a long queue of hot, sandy customers clamoring for something cold. So I shook myself out of my daydream and smiled at Will. Adopting my best aren't-you-a-pathetic-little-puppy voice, I said, "It's a *great* ribbon, honey. Now what I can I get you? The Greek Holiday's going quick."

"Mmm," Will said. "How about Pineapple Ginger Ale."

Oh, great. That only made more memories wash over me. I looked away from Will. If he added anything else to this bitter-sweet brew of mine, I was going to have to retreat to the cooler, where I could become a puddle in private.

Instead, I was jolted out of my brooding by the high-pitched whoops of a gaggle of girls coming into The Scoop. When I turned, I saw that one of them was my sister, waving a red ribbon over her head. Her friends surrounded her, pumping their French-manicured fists in the air and shimmying their hips.

"Se-cond place!" they chanted. "Se-cond place!"

"Sweetie!" cried my mom, who was working the cash register. She waved at Sophie. "That's wonderful!"

As a fellow castle builder, I finally understood *just* how wonderful second place was. A simple thumbs-up wouldn't do. I handed my ice cream scoop to my mom and scooted around the counter. Then I gave my sister a big hug.

"Congratulations!" I exclaimed. "We saw your opera house. It really was amazing."

From behind me, Will added, "It was awesome, Sophie."

"Thanks!" Sophie said. She glanced down at my arms, which were still wrapped around her, and gave me a look that meant, *You're weird.*

But she quickly followed it up with a sweet smile.

"I saw your castle too," she said. "It was . . . well, it was nice? Um, what was it?"

"The Flatiron Building," Will piped up. "It's the third most famous . . ."

Will trailed off as Sophie's teammates began chanting again and my sister, as always, got sucked into the center of her social circle.

Through the crush of girls, I gave Will a *don't sweat it* smile.

He returned it with a smile I'd learned to recognize. The one that meant *I'm crazy about you.*

Me too, I thought with a deep, shuddery breath. *Me too.*

Then I went back behind the counter to make Sophie a Diet Coke float with chocolate chip ice cream, and scoop up some Pineapple Ginger Ale for Will. His favorite.

The next thing I knew, I was waking up and it was August 28.

It was a day when all I wanted was routine. I wanted to go with Will for a lazy swim and a long, luxurious bike ride. I wanted to go to work and have him show up at nine like he always did.

But there was nothing routine about this day. Instead, there would be Will returning Zelig to the bike shop and packing and cleaning the cottage and having his last Dune Island moments with his family.

And me there for all of it, my heart threatening to explode.

In the morning, I went to Will's house. When I got there, his T-shirts were in a neat stack on the bed. I *loved* Will's T-shirts, so soft and worn and perfect-fitting.

When Will left the bedroom to help his mom with something in the kitchen, I sat down next to the T-shirt stack and gave it a little pat.

Then I laid my cheek down on it. The shirt on top—a light blue tee with a faded navy crew neck—was as soft as always. But without Will's torso inside of it, it didn't move me at all.

In fact, it made me feel unspeakably empty.

"Anna?"

I bolted upright to see Will standing in the doorway, trying not to laugh.

"Shut up!" I said. "Hey, at least I wasn't *smelling* your shirts. They always do that in the movies, have you noticed?"

"I know," Will said shaking his head. "Cheesy."

"So do you want to say good-bye to The Room?" Will said, pointing across the hall to his mother's orange-and-brown lair.

"Eh, that's okay," I said. "I'll say good-bye to your mom and Owen, though."

They were eating breakfast on the deck. As we walked through the tchotchke-clogged living room to the back door, I felt a wave of grief wash over me. This house, with a suitcase by the door and another splayed out on the dining room table, already felt stale and empty. Lifeless. Will-less.

Out on the deck, Owen took a break from a massive bowl of cereal to give me a bear hug.

"Hell of a summer," he said, shooting Will a not very Owen-ish look of concern. "Anna, I will think of you every time I see a ghost crab."

"I think I've just been insulted," I said with a laugh.

"Definitely not," Owen said, giving me his usual devilish grin. "Definitely not."

Ms. Dempsey's good-bye hug was more fragile. When we looked at each other, both our lower lips were trembling.

"Oh, Anna," she said, her voice filled with lots of things— sympathy and worry, but also joy and maybe a vicarious twinge.

"Are you glad you came back?" I asked her. "Was the summer what you hoped for?"

"I think I'll need to ponder that for a while before I know," Ms. Dempsey said. "But you know what? I think so.

"And it was *lovely* knowing you, my girl," she added, her smile looking more mommish now. "Now, you guys go on. Have a good day."

She gave my hand a quick squeeze.

I wondered for the first time if Ms. Dempsey knew exactly what I was going through; if she'd fallen for a boy on Dune Island, too, long, long ago.

If I'd had more time maybe I would have asked her. But there was so little time left. And Allison and Zelig had one last ride in them.

"Are you ready?" Will asked.

I nodded eagerly, and with a last little wave to Will's family, I followed him down the steps to the road.

We rode up and down Highway 80. We swooped back and forth across the highway, passing each other at the road's center line. It was a habit we'd developed during our many bike rides that summer, in which the destination had mattered so little that half the time, we'd just given up on it and kept pedaling.

We'd become experts at that center-of-the-road crisscross, even high-fiving sometimes as we passed each other. But today we were clearly off our game. At one point, we came so close to each other, we almost crashed. Will skidded to the side of the road and had to jump off his bike to avoid falling. He took a few stumbling steps, then stopped himself with his hands to keep from face planting into the gravel.

We looked at each other and shook our heads at our own pathedicness.

I motioned northward with my head.

"Let's go, huh?"

Will nodded, picked up his bike, and we headed to the North Peninsula.

Our beach.

I was happy to see that it looked as deserted as ever when we got there, maybe even more desolate than usual with its sun-fried dune grasses and the CLOSED sign on Angelo's door. (Angelo always took his vacation between the tourists' departure and Labor Day.)

I unfurled my desiccated wrap from around Allison's handle-bars and dropped it on the sand near the water. I quickly peeled off my shorts and tank top. Underneath I was wearing my blue flower-print two-piece, because it was my favorite—and I knew it was Will's favorite too.

We were silent as we waded out past the breakers. Then, once we were up to our necks in the water, we circled each other, our faces somber. Will swallowed hard. Then *I* swallowed hard.

But just as I thought we'd both buckle under the weight of all these *lasts*—last bike ride, last swim, last date—Will lifted his feet and swam splashily toward me. And I remembered—in the water, you're weightless.

So I floated too. And then we were floating together, kissing and kissing, our arms and legs tangled up, hanks of my long, wet hair sticking to Will's bare shoulders. I didn't quite know where he began and I ended. I was only aware of his lips on my lips, on my neck, on my shoulders, his hands skimming over my body, memorizing it, while I did the same.

I love you, I love you.

We said it over and over again.

I felt a quick flutter of my old desire—to just duck beneath the waves, do my mermaid kick, and head out to sea. This time I wanted to take Will with me.

But instead, I looked at the sun, which was already going slanty in the sky, and told Will that it was time to go.

We'd floated a good bit away from our shoes and clothes, and the walk back to them gave our swollen lips a chance to start returning to normal.

We rode back to the boardwalk together, but I headed for home before Will went to return Zelig to the bike rental shop. For some reason, *that* was a "last" I couldn't bear to watch.

While Will had a last Dune Island supper with his mom and Owen, I took a long bath to get ready for our date that night. As I combed out my hair and put on makeup at the vanity, I opened my little keepsake drawer, dug beneath the note paper and the sea glass, and found that little plastic toothpick from the Dune Island Beach Club.

It was hard to imagine how guarded and clueless and terrified I'd been on our first date; hard to fathom the fact that I hadn't *always* known Will, and loved him, the way I did now.

It was even harder to believe that I'd known him for less than three months.

The fact that after tomorrow I might never see him again was the most difficult to envision. I didn't want to, anyway. Like Will always said—there'd be time for that later.

Instead, I slipped on my silver bangle and a swishy,

long-skirted white sundress and headed out the door, feeling the same flutter of comfortable excitement I always felt when I left for a date with Will.

And I went right on feeling fluttery and excited until Will and I sat down for dinner that night. We'd decided to go to Fiddlehead, one of Dune Island's fancier restaurants. (Will had promised to eat light with his family.) We sat at a low-lit, imposing table, complete with burning candle, basket of artisanal bread, and massive, leather-bound menus.

The place was beautiful.

The menu was impressive, too, all iced platters of raw oysters, high-grade steaks, and buttery pastas. The ambiance was pure, manufactured romance.

It was also purely *wrong*. For us.

"I feel like I have to whisper in here," Will whispered, leaning across the table.

"I feel like I should be wearing a corset," I responded.

I threw my head back, looked at the bronze-painted, pressed-tin tiles on the ceiling, and felt miserable.

And I didn't want to feel miserable tonight. We didn't have *time* for that. So suddenly I stood up. I grabbed my purse from the back of my chair and rifled through it, pulling out a ten-dollar bill. I tossed it on the table.

"What are you doing?" Will sputtered.

"That's for the bread and the waters and a tip for the server," I said, grinning at Will. "You've already eaten with your mom and Owen anyway, and I'm not hungry. Let's go!"

Will got to his feet so fast, he almost tipped his chair over.

We gritted our teeth to keep from guffawing into the ambiance, then dashed out the door.

We made a quick, surreptitious stop at The Scoop for a soft cooler with a long strap, an ice pack, and a couple of pints of ice cream.

And then, holding hands, we headed south.

"Where are we going?" Will said as we walked down the sandy sidewalk that led from the boardwalk toward the lighthouse.

"I can't believe I never got around to taking you here," I said. "I'm just glad it's a clear night."

"Where?" Will almost yelled.

"You'll see," I said. "We're almost there."

Before we reached the lighthouse parking lot, we veered left onto a gravel road, which culminated after about a quarter mile at . . .

"The water tower?" Will said, peering up at the giant, oblong tank on top of a crisscrossing network of steel stilts. "Seriously?"

"Oh yeah," I said. "It's great during the day, but it's magic at night." We walked around the tower until we reached its ladder. I kicked off my sandals, slung the long handle of the ice cream cooler across my chest, and started climbing.

"You're not afraid of heights, are you?" I thought to ask when I was halfway up the ladder.

"I'm a New Yorker!" Will scoffed.

"There *are* a few tall buildings there, aren't there?" I laughed.

We crab-walked up the curved side of the water tower until we were in the center of the tank, which was spacious and fairly flat.

Then we sat with our backs to the lighthouse and the ocean. We gazed out at the skinny, bent-leg shape that was Dune Island. In the moonlight, the swamp grasses undulating in the breeze looked almost mystical, like a fluttering golden cloth. The swamp pools were like tiny islands themselves, black shapes stretching out toward the mainland, looking like a work of abstract art.

"See what I meant about the shapes in the pools?" I said to Will. "They're better than clouds."

"Huh," Will said, squinting at the landscape. "All I see are a whole lot of Jesuses!"

I burst out laughing and threw myself at Will, hitting him so hard that he fell backward. He laughed too, and coughed a bit when he hit the tank.

We lay there for a moment, with my top half laying on his, looking into each other's eyes. And then we were kissing, our bodies pressed together as close as we could get them. But after a moment, the sobs that I'd held in so valiantly all day broke free. I buried my face in Will's shoulder and cried so hard, I could barely speak. He stroked my hair, held me tightly, and didn't try to quiet me.

"I can't do this," I cried.

It was the same thing I'd said to him the night we broke up. Then I didn't think I'd had the strength to be with Will.

Now I didn't think I could be *without* him.

But I had to.

The thought threatened to set off another bout of tears, but instead I turned to Will and put my hands on his shoulders. I looked into his eyes, which were drawn downward by a new sadness now, and got pragmatic.

My curfew was at eleven. I had ninety minutes left with Will. And I didn't want to waste them.

I swiped the tears off my cheeks. Then I peered over Will's shoulder at the swamp and said, "I actually do see a shape. I think it's a canoe."

Will nodded slowly. He understood what I was doing. So he looked too.

"Um, I see a turtle over there," he said, pointing at a round patch.

"Oh, please," I scoffed, "turtles are the easiest ones to spot. Hey, do you see that trombone?"

"Seriously? A trombone?" Will laughed. "Now you're just being ridiculous."

"I know," I said, snuggling into him, my arms wrapped around his waist.

"I can picture you at your school in New York," I said. "I'm seeing a blazer with a crest and a striped tie."

"Sorry to disappoint you," Will said, "but we don't even wear uniforms."

After a pause, Will said, "I wonder if I'll be different now. At school. At life. You know, after you."

I squeezed Will a little harder and thought of my own life before this summer. I'd held so much, and so many, at a distance lest they prevent me from breaking away from Dune Island. Would *I* be different?

I hoped so, at least in some ways.

I looked into Will's eyes again.

In a good way, I thought before I closed my eyes and kissed him.

When it was too dark to see anything but Will's watch, which said ten forty-five, we carefully climbed back to earth.

"We forgot to the eat the ice cream," Will said, pointing at the cooler hanging from my shoulder.

"I know," I said. I handed it to him. "Take it home with you. For your mom and Owen. Maybe they're still awake."

We held each other for a long, long beat. Our kisses felt endless, but also way too brief. Tears streamed from my eyes, but I managed not to sob for this moment.

Finally, Will cleared his throat.

"I think I need to walk home by myself," he said. "I don't want to say good-bye with suitcases and boxes and stuff all around us."

Our eyes were open during our last kiss. Will's lips were so soft, so delicious. His eyelashes fluttered with the pain he was feeling and I felt them brush my own. I pulled away and smoothed his hair back from his face so I could look at him, really look at him, one last time.

Will kissed my forehead, softly and sweetly and so, so sadly. Then we drew away from each other, our arms outstretched and our fingers touching until we finally pulled them apart.

I watched Will walk away until I couldn't see him anymore.

Then I went home myself, crying until I literally couldn't anymore.

That feeling, of having no tears left, somehow felt even worse than all the crying. I felt dry. Passionless.

I wondered if I'd ever feel passionate about anything again.

After every date with Will, I'd fallen into a deep, heavy, happy sleep.

After this one, of course, I couldn't sleep at all. I don't think I even *tried*. I just lay on my back under my skylight, staring through the clear night sky at the stars.

At two a.m. I got out of bed without even really deciding to. Suddenly I was just up and slipping into a pair of cutoffs and a tank-top. As I tiptoed across the room, carrying my flip-flops, I stared at my sister in her bed, willing her to stay asleep. Then I slipped out of our room.

My parents slept with a machine that piped the sound of waves and gulls into their room, as if they didn't get enough ocean sounds living on an island. So it was easy to tiptoe my way out of the house without them hearing. I didn't feel even a twinge of guilt. I was certain I wasn't doing anything wrong.

As I pedaled down Highway 80, I also didn't worry about how I was going to rouse Will from his bed. I think somehow I knew he wouldn't be in it.

Sure enough, when I arrived at his stretch of beach, there he was. He was gazing out at the waves with his hands dug deep into the pockets of his khakis, his bare feet scuffing at the sand.

He didn't even seem surprised when I came up behind him and touched his shoulder. He simply wrapped his arms around me and buried his face in my neck. We stood there, swaying slightly in the wind coming off the waves, breathing each other in.

We walked along the beach for a long time. And when we were tired of walking, we lay down, Will's arms around me, my head on his chest.

There was nothing left to say. We just lay entwined on the sand, listening to each other's heartbeats during the pauses between waves.

We fell asleep like that, and didn't wake until the sun began to rise. We sat up to watch it, all flaming, pink-orange shimmers and golden beams. I rested between Will's legs, leaning back against his chest. He clasped his arms around my shoulders, holding me close.

Just as the sun broke free from the horizon, Will spoke. His voice was gravelly.

"I don't know what's going to happen with us, Anna," he said. "But I'm always going to love you. *That* I know."

I knew it too—that I would always love Will, even if I never saw him again.

I knew it as I walked him back to the rickety bridge that led to his cottage.

I knew it as we luxuriated in one final, delicious kiss and as we said good-bye for real this time. In a few hours, Will would go back to that foreign country of subways and elevators and I would remain in this lush habitat where it never snowed and you could hear the sizzle of the surf everywhere you went.

As I pedaled my bike slowly home, I realized one more thing. I didn't have to wonder if I'd ever be passionate or happy again. I *was* happy, even as I tasted tears on my lips, along with Will's last kiss; even though part of me dreaded this day, my first without Will.

I was happy because I knew I'd never forget Will. Even if parts of this summer faded from my memory over time, even if Will's face grew vague in my mind, I'd never forget what it had felt like to be with him for a few short months. What it had been like to be sixteen and in love for the first time.

I wouldn't forget *that*—not ever.

Many thanks to . . .

Emilia Rhodes, for giving me quite the summer.

Micol Ostow, for being a lovely yenta.

Sonya McEvoy, Katherine Moore, Laurel Snyder, Melanie Regnier, and Alissa Fasman, wonderful friends who pitched in with playdates.

Morelli's Gourmet Ice Cream & Desserts and King of Pops in Atlanta, for the ice cream inspiration.

Our beloved granny nanny, Bunny Lenhard, who did too many above and beyonds to list.

Mira and Tali, who bounced through this crazy summer with so much cheer and charm.

And Paul, who kept me going with tremendous support, lots of housework, and most of all, inspiration for a love story.